DEATH RIDES
THE MIDNIGHT OWL

DEATH RIDES
THE
MIDNIGHT OWL

Agata Stanford

A JENEVACRIS PRESS PUBLICATION

DEATH RIDES THE MIDNIGHT OWL
A Dorothy Parker Mystery / November 2011

Published by
Jenevacris Press
New York

This is a work of fiction. Names, characters, places, and incidents either are the product of the author's imagination or are used fictitiously. Any resemblance to actual persons, living or dead, events, or locales is entirely coincidental.

———◆———

ISBN 978-0-9827542-7-6

Printed in the United States of America

www.dorothyparkermysteries.com

For my parents, Angelo and Angela Puccio

Also by Agata Stanford

The Dorothy Parker Mysteries Series:

The Broadway Murders
Chasing the Devil
Mystic Mah Jong

Acknowledgments

I'd like to extend my thanks to Ray Cooney, of the National Railroad Historical Society, for answering my long list of questions about the New Haven Line's Midnight Owl Pullman service during the 1920s. Thank you, Stanley Werner, for many years of encouragement and for helping to make it possible for me to write this mystery series. My appreciation goes to Eric Conover, without whose design talents my books would not look nearly so good. I give a special thank-you to my friend and editor, Shelley Flannery, for her expertise as copyeditor, proofreader, and historian. She is also responsible for the title of this novel. My appreciation goes to artist Rob Smith, Jr. for the wonderful illustrations of Dorothy Parker, Robert Benchley and Heywood Broun for this book. www.robsmithjr.com

Contents

Who's Who in the Cast of
Dorothy Parker Mysteries

The Algonquin Round Table was the famous assemblage of writers, artists, actors, musicians, newspaper and magazine reporters, columnists, and critics who met for luncheon at one P.M. most days, for a period of about ten years, starting in 1919, in the Rose Room of the Algonquin Hotel on West 44th Street in Manhattan. The unwritten test for membership was wit, brilliance, and likeability. It was an informal gathering ranging from ten to fifteen regulars, although many peripheral characters who arrived for lunch only once might later claim they were part of the "Vicious Circle," broadening the number to thirty, forty, and more. Once taken into the fold, one was expected to indulge in witty repartee and humorous observations during the meal, and then follow along to the Theatre, or a speakeasy, or Harlem for a night of jazz. Gertrude Stein dubbed the Round Tablers "The Lost Generation." The joyous, if sardonic, reply that rose with a laugh from Dorothy Parker was, "*Wheeee! We're lost!*"

Dorothy Parker set the style and attitude for modern women of America to emulate during the 1920s and 1930s. Through her pointed poetry, cutting theatrical reviews, brilliant commentary, bittersweet short stories, and much-quoted rejoinders, Mrs. Parker was the embodiment of the soulful pathos of the "Ain't We Got Fun" generation of the Roaring Twenties.

Robert Benchley: Writer, humorist, boulevardier, and bon vivant, editor of *Vanity Fair* and *Life Magazine,* and drama critic of *The New Yorker,* he may accidentally have been the very first standup comedian. His original and skewed sense of humor made him a star on Broadway, and later, in the movies. What man didn't want to *be* Bob Benchley?

Alexander Woollcott was the most famous man in America—or so he said. As drama critic for the *New York Times,* he was the star-maker, discovering and promoting the careers of Helen Hayes, Katherine Cornell, Alfred Lunt and Lynn Fontanne, and the Marx Brothers, to name but a few. Larger than life and possessing a rapier wit, he was a force to be reckoned with. When someone asked a friend of his to describe Woollcott, the answer was, "Improbable."

Frank Pierce Adams (FPA) was a self-proclaimed modern-day Samuel Pepys, whose newspaper column, "The Conning Tower," was a widely read daily diary of how, where, and with whom he spent his days while gallivanting about New York City. Thanks to him, every witty retort, clever comment, and one-liner uttered by the Round Tablers at luncheon was in print the next day for millions of readers to chuckle over at the breakfast table.

Harold Ross wrote for *Stars and Stripes* during the War, where he first met fellow newspapermen Woollcott and Adams. The rumpled, "clipped woodchuck" (as described by Edna Ferber) was one of the most brilliant editors of his time. His magazine, *The New Yorker,* which he started in 1925, has enriched the lives of everyone who has ever had a subscription. His hypochondria was legendary, and his the-world-is-out-to-get-me outlook was often comical.

Jane Grant married Harold Ross but kept her maiden name, cut her hair shorter than her husband's, and viewed domesticity with disdain. A society columnist for the *New York Times*, Jane was the very chic model of modernity during the 1920s. Having worked hard for women's suffrage, Jane continued in her cause while serving meals and emptying ashtrays during all-night sessions of the Thanatopsis Literary and Inside Straight Club.

Heywood Broun began his career at numerous newspapers throughout the country before landing a spot on the *World.* Sportswriter and Harlem Renaissance jazz fiend, he was to become the social conscience of America during the 1920s and beyond through his column, "It Seems to Me . . . ." His insight and commentary made him a champion of the labor movement, as did his fight for justice during and after the seven years of the Sacco and Vanzetti trials and execution.

Edmund "Bunny" Wilson: Writer, editor, and critic of American literature, he first came to work at *Vanity Fair* after Mrs. Parker pulled his short story out from under the slush-pile and found it interesting.

Robert E. Sherwood came to work on the editorial staff at *Vanity Fair* alongside Parker and Benchley. The six-foot-six Sherwood was often tormented by the dwarfs performing—whatever it was they did—at the Hippodrome on his way to and from work at the magazine's 44th Street offices, but that didn't stop him from becoming one of the twentieth-century Theatre's greatest playwrights.

Marc Connelly began his career as a reporter but found his true calling as a playwright. Short and bald, he co-authored his first hit play with the tall and pompadoured *George S. Kaufman*.

Edna Ferber racked up Pulitzer Prizes by writing bestselling potboilers set against America's sweeping vistas, most notably, *So Big, Showboat, Cimarron,* and *Giant.* She, too, collaborated with George S. on several successful Broadway shows. A spinster, she was a formidable personality and wit and a much-coveted member of the Algonquin Round Table.

John Barrymore was a member of the Royal Family of the American Stage, which included *John Drew* and *Ethel* and *Lionel Barrymore*. John Barrymore was famous not only for his stage portrayals, but for his majestic profile, which was captured in all its splendor on celluloid.

The Marx Brothers: First there were five, then there were four, then there were three Marx Brothers — *awww, heck,* if you don't know who these crazy, zany men are, it's time to hit the video store or tune into Turner Classic Movies!

Also mentioned: *Neysa McMein,* artist and illustrator, whose studio door was open all hours of the day and night for anyone who wished to pay a call; *Grace Moore*, Broadway and opera star, and later a movie star; Broadway and radio star *Fanny Brice* — think Streisand in *Funny Girl*; *Noel Coward*, English star and playwright who took America by storm with his classy comedies and bright musical offerings; *Condé Nast,* publisher of numerous magazines including *Vogue*, *Vanity Fair,* and *House and Garden; Florenz Zeigfeld* — of "*Follies*" fame — big-time producer of the extravaganza stage revue; *The Lunts*, husband-and-wife stars of the London and Broadway stages, individually known as Alfred Lunt and Lynn Fontanne; *Tallulah Bankhead* — irreverent, though beautiful, southern-born actress with the foghorn drawl, who later made a successful transition from the stage to film—the life of any party, she often perked up the waning festivities performing cartwheels sans bloomers; ***Irving Berlin, George Gershwin,*** and ***Jascha Heifetz***—famous for "God Bless America" and hundreds more hit songs; composer of *Rhapsody in Blue* and *Porgy and Bess* and many more great works; and the violin virtuoso, respectively.

DEATH RIDES
THE
MIDNIGHT OWL

"*I would not wish to a dog or to a snake, to the most low and misfortunate creature of the earth — I would not wish to any of them what I have had to suffer for things that I am not guilty of. But my conviction is that I have suffered for things that I am guilty of. I am suffering because I am a radical and indeed I am a radical; I have suffered because I am an Italian and indeed I am an Italian . . . if you could execute me two times, and if I could be reborn two other times, I would live again to do what I have done already.*"

— **Bartolomeo Vanzetti**

"*If this is a lynching, at least the fish peddler and his friend the factory hand may take unction to their souls that they will die at the hands of men in dinner coats.*"

— **Heywood Broun (New York World)**

Chapter One

There was death that day, whichever way we turned, coming and going. We couldn't escape it. Like the oppressive August heat wave, death hung heavy on the air and would not relent. What a way to spend my thirty-fourth birthday.

Suicide tomorrow.

"By golly," said Mr. Benchley as our taxi pulled up to the curb, breaking the long, funereal silence of the cab ride from my hotel to South Station. "Why, I could swear that that's Roger Mellon."

"Don't swear; I do enough of it for both of us," I said, mindlessly.

"What's he doing taking the train with us plebes?"

"Slumming, I suppose," I replied, not really interested, but craning in the direction in which he pointed, glad that something, someone, had brought my friend out of the funk of the last few hours, if only temporarily. Once out of the taxi, a Red Cap leading the way through the terminal with our luggage, we walked toward the departure platform of the New Haven Line.

South Station was unusually crowded for the late hour, but of course that was to be expected, given the events of the past week—the events of the past seven years!—when all that had been dreaded by observers and critics around the world, would, at the stroke of midnight and the very same hour of our train's departure for New York, most tragically culminate with the executions of Nicola Sacco and Bartolomeo Vanzetti.

The world press had converged on Boston, as had thousands of protesters from all walks of life and political persuasions. Among those represented were leaders and organizers of labor, communism, socialism, and syndicalism and celebrated artists, poets, authors, representatives of the ACLU and the IWW, and persons from all social classes possessing a conscience and who wanted to add their voices to the protests. Sacco and Vanzetti were to be executed, convicted of the murder of a paymaster and his guard during the robbery of a factory payroll on an April morning of nineteen-hundred twenty, in the small industrial town of South Braintree, Massachusetts.

The trial from beginning to end smacked of prejudice, miscarriage of justice, and blatant disregard for the civil liberties of the two men, and, as repeatedly pointed out by tireless supporters of the Bill of Rights as well as by our friend Heywood Broun through his column in *The World,* so threatened the rights of all Americans.

From what I'd been hearing over the radio as I was packing my bags in my hotel room, protestors were demonstrating all over the world: New York, Amsterdam, London, and as far away as Tokyo. There were riots in Paris—the façade of the Moulin Rouge had been defaced; there were uprisings in Germany, Switzerland, and in South Africa; factory worker walk-outs were happening throughout South America. But nothing could stop the executions, except, perhaps, to bomb the jailhouse, and that was too radical for me to imagine anybody doing, although there had been many bombings attributed to anarchists in New York and other cities of late.

I wanted to get out of town before the stroke of midnight, away from the calamity, not because I was afraid, but because *there was nothing I could do to stop the madness!* I'd tried, in my own way; I'd stuck my nose into the nasty business, and where did it get me—what did I accomplish after two weeks of protests? Getting arrested and hauled down to jail for leading the march down Beacon Street and belting out "The Internationale," while that glory-seeking John Dos Passos, covering the execution for *The Daily Worker,* nearly knocked me over to assume the lead, and then, with a not-so-tuneful booming of "The Red Flag," tried to turn the entire march into a Communist Party rally! Really!

Mr. Benchley and I were glad for *any* distraction from the gloom of the sad events about to take place, so as we waited for the porters to load our valises onto the train, we watched as the Mellons, one of the richest couples on the planet, began boarding. Roger spied Mr. Benchley through the crowd and raised a hand in recognition. The old schoolmates exchanged words of greeting to the effect of an invitation from Roger for Mr. Benchley to stop in for a nightcap in his drawing-room once everyone was settled. Camera flashes lit up the gloomy platform, as press photographers shot pictures of the couple for the morning papers. Hermione Mellon shielded her face and, in spite of a hat pulled low and dark glasses, visibly winced from the terrible onslaught of flashbulbs as she climbed into the car, porters fussing over her.

I dreaded being spotted by the reporters in the state I was in. Tired, hot—the ninety-degree-plus August heat had left me wilted. My disappointment and frustration with a judicial system gone bad had left me spiritually spent. For a woman who was famous for her quick wit, it was the first time in my life I'd been rendered speechless. A photographer would expect me to smile and say something clever for the caption. The irony was that this was the perfect time for gallows humor and I couldn't find anything funny to say tonight.

Heywood Broun, Crusader!, appeared on the platform, having taken a cab with several other reporters who would not remain for the execution. "I just saw Roger Mellon and a woman who must be that strange wife of his, Hermione, is it? The Kenyan Coffee woman?," he said while tipping the Red Cap for his services.

Struggling in my closely fitted skirt in order to ascend the dropped step before being spotted by the reporters, I felt hands encircling my waist, and soon I was hoisted into the waiting arms of Mr. Benchley, who had already boarded.

"Thanks for the lift, Hey," I said to Broun, who smiled up winsomely, yet with an under-painted hangdog expression bleeding through. I ached in my heart for his wretchedness, for the sad state of his body and spirit.

During the past few weeks Heywood had spent much time in the same sorry suit. Boston's steamy weather—and no doubt the waistcoat's multiple uses as pillow and bib—had stretched and curled the garment's fabric, making him appear to be dressed in wilted lettuce, like a character out of *A Midsummer Night's Dream,* a vision faithful to the very fitting description of him by a fellow journalist as "an unmade bed." In spite of the ink smudges from cuffs to elbows, the shine of well-worn trousers, the unidentifiable remains of Tuesday's dinner on his tie, and Wednesday morning's egg on a lapel, he smelled not unpleasantly of tobacco, whiskey, and shaving lather.

But the man looked even more deflated and defeated than did the suit. He had tried so hard, for so long, to change the fate of the two Italian immigrants. We believe wholeheartedly in their innocence, and it is principle that drove Broun to write about the miscarriage of justice in the case against them. He'd been warned by Pulitzer, his publisher, to quit the campaign he'd been waging through his column, *It Seems to Me . . .*, to bring to light the injustices carried out against Sacco and Vanzetti, and to save the lives of the convicted Italians. Heywood said he'd quit before he would stop. Last week he wrote a letter to his publisher in his column and resigned his position at *The World.* I am so proud to know him! He turned at the sound of his wife's voice.

Ruth Hale, my traveling-companion-slash-jailhouse-cellmate (we were arrested, after all), appeared through troops of travelers to announce, "Wonder of wonders! I just spotted royalty boarding the train. Roger Mellon finally brought his wife here to the States."

"Ain't that just dandy?" I said. "But are you

certain that's his wife, and not just a current par-
amour?"

Ruth laid a narrow-eyed expression of contempt
on me. "Of course it's his wife, Hermione; he's not
the type to—"

"Awww, c'mon!" I said, shaking my head as Heywood offered a hand to help Ruth onto the car, "He's
a man, is he not? And therefore he is the type."

"Really, Mrs. Parker," said Mr. Benchley, leading the way toward the compartment, "your cynicism
increases with your years."

"What are you trying to say, you old bum?"

"Now, now, my dear, I am saying nothing at all,
at all."

"That's better," I replied testily. "We don't need
you to attest the virtue of monogamy."

Mr. Benchley uttered no retort. I'd spoken
only the truth. He and Gertrude had what you'd call
a "modern marriage": They lived mostly separate lives,
Mr. Benchley taking the train home to Scarsdale for
Sunday dinner and to play "Papa" to his sons, and
lord of his manor, before returning to his apartment
at the Hotel Royalton, in Manhattan, where he lived
weekdays. I was sorry that I was short-tempered with
him, even if he had suggested that I was getting old
and brittle with the passing years. Maybe I was.

"I see you're rather chummy with Mellon," I said, trying to draw him out.

"Harvard, Class of 1912, a Delta Upsilon fraternity brother." He chuckled gaily at some secret knowledge, and then shook his head. "Up to no good, we were."

"You see, Ruth, I didn't need to go to college like Mr. Benchley, here; I've learned 'up to no good' all on my own."

"Those were the days! Joe Kennedy, Johnny Reed—"

"Ah! A bootlegger and a Red! Good company!"

"And successful in their chosen fields!" he defended.

I laughed. "Successful? One's a traitor, buried at the Kremlin, and the other's a criminal."

"It's all how you look at it, I suppose . . . ."

"Well, it doesn't look good for you."

"Mellon and I perfected the game, 'We've come for the davenport.'"

Ah-ha! I thought, remembering only last year, when Mr. Benchley had led the Marx Brothers through the Dakota Apartments, switching out davenports from one apartment to another. They didn't stop at sofas, however. Pricey carpets were rolled up, carried out, and delivered to a neighboring household in exchange for a shabby rug. The draperies would have been pulled down if Groucho hadn't strained his back. A knock on a door—a maid answers— *We're here for the davenport*—and the furniture is carried out while a compliant, if confused, maid looks on.

Ruth laughed and let out an unattractive snort: "Let's hope the beds of this Pullman are bolted down."

"We had a grand time . . . ."

"Glad to know your time at college wasn't a total waste," I sniped.

"Really, Dottie, you are out of sorts," broke in Heywood, as Ruth and I took seats opposite each other in the Brouns' compartment.

I am rarely shamed, but Heywood could do it with a look.

"I am a bit—off, and I'd apologize, but I'll wait until morning if you don't mind. That way I can do it just once."

"You've spent too much time with Ruth these past weeks."

"I heard that, you brute," said Ruth, who then, with meticulous deliberation, proceeded to dramatically remove her pristine white gloves, one finger at a time, as if ready to slap one across the face of her husband in challenge for a duel. Instead she folded the pair and placed them in her purse, daintily removed the hatpin from her chapeau, and, smoothing her skirt, sat down next to her husband.

Ruth Hale, small, frumpish, if well tailored, is a little hellcat in the arena of women's rights, starting with the suffrage movement of the past decade. She, like my friend, Jane Grant, refused to take her husband's name upon marrying. She hates being referred to as "Mrs. Heywood Broun." I don't know what the hell she expected when she married him. His reputation as a sportswriter, political journalist, columnist, and prolific author of best-selling books had made him a household name. His fame precedes him, and the little woman who trots three steps behind trying to keep up is referred to, much to her frustration, as "Heywood Broun's wife." Poor dear, she was a passionate crusader and worked hard to stand as tall (figuratively) as her husband. To be married to such a powerful and influential man is not enough for Ruth. She is the modern woman of our new generation: the female who not only can survive without a man, but can live and thrive without his protection, interference, or dictates. Such is Ruth's continuous mantra, which at times can get a bit tiresome. That she is ambitious in her own right, that she is outspoken on issues both political and social, is probably what endeared her to Broun. But Heywood, competitive as he is, did not foresee a contest at home. My blunt and outspoken friend can be rendered quite contrite just to avoid an argument with his wife, and this deliberate reticence often serves to egg Ruth on even more rather than subdue her waspish tendencies. Aside from the argumentative suffragette pose she wears like impenetrable armor, and her disdain for the constraints on women imposed by men for thousands of years, I pretty much agree with her philosophy. Although the battle for the vote has been won, there is still a war going on. But, Ruth would fare better toward a victory if she used a modicum of wit and charm to grease the rusty, outdated machine of our male-dominated society. In many ways I envy the life she lives: home, children, and a husband who loves her . . . .

I never really suffered many restrictions for being a woman, so I suppose I am not as militant in my approach on these issues as Ruth or Jane Grant. Rather, I have made the most of my petite stature and my soft-spoken voice, and these qualities have served me well. Because my demure demeanor is in stark contrast with my often-caustic words, I don't come off as brashly outspoken, but rather as disarmingly funny.

The secret of my success began some years ago and, giving credit where credit is due, may be attributed in part to the men in my life. My best friends are men, and I am accepted as an equal. Talent and wit make for equal rights in the gang I hang around with; whether female, Jewish, or Negro, it matters not with my Round Table friends. I manage to keep in step and, in spite of my five-foot height, on the same imposing level.

Mr. Benchley tipped the porter and instructed him to place our valises in our respective single bed-rooms down the hall. I pulled my Victrola off the cart. We'd need music, I figured, or this journey home would be reminiscent of Lincoln's funeral train to Springfield.

Passengers plowed slowly through the hallway, some porters toting hand-luggage on their way to drawing-rooms, compartments, and bedrooms in our car, and others toward the sleeper cars where at a substantial savings you could retire onto a curtained bunk. I had a single bedroom a few doors down from the Brouns' compartment, but I doubted I'd ever hit the sack this night.

I stood near the open door, hoping to catch a breeze from the hall fans, watching the parade of tired travelers: a father toting a sleeping child over his shoulder, a matron carrying a small birdcage, a group of fresh-faced Harvard boys charging noisily into the compartment next door. I recognized a young couple who'd marched with me the day of my arrest, and had themselves escaped arrest. There followed a man in a tan gabardine suit, sporting a rakish beret. He was tall enough to peer over the heads of those in front of him, and because he'd caught my eye he nodded before moving on down the car. Then there appeared a tall, wiry man with patrician features who had spoken at a rally in the park. He'd attained fame as a muckraker, exposing the conditions of coal miners and slaughterhouses, as well as a speaker for the socialist cause. Following him was an entourage of half-a-dozen men chatting fiercely with the rat-tat-tat rapidity of their native Italian. Pushing through the line was a slight, young fellow with suntanned Italian good looks and the air of an immigrant about him. It was written all over him in the cut of his suit, the old-fashioned collar, and the fact that he possessed that just-off-the-boat look—a mixture of wide-eyed wonder, an expression of easy compliance with authority, and a healthy dash of the fear that all immigrants naturally assume when they hit the shore. He pressed forward in a zigzag fashion through the line, whispering, "*Scusi, scusi,*" waking the old gal's canary as he brushed the cage cover, which resulted in a series of startling chirps, and knocking off-kilter a Harvard boy's boater.

"Hey! You there! Watch where you're going!" shouted the Harvard boy, with haughty condescension.

"*Scusi, scusi,*" said the Italian, his head bowing in a gesture of respect, one hand clutching his hat to his chest, the other, a small brown leather valise. There was a spark of contempt in his expression as he threw a glance at the back of the boy who'd moved on with his friends, and he caught me watching when he nearly fell in through the door to our compartment. He quickly lowered his head. *"Forgif, pleez*, lady," he whispered, before passing on down the hall.

The Harvard contingent fell into drunken song in four-part harmony, and within seconds came a ukulele accompaniment of "Sweet Georgia Brown."

"I'm in a funk," I said to no one and everyone. "I've been jailed, tailed—by G-men in dusty shoes—suspected of trying to set off bombs in the town square, and been called all sorts of names—and even though some of the names fit, it's not nice to air someone else's dirty laundry in public. This town stinks; it's not only full of beans, it's full of—"

"Now-now, Mrs. Parker," cut in Mr. Benchley, soothingly patting my shoulder. "Let's not get into personalities, my dear."

"They would have framed me for the Boston Tea Party if they could have gotten away with it! I've been pushed around this town long enough! What time is it? How long before we get the hell out of here? Somebody put on that fan and open up the windows; it's stifling in here!"

Heywood did my bidding, but I didn't expect a reply about our departure. We were, after all, on the Midnight Owl, leaving at twelve-oh-one A.M. A terrible time to depart; a terrible hour in the history of our nation! I was in a hurry to escape, and yet I

knew there was no escaping for the two Italians awaiting execution at the Massachusetts State Prison in
Charlestown. Right now, more than two hundred city
and state mounted police were guarding the walls of
the prison against attack from protesters. Once the
train's warning whistle blew it would be midnight; the
sound would be like a long-dreaded death knell. The
two men would be escorted out of their prison cells for
the walk to the electric chair. The first of the executions would begin at the stroke of midnight. When
the switch was thrown, the lights would flicker and
buzz, the smell of ozone and burnt hair and flesh and
fear would permeate the air—I winced at the horrific
scene playing out in my head. I cringed, not only at
the thought of the terrible deaths but that their murders by the state could ever be *justified*.

I touched Mr. Benchley's arm. He, too, was in
a dark mood. It was, after all, he who tried to bring
to light, during these last months of appeals, through
letters, affidavits, and testimony, the knowledge he
possessed of the blatant prejudicial conduct of Judge
Webster Thayer, who had presided over the trial, later
denied the appeals, and sentenced the men to death.
Thayer took every opportunity to air his bigotry. He
viciously voiced his hatred of the "wops," bending the
ears of the Boston bluebloods who he thought might
be of like mind in wanting to rid America of "those
Red bastards," those labor agitators who were the
bane of corporate and big banking interests in the
city—and in the country! He'd been shooting off his

mouth these past seven years in an attempt to ingrati-
ate himself with these pillars of the community, as if
to justify his bias to any upstanding fellow he could
corner at the Union Club, University Club, dinner
parties, and society functions. Thayer engaged in this
despicable conduct while sitting on the bench. When
not busy bullying defense witnesses, he was steering
witness testimony against the defendants, obstructing
justice by assisting the district attorney at every turn
and aiding and abetting the prosecutor's intimidation
of defense witnesses. He spread his venomous hatred
at every turn. And then there was the brazen editing
of court transcripts, the dismissal or distortion of
the facts given in favor of the defense by expert witnesses, and the deliberate suppression from the jury
of the Pinkerton reports with their sworn statements
from eye-witnesses that Sacco and Vanzetti were *not*
the men who had committed the robbery and shooting death of the paymaster's guard. For seven years,
Web Thayer could be heard publicly spouting: "Did
you see what I did with those *arn-y-cist* bastards the
other day? That will hold them for a while!"; "Those
bastards down there, I'll get them good and proper!";
and "I'll show them and get those guys hanged, and I'd
like to hang a few dozen of those radicals!"

A burning, angry fury took hold of me when I
first heard about what Thayer had been saying. Now,
when there was no longer anything any of us could do
to stay the executions, no action to take, no protest
to voice, I felt a sinking in my stomach in fearful an-

ticipation of the travesty about to occur in just a few minutes, when the struggle for justice of the past seven years would shudder to a bitter end with the throwing of a switch. Two good, hardworking, kindhearted family men, two Italian immigrants, were about to be put to death, about to be murdered by the Commonwealth of Massachusetts on circumstantial evidence because of their anarchistic beliefs, the propaganda literature they distributed, and their efforts to increase the wages of their fellow laborers.

I was sinking into a mire of despondency. Woodrow Wilson, my Boston terrier and canine companion, reacted to my despair and the heavy, gloomy mood cast over all of us in the compartment. He whined and leapt up onto my lap to stare into my eyes with questioning concern.

I readjusted my attitude. Although beaten (figuratively) and abused (verbally) for my protests (the feds actually suspected me and Ruth of planning to set off a bomb at the courthouse, so we were watched), I needn't whine my discontent to my friends. We were all feeling ineffectual in not having achieved justice for Vanzetti and Sacco. Although I was brokenhearted, I would not cry! *I must not cry!*

The train whistle blew, long and shrill, announcing imminent departure.

Ruth and I clutched each other, hankies fluttering at our faces, Woodrow Wilson caught in the snare of our tangled arms; Heywood, his usually vibrant and powerful bulky figure caved in a heap of sadness, sat facing the window looking out blindly at latecomers rushing to board, lovers in parting embraces, conductors, porters, and Red Caps loading on stray luggage and passengers, all the while seeing none of the frantic activity, only the slow, terrifying death-walk taking place three miles across the river.

Suddenly, all our attention was fixed by yells and a scuffle out on the platform, as the scene of flurried farewells transformed into a startling play of chase-and-capture as policemen converged to restrain a young man we had not seen before.

"*Viva l'anarchia!*" he screamed, and the anguish in his cry sent chills through me. "*Viva* Vanzetti!" he continued as he fought off three big men. "*Viva* Sacco and Vanzetti!" he sobbed as he was tackled down, his beautiful dark features pressed to the ground as the policemen cuffed his wrists behind his back. They brought him up to his feet, and as the train whistle sounded its urgent cry once again, he threw back his curly head with a gesture of intrepid defiance and screamed out loudly over the din, "Never forget Sacco and Vanzetti!" He was punched and battered by the policemen. We watched in horror as the train jolted forward and he passed from view.

I glimpsed Mr. Benchley, a rare morose expression creasing his handsome brow. He rose slowly to his feet, as if an additional burden pressed down upon him. He reached for his traveling case, from which he retrieved a bottle of Dewar's. The whistle sounded again like a terrible warning. My friend, with shaking hands, filled paper cups pulled from a dispenser beside the little sink, and solemnly, respectfully, we toasted the lives and memory of Nicola Sacco and Bartolomeo Vanzetti as the Midnight Owl began its steamy, thunderous chug out of South Station.

———

One cannot sustain for long a state of misery, nor dwell in the darkness of the mind's despair without becoming morose and suicidal. Believe me; I know.

So as the train barreled into the night, Heywood produced a pack of cards, which he shuffled violently, and from which he dealt a game for diversion from our grim thoughts. Mr. Benchley was assigned scorekeeper, and he took out his little notebook and pencil from his coat to tackle the mindless job. There followed a long and weighty silence as we feigned concentration on our hands, the quiet a rarity for so vocal a gang of friends. The moronically happy plunking of ukulele music seeped through the walls. The music was just too gay to stand any longer, so I turned on the compartment's radio, and the only broadcast that came in clearly was the *Boston Evening Transcript* on WBET.

Boots and His Nighthawks were playing dance music, and after Doc Wassermann's Orchestra played a turn, "the time at the tone" sounded twelve-thirty A.M. I got up and fetched my portable Victrola case that I'd lugged along for the trip, and in which I had stacked half-a-dozen or so records on the turntable. I'd not had the time or inclination to play the thing all the time we were in Boston, and I now realized that none of my choices would serve to lift our sullen spirits. Bessie Smith would make us cry; the Duke would make us bluer.

I listened with one ear to the news of the day broadcast on the radio as I leafed through my record selections: St Mark's Church had been the beneficiary of a millionaire's will; the amateur cracksman long suspected of stealing museum masterworks throughout Europe was arrested at the Metropolitan Museum of Art in New York City; a terrorist plot foiled in Chicago earlier today points to anarchist activity; Ed Farrell's slugging is the reason why the Braves won the last three games from the Cubs; the French Davis Cup had arrived in Boston earlier in the day; three were found dead in a cargo-hold fire aboard the HMS *Victoria*, including the body of a stowaway; and Charlie Chaplin agreed to pay the astronomical sum of eight-hundred-fifty-thousand dollars in a divorce settlement.

And then, to wrap things up:

The juice was turned off, and Vanzetti was officially pronounced dead at twelve-twenty-

*six-fifty-five. The orchestra will now play,
"The End of a Perfect Day."*

"*Sons of bitches!*" I hissed with a little cry, slamming off the radio and then looking at the forlorn friends who sat there in a motionless tableau of grief. "I'm taking Woodrow for a walk through the cars," I said while opening the drawing-room door.

The nightmare in my head ended abruptly as I faced a familiar and spectacular vision in the hallway.

Black veiling almost obscured the detailed edging on the brim of an elegant black chapeau that concealed the face of the woman who floated through the corridor, a porter leading the way. The pair had stopped abruptly in front of the door to allow an elderly woman with a cane to pass through from the opposite direction.

That hat! I knew that hat! We were on intimate terms!

Despite the black veiling, the most wonderful expanse of organza unfolded from angled pleats at the crown. Narrow at the forehead, the tautly stretched silk "wings" widened at the sides. White egret feathers swooped up from the band, and draped downward, forming an extravagant "S" as they brushed along the shoulder for a final caress of her chin. A large brooch, fashioned with white diamonds into the design of an egret in flight, secured the veiling to her suit; its refractive brilliance flashed like miniature fireworks in the dull lamplight.

I'd seen that saucy confection that floated upon this woman's head at *Madame Charlotte's Chapelier*, on Madison Avenue. Jane, the voice of reason, had talked me out of buying it: "It is a glorious creation, Dottie . . . but, well, it makes me think of one of those fancy prize layers—"

"Ah-ha! Then it's perfect for me, as *I*, too, am a rather fancy prize layer, don't you know?"

She murmured audibly under her breath. "More like the barnyard variety."

"Are you suggesting that I look like a *chicken*?" I clucked, rustling the long expanse of feathers tickling my neck.

"Well, it's just—"

"Don't think I can carry it off?" I said point blankly while bobbing my head and strutting before the mirror, hands behind my back, and fingers fanned.

"It's disproportionate with your petite stature, is all." I was too short, she insinuated, for a hat that large, and the feathers were just over-the-top. I picked a piece of fluff from off my tongue.

"Oh, crap, Dottie!" said Jane, throwing off any

further attempt at being tactful, "You look ridiculous!"

"I don't think I look at all—*bruk-bruk-bruk-BRUK!*—ridiculous!" I insisted with a straight face, and then sighed, abandoning all fantasies of purchasing such a confection. Oh, to be long-legged and lithely graceful!

Well, the woman in the corridor, standing aside as the elderly woman shuffled slowly past, was both long-legged and graceful, damn her eyes! But of course, I couldn't see her eyes—or her face—for the dark veiling. I supposed she was mourning the executed men.

I lifted Woodrow in my arms and followed the veiled lady along the corridor past the cheerful, raucous music in the Harvard boys' compartment and past the larger drawing-room occupied by the Mellons. The corridor curved, and ahead were the rows of single bedrooms flanking a narrow center hall. The porter unlocked the door of the room across from mine, and The Hat disappeared from view.

"It stops there!"

I turned to see who was addressing me, and then realized the woman's voice had come from behind the Mellons' drawing-room door and that the lock was not fully engaged.

"I'm not doing that, Hermione!" A man's voice;

obviously Roger Mellon's. "You're on the wrong track!"

"Margie Seldes says—"

"Margie Seldes says a lot of things—"

Ahhh, I thought, *wedded bliss!*

Perhaps I am the original *Nosey Parker*, so I've been called, and the truth is, I am not above eaves-dropping from behind drapery, behind a potted palm, or from within a closet, usually to avoid being caught where I don't belong. Often, I am in the company of Mr. Benchley or Aleck Woollcott, who help to pass the time with a stick of gum until the coast is clear. But tonight I was innocent, just passing through, so when Woodrow scratched at the drawing-room door and Roger Mellon threw it open to glare daggers at me, all I could do was to swallow hard, pick up my pooch, and whisper a hesitant "Hi." He slammed the door in my face.

Having been given my comeuppance I walked the few remaining feet to my little bedroom and rum-maged through Woodrow's bag, filled his water bowl, and fed him beef stew brought from the hotel. As he filled his belly, I threw off my shoes, sat on the bed, unpacked my overnight case, set out my kimono, toothbrush and powder, night cream, and comb. By the time I had finished setting up for the night, Wood-row was ready for his evening constitutional. The train would be pulling into New Haven in a few minutes to change from steam locomotive to electric engine, and the conductor would allow us to disembark so that Woodrow might "conduct his business." I slipped on my shoes and out we went, I having locked the bedroom door. I stood for a moment, deciding whether to walk forward or aft through the car, dropping my key into my purse and searching for change to buy a paper when we got to the station.

The famous muckraker came out of a bedroom a few feet away, and leaned against the doorjamb to engage in conversation with the man I saw earlier boarding the train, the man in a tan gabardine suit sporting a blue beret, only now he stood hatless. The men caught sight of me, nodded, and then they continued their talk in more hushed tones. Woodrow, ever curious, followed his nose to the door across from mine. A thin line of lamplight bled out through an inch-wide line around the door; it seemed like no one was locking their doors in this car. I was tempted to knock on the door, as the light and the open door obviously meant that the room's occupant was awake. We had a hat in common, and I really wanted to say, "Hello, you have my hat, you bitch." Ridiculous as it seemed, the compulsion to see the face of the woman under The Hat, under the veil, was strong.

Helplessly, I followed through with a light tap on the door.

"*Yoo-hoo!*" I called out lightly, and then again, in a friendly sing-song soprano.

I encouraged Woodrow to edge around and through the open door so that once he'd entered I could follow. "Woodrow, come back here, you naughty boy," I gently scolded my innocent little scapegoat, who looked back at me like I was crazy. But once through the door, and despite the evidence of valises and various items of clothing flowing out from an overnight bag, I could see that my Veiled Lady was not in her room. Only the faint wisp of the very popular perfume, *Shalimar*, wafted through the air.

I realized the folly of my ways and was about to exit the bedroom when I spotted The Hat in elegant repose on the overhead luggage rack. I was tempted, but I recovered my self-control and left the room, returning the door to its approximate condition before my intrusion.

As I was about to walk around the curve where the hall widened and led to the two compartments and larger drawing-room, I turned. The young Italian man who'd made his flustered apologies earlier walked past me and then toward the next Pullman sleeping car, and walking toward me was the famous socialist.

Woodrow cares not a fig about the social graces—introductions, and all that. He turned to meet the gent, sniffed at his trouser cuff, and then begged for a pat on the head.

"Behave yourself, Woodrow," I said without conviction, as I smiled upward nearly a mile and onto the rugged features, shamelessly wanting a pat, too, proving I was no better-mannered than my dog. For, although this fellow was far from handsome, he possessed a face infused with character; his features were strong and angular. The prominent nose had been chiseled to a fine hook; eyes, light green or gray—hard to tell in the dull light of the hall—set within dark hollows and winged with heavy brows. His mouth—well, it was that feature that betrayed him, for although set with determination, the fullness belied a compassionate nature, as did the ridiculously curly brown locks of hair that softened all the other sharp edges of his face. If one could judge a man's trustworthiness by looking at his face, this man would be the keeper of great secrets. But, what I knew of him from his books and articles was that he was also a deliverer of great and controversial revelations.

We were poised to speak but were interrupted by a shuffling noise followed by a heavy thud, like the toppling of a bookcase. Of course no bookcases graced the Pullman. Everything on the train was bolted down, I knew, as Mr. Benchley and his band of movers had been warned. With the abrupt ceasing of ukulele strumming, followed by high-pitched hoots and language appropriate to an adolescent gathering, I figured the lads must have been tossing their luggage about like footballs.

"Sounds like a grand time," I said, smiling up at the man.

"I'm glad they can find something to laugh about tonight."

The drawing-room door cracked open, revealing Roger Mellon's head peeking out, an expression of query on his face. "Dottie Parker," said Mellon, almost accusatorily, at seeing me standing at his door once again. He probably thought I had been lurking about all this time since he'd slammed the door in my face half an hour ago!

"Not me!" I protested, believing the industrialist thought I was creating the disturbance. "The college boys next door," I said, "tearing-up the compartment, I wouldn't be surprised."

"Uh, yes, of course," he said, easing his head back in to shut the door, gently this time. Before I could walk away he reappeared and said, "You're traveling with Bobby and the Brouns, I believe. Come in for a nightcap in a little while, won't you? I'll tell the porter to fetch you."

I hesitated. "Sounds . . . swell."

"Right," he said and, after a glance at the fellow by my side, added, "Bring your friend," and the door slammed shut.

In reaction to the curt invitation, my companion frowned; a look of skepticism raised one eyebrow. "Capitalist," he murmured under his breath, thinking I didn't hear.

I had met Roger Mellon several years ago, at a Swope weekend, before his marriage. I'd heard that he'd wed a spinster type whose parents had died in an avalanche while skiing in the Swiss Alps. I thought Roger a nervous, rather sullen character, and was surprised to hear that he and Mr. Benchley were bosom buddies at Harvard, because my friend is such a warm and loveable sort. The man and I walked past the Harvard boys as they began a cacophonous rendition of "I'm Looking Over a Four Leaf Clover," past the Brouns' compartment, and finally, the women's lavatory at the car's end. We stood on the open platform between cars silently smoking cigarettes. We really didn't know what to say to each other, although our private thoughts and sentiments about the evening seemed to hang heavily in the air. Smalltalk seemed like vacant chatter, so through some sort of mutual understanding, we didn't bother with it. We said "good night" when the conductor appeared to announce our arrival in New Haven, the socialist back-tracking to his bedroom, and I to depart the train. I was warned not to dally; the engine exchange would take only seven minutes. Woodrow Wilson was anxious to see the sights and leave his mark on Connecticut.

South Station, Boston

All Aboard!

Yours truly, Dorothy Parker.

Mr. Benchley, Frat brother

UNDER
GROUND
HOLE
FOR THE
UNDER
DOG
HEYWOOD
BROUN
Rob
Smith,
Jr.

Rob Smith, Jr.

Heywood Broun, crusader!

Chapter Two

Having completed his appointed task, Woodrow led the way along the platform toward the entrance to our car. A newsboy appeared with his sack of papers — special editions of the *New Haven Register* — shouting, "Read all about it! Anarchists executed!"

No passengers were boarded at this station, so the teenage newsy was selling papers to people on the train, handing papers in through the opened windows of compartments. Mr. Benchley flipped the kid a coin. Spotting me, he said: "Dottie Parker, it's time you came in from play."

"Coming, Mother," I said with a smile, before my attention was diverted to the window next door— the Harvard boys hadn't bothered to pull down their shade. They were engaged in the less-rambunctious pastime of touch football.

Woodrow was leaping up and down on hind legs with the rhythm of a pogo stick as Mr. Benchley tossed peanuts from his perch at the window. Woodrow never failed to catch his treats. I glanced at the shade-drawn window that was the Mellons' drawing-room. The narrow line of light that had been peeking out from the bottom of the shade was gone, and I thought, *Well, that's that for Roger's promised nightcap. They've gone to sleep.*

It was one-forty-three A.M. when we left New Haven, and at about two o'clock I no longer fancied sitting around the Brouns' compartment watching them grimly playing card games. All was quiet next door; the college boys were, no doubt, exhausted from their boisterous antics and had fallen into drunken stupors. The steady, rhythmic chugging of the Midnight Owl racing along the tracks was uninterrupted.

Although I needed the companionship of my friends, I needed sleep even more, and was about to tote my pup back to my bedroom when the porter knocked on the door, bidding us come to the Mellons' drawing-room.

"Now we shall meet the *Mrs.* Mellon, Mrs. Parker," Mr. Benchley said.

"What's she like?" I asked.

"I've no idea; never met the woman. But I hear that she has suffered from melancholia, and has been in a sanatorium in Switzerland for the past year."

"I suppose you are telling me to behave myself?"

"Not at all."

Ruth and Heywood begged out; time for bed.

Mr. Benchley tapped on the door.

"We've come for the davenport!" said Mr. Benchley when the door was opened by Roger Mellon.

"You're welcome to it, only it's bolted down!"

The men reverted to their youthful schoolboy camaraderie, slapping each other about in club greetings long ago rehearsed and affectionately sophomoric, if asinine. I expected them to break out in the school song or some such nonsense, but I was spared that, I'm glad to say. In his blue silk smoking jacket and red ascot, Roger Mellon appeared relaxed and friendly, a sharp contrast from the man who'd popped his head out the door earlier to chastise me.

On the sofa was his elegant wife, a good-looking full-figured blonde draped in a sky-blue silk wrap. She had a substantial, cushy appearance, like that of a plumped pillow. In spite of living in a world where women no longer cinched their waists, her voluptuousness was very attractive. Standing near her I felt plain and as brittle as a stick. She offered her hand to Mr.

Benchley and he made a gracious gesture of taking it in both of his own.

"Delighted," he said.

"Charmed, I'm sure," was Hermione Mellon's reply.

She turned to me with a smile, and I could swear she quivered, like a swan rustling her eiderdown. She rose up on little feet encased in powder-blue satin slippers and embellished with puffs of marabou feathers dyed to match. *Why, she's a creature right out of the moving pictures!* I thought. *Dripping glamour, mascara, and jewels!* I searched her face for a ghost of her past maladies, but found only great enthusiasm.

"Oh, Mrs. Parker—may I call you *Dorothy*?"

"Yes, of—"

"Good, Call me *Hermione*, why don't you?"

"Yes, of—"

"It's so exciting meeting Roger's American friends. I can't wait to see the United States. We are going to be great friends," she gushed, taking my arm, patting my hand, and leading me to sit beside her on the sofa. She had a way of speaking, an affectation of a clenched-jaw monotone voice. *Oh, my,* I suddenly thought, perhaps the clenched jaw was a result of her illness?

Woodrow became fascinated with the feathery puffs on her slippers. "Oh! Isn't it adorable!" she drooled as she picked up Woodrow and held him in her arms. She checked out his hardware: "Why, it's a boy doggie! He is a big little fella!" Nuzzling her face into Woodrow's wiry fur she lapsed into babytalk: "*Ain'cha a bi-i-i-ig wittle feh-wah?*"

Mellon, with an air of detachment, began filling glasses with warm, caramel-colored liquor—cognac.

"*Ain'cha? Ain'cha? Why, wes yew ahwr, wes yew ahwr. . . .*"

Hermione threw a glance in my direction and continued, "We are going to be the very best of friends, *ahw-ent we?*"

I thought she was awaiting a reply from Woodrow, but, caught under his front shoulders in the woman's firm grip, and dangling both hind legs and other parts, all he could do was whine pathetically at the face staring into his, millimeters from his own.

"Aren't we, Dottie—Oh! You don't mind if I call you *Dottie*, do you?"

"If you—"

Mr. Benchley looked on with amusement.

"That's just great, then, Dottie! Now, I want to know all about you, *all* about you!"

This woman is not depressed so much as she is manic, I thought.

A slightly dour Roger Mellon handed around the drinks.

"Because, I want to hear all about it!"

"All about wha—?"

"Not to say that I don't already know lots of things about you, Dottie, pet, but what I do know is only what I've read in the newspapers."

"That should suffice—"

"Y'see, I know you like to scribble and say funny things—"

"A regular idiot savant is our Mrs. Parker," cut in Mr. Benchley. "Did you know she can walk on her hands?"

"How thrilling!—and oh! I heard you got arrested! Along with those Greenwich Village Reds? Imagine! How romantic! What an adventure!" And then with a frown of dismay—her eyebrows forming conjoined squiggles, her voice modulated down an octave—she asked, "But, you're not a Red, are you?"

"Well—"

"Anarchist? Same thing, isn't it? Reds, anarchists, Italians!"

"Not the—"

"You know that they electrocuted those Bolshies."

Roger Mellon, suddenly engaged, found an opening in the monologue: "We narrowly missed getting blown up in London, you know."

"How unfortunate," I said.

Hermione jumped in: "And then, when we were in Italy, there was a bomb went off in the next street from our hotel. When I think it might have been us!"

"*Tsk-tsk!* What do you think about that?" clucked Mr. Benchley.

"I think they need glasses," I whispered.

"What was that Dot? You don't mind if I call you *Dot*, do you?"

"Certainly."

"Only *I* am allowed to call her *Mrs. Parker*," said Mr. Benchley.

The woman was a runaway train, and there was no stopping her: "Did they feed you bread and water— I mean, when they threw you in jail? Were they rough with you? I can't imagine how horrible, horrible—Isn't the thought just horrible, Roger? Being thrown in jail like that? Did they manhandle you?"

"It wasn't the way I would have preferred—"

"What exactly did you do that got you thrown—"

"—in the clink?" I asked.

"The clink! Horrible, horrible! I don't think I can bear to hear—tell me all about it! Did they put handcuffs on you?"

"Well, they tried to put me in the paddy wagon—"

"Horrible, horrible!

"—but I insisted on—"

"Did you know that I knew Houdini and he showed me how to get free of handcuffs?"

"So, if I were to cuff you to that towel bar over there—"

"I'd be free in a few seconds—"

"Pity . . . ."

"I'm what you call *double-jointed*."

"Is that the problem?"

"And that means I can get out of lots of tricky situations."

"That I should be so talented."

"But, you have to be double-jointed, you see. Pity about Harry, though."

"Harry?"

"Harry. Harry Houdini. Dead, you know, and just when I was getting to really know him."

"What people will do when desperate . . . ."

"What? Oh, it was easy for him! He always got himself free, did Harry. Nothing could trap him for long! He never failed at an escape, now did he, Roger?"

"Never failed," confirmed Roger Mellon.

"And the man could hold his breath for the longest time—he had to practice all the time—holding his breath, that is, because he was doing his underwater escape?" She barely took a gulp of air before continuing, "Remember that time he just up and disappeared from our dinner party, Rog, said he needed a breath of fresh air? That's when he was getting ready for the water tank."

"I should have paid him more attention," I said.

"Why, he could hold his breath—"

"Show me, show me, dear frantic Hermione," I implored with a great big grin, talking through clenched teeth in the manner of my hostess, "show me how he held his breath."

"Well, you see, first, he would take several big breaths—inhale and exhale—like this, and then—Oh!" She guffawed like a gagging goat, "Don't be an Airedale! Silly! I can't hold my breath *that* long."

"How can you know if you haven't tried?"

Her mood switched without transition. "Poor, dear Harry, gone now, forever to roam the great unknown."

"So true, so true," *tsk*ed Mr. Benchley.

This scintillating conversation was giving me a headache. As there was a momentary lull in the chatter, I handed Roger my glass for a refill.

"But, you are out now," said Hermione.

"Out? Out of what?"

"Don't be an Airedale! Jail, silly!"

"Yes, but I must say it had its advantages and here with *you*, now, I look back affectionately at the experience and long for the peace and quiet of my little chigger-infested cell."

Hermione giggled coquettishly and then slapped

me on the back like a politician before turning her attention back to Woodrow, who'd sought solace on my lap with his head tucked under my arm. "You *godda siwwy mama*, a *siwwy mama!*"

Woodrow whined.

If Woodrow were to snap, right now, and take off Hermione's pretty little nose, Roger could sue me, I thought, but he'd get nothing. For I have nothing—no house, no car, no stocks or bonds.... Go for it, Woodrow! There are advantages to being poor like me.

"Oh! I forgot to ask! What is *dis wittle feh-wah's* name?"

"Wood-wow Wilson."

"No! Don't be an Airedale, D! You don't mind if I call you '*D*,' do you? Come on, what's his name for real?"

I repeated myself.

She chortled like a sneezing horse. "Why not Al Jolson? Why not Groucho Marx?"

"Woodrow croons better than Al—"

"And we already have one 'Groucho' in our little gang; two might prove confusing," said Mr. Benchley.

"*Tsk, tsk*," she said, shaking her index finger at my friend, "Don't be an Airedale!"

"Boston terrier, I believe."

Mr. Benchley envisioned my imminent explosion, because he turned the topic of conversation to train travel.

"I'm getting a headache . . ." I said.

"And who can blame you?" replied Mr. Benchley, with a patient pat on my shoulder, before turning back to ask, "I suppose you are glad to be in back in the States, Roger?"

"It's grand to be home, Bobby. We did the grand tour these last three months, and it's done wonders for my darling."

"Oh, it was grand, all right!" said Hermione.

"But, it is good to return to good old American plumbing," said Roger.

"But Roger tells me there are no bidets, in this country."

"They were outlawed in New York," I replied. The absurdity of the quality booze and the inane conversation made my head swim.

Mr. Benchley said, "I was surprised to see you on the train."

"The Rolls—radiator burst a leak, you see?"

"I'm putting the boy to bed," I announced, as I

rose to my feet, a sleeping pup in my arms. "Thanks for the drink, you all."

"A pleasure meeting you, I'm sure," said Hermione Mellon. Her voice was at a lower pitch, less strident, her demeanor calmer, as if all of her energy had been spent.

Mr. Benchley wished the couple well, and we were about to depart when Hermione, recovering a bit of her former zeal, said:

"Oh, D, Bobby—we'd love to have you come out to the Island on Saturday."

Mellon jumped in with, "Of course! Bobby, won't you and Dorothy come to our place on the North Shore? It's a little celebration—you know, old sport—my darling home again with a few of the crowd?"

"I can't wait to see Rogie's little bungalow that he built for me on Long Island. He's named it 'Last Call,' ain't that a laugh? He's told me all about it, and it sounds just grand!"

"It is *grand*, all right. *Grand* Hotel, if you want to know," I warily chuckled, trying to slip away, but they were blocking the door.

Mr. Benchley, ever the gentleman—the same cannot be said of me—hedged gracefully. "Well, I will have to—"

"Bring your wife, Bobby; I'd love to meet her— you are still married to that girl you were courting while in school?" asked Roger.

"Gertrude—yes, well, I just visited her and the boys; they are spending the rest of the summer on Nantucket. They won't return home for another ten days. That's why I'm on the train from Boston, returning to the old work grind."

Hermione touched my shoulder in a pleading way. "You'll join us, won't you, Dot?" The heady scent of her Guerlain overpowered me.

For a long second I sought a clever retort, but was too tired, off my game, and my ears were still ringing. Tragic heroine or not, I could feel the soles of my feet itch at the very idea of spending time with this abrasive cow. Perhaps I should be more charitable, but being stuck all evening at a small dinner party and having to listen to Hermione chattering on inanely was low on my list of preferred activities, just above sticking a fork in my eye. I was about to beg off with something like, "I'll be brushing my teeth on Saturday," when it dawned on me that a summer weekend on the Long Island's North Shore was preferable to one spent in my sweltering apartment at the Algonquin. And the champagne would be flowing . . . .

"A *small* dinner party, didjasay?"

Mellon said, "No, Dorothy, if you were hoping

for a quiet dinner party, it won't be at Last Call this weekend. There'll be scads of people."

Last Call. Clever name for the place. A big party, *and there was safety in numbers*, I thought. "In that case, I'd love to come."

We left the drawing-room, and Mr. Benchley and I walked around the curve in the corridor that led to the bedrooms.

He scrutinized me holding Woodrow, a babe in arms. "Pretty little fellow; resembles his mother. Wonder what he'll be when he grows up?"

"Don't be an Airedale, you fool. President, no doubt."

"They say, 'Let sleeping dogs lie,'" said Mr. Benchley, as we approached my room, Bedroom Number One, the first on the right side of the hall. "Key?"

Mr. Benchley took the key from my pocket, unlatched my door, and then bade me good-night.

I splashed water on my face, brushed my teeth, and, before throwing my weary body onto the bed, opened the newspaper I'd bought at New Haven to accommodate any emergency Woodrow might have during the night. I pulled off the front page—photos of the men under the headline declaring the execution— which I gently folded and tucked in my purse. What remained of the paper was page three and beyond, which I placed on the floor, and there, looking up at me, was a press shot of the Mellons walking down the gangplank of the HMS *Victoria* docked in Boston Harbor earlier in the evening.

"Be a *good wittle boy*, *wittle doggie*, and do your business here," I said, turning off the lamp.

———•———

I awoke with a start. I don't know what startled me. I don't remember hearing a noise, and the rhythm of the train felt steady, uninterrupted. Woodrow, who'd been sleeping at the foot of my bed, sat up, stared at the door, his head tilted in canine query. He leaped off the bed and sniffed at the door, then stepped back and assumed a pointer's pose.

"Go back to sleep, Woodrow," I said, after I glimpsed the time on the bedside clock: three-twenty-two. Woodrow rolled out a low growl.

"Woodrow?" I said, and then lent an ear to what was going on outside my bedroom door. I heard a tapping—two taps, as if someone had knocked on a door. I was about to lay my head back down on the pillow when I heard the taps repeated.

"Come back to bed," I hissed at my pup, who whined in response. I fell back on my pillow, and within seconds the rocking of the train pulled me gently back into unconsciousness. But, not for long.

Two taps, and Woodrow's head popped up again, and then he pirouetted around the floor, repeating his rendition of *Whine and Growl.*

Annoyed and uncomfortable — the events of the day, the heat and general exhaustion made me irritable — I threw off the damp sheet and threw on my kimono while mumbling various expletives on my way to the door. Woodrow had the curiosity of a cat and I'd get no rest until I showed him that nothing was amiss.

"*Awwight, awweady!* I don't know what's so interesting out there, but *look,*" I said, throwing open the door to allow Woodrow to investigate. Like a brave little soldier he stepped out into the hall. He turned left, then right, and then looked up at disgruntled me. "Nothing! Nobody!" I hissed, as I blindly peered out into the dimly lit corridor. The hall was cooler than inside my room. I turned on my heel and stepped back in and like a stiff-jointed zombie I started for the window near my bed.

Although the knob was turned for a full blast of cool conditioned air, the result was no better than the fan circulating the hot air. Better to sleep with the window open, even if I woke up in the morning with a dusting of soot all over me. Better than to awaken drenched in sweat. I leaned over to pull up the window sash, but as I was about to yank the sticky frame upward, I saw reflected in the glass against the black night a peculiar glint of light and the fleeting glimpse of a figure passing in the hallway. I turned quickly to see who was standing at the threshold, but no one was there. *Probably a porter passing through*, I thought. I forced the window open, pulled down the screen, and then went to close my door, but not before peeking out into the hall to see who was out there: No one.

I heard a click, the sound of another door closing somewhere down and around the curved hallway in one of the compartments or the drawing-room. Perhaps a Harvard boy returning from using the men's lavatory, which was situated beyond the bank of bedrooms at the front of the car. I closed the door and went back to bed. The breeze through the window was an improvement over the insipid air from the vent, and I thought that if I laid in bed with only a sheet for a cover, I had a chance for sleep.

Before I drifted off to Dreamland there came a scratching noise at the door. I sat bolt-upright to scold the little bastard, but when I looked about the tiny room he was nowhere to be found. I'd left him out in the hall! Up from the bed, once more, throwing on the kimono, I opened the door. I spotted Woodrow's little rump turning the curve toward the drawing-room section of the car, and when I followed I saw that he was tailing a man down the hallway. The fellow made a gesture to shoo Woodrow away from his heels, but Woodrow only continued in pursuit.

"Woodrow, come here!" I commanded, and my dog froze. The man's attention turned to me for a second, and then he broke into a run, disappearing into the next car.

Head low, Woodrow made a slow, hesitant return, but not before my next-door neighbor, Mr. Benchley, stuck his head out to investigate.

"Is everything—"

"*Yes!*" I hissed. "*Go back to sleep!*" I said, rather rudely to my friend, who looked taken aback, and then confused. Shaking and then scratching his head, he blinked a couple of times, mumbled something under his breath, chuckled at some private joke, and then retreated to his room.

I ushered Woodrow back into mine and was about to close the door when I noticed that the door across the hall was slightly ajar. Aside from a fleeting impression that the lady with "my hat" had, like Mr. Benchley, peeked out to see what the fuss was all about, I dismissed further thought of knocking on her door. It was the middle of the night, no time for socializing, and I was determined to get another couple of hours of sleep before the Midnight Owl arrived at Grand Central Terminal. But sleep was not to be had.

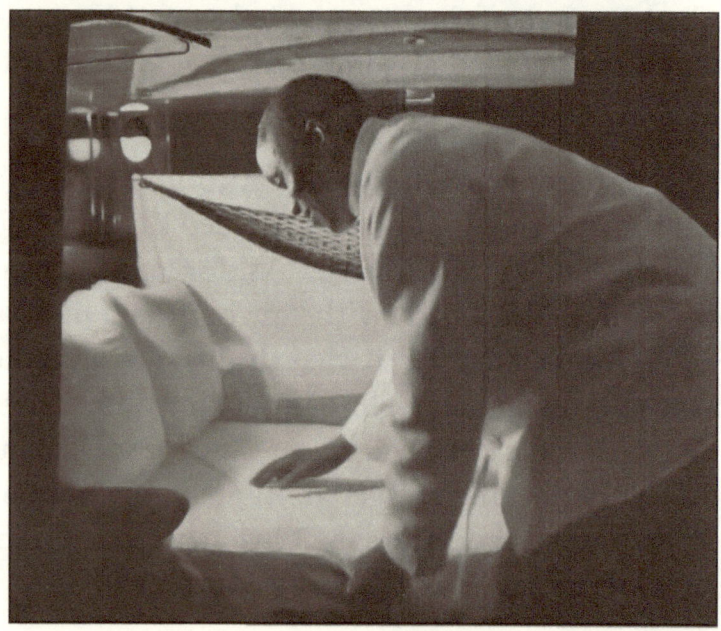

Our Pullman porter on the Midnight Owl

Chapter Three

It wasn't Woodrow this time, not at first.

It began with sounds like someone shuffling about, and then deep voices penetrated the edges of sleep. The train had stopped.

Soon, Woodrow joined in with excited yaps and leaps. My nerves were shot as I made for the door, this time leashing my little monster before venturing out into the hall.

My first thought was that we'd pulled into New York and the porter had failed to awaken me for the arrival. But the group of men hovering around my door and speaking in hushed tones stood in their night robes, and I realized we were still hours away from our destination, and that their interest was in the room across from mine.

Through squinting eyes I was about to growl "What the —" when a tousle-haired Mr. Benchley stuck his head out the door.

"Is everything—"

"How should I know?" I barked.

Silenced by contrition and meekly retreating behind the door, he was stopped by a ruddy-faced, burly-bellied man of fifty years who referred to a clipboard and asked, "Mr. Robert Benchley?"

"I think so," said my friend, noncommittally.

The big man persisted: "Are you, or are you not, Robert Benchley?"

"Last time I looked," he chuckled, and then seeing that his jaunty remark had not worked well to sweeten the sour expression on the face of the man who had addressed him, he said, "Yes."

The man nodded, studied what appeared to be a floor plan and passenger manifest on the clipboard, and then turned toward me. "Mrs. Parker, Dorothy Parker?"

"Who wants to know?"

"My name is Gum, and I'm a detective with the Pullman Company."

I was expecting to hear that there had been a complaint about Woodrow nipping at the heels of the passenger I'd seen earlier, but then I realized that the detective would not be conducting that kind of business at this hour of the night.

"Yes, yes. What is going on here?" I asked. "The commotion is disturbing Woodrow Wilson's sleep."

"Excuse me?" asked the detective.

"It's true, you know," put in Mr. Benchley. "Why, the racket's enough to raise Warren Harding from his eternal rest, too."

Heywood appeared, a pillow track creasing his face and as rumpled from sleep as from life in general. He didn't say anything, just tightened the sash of his robe. He might have been sleepwalking for all I knew, because he stood expressionless, his eyelids droopy, a silent, observing witness. Ruth came bustling to his side, chattering a dozen questions and complaints.

Roger Mellon joined the fray, offering his cigarette case around and lighting us all up. "I heard a fuss in the hall," he said. "Hermione is dead asleep, and I don't want her disturbed."

The Harvard boys snored behind closed doors, enjoying the deep slumber of stupefied minds.

"What is going on here?" asked Roger Mellon. "Somebody sick?"

But before he had his answer, the grim Gum turned to face an odd-looking little fellow, who was obviously a physician because he carried a black medical bag and wore a pince-nez that teetered on the tip of his nose and threatened to tumble off into his substantial moustaches. He had appeared, suddenly, from the room opposite mine, Bedroom Two, occupied by the lady with my hat.

Oh, shit! I thought. *The Hat Lady must have witnessed Woodrow's romp down the hall when she'd peeked out of her room earlier.*

After a quiet consultation with a conductor, and lots of frowning and nodding, the men appeared to reach a consensus. They turned to face me.

"*What?*" I whined, on the defensive, if not the offensive. I picked up Woodrow, expecting a scolding by the way the three men stared at us. If Woodrow had peed in the corridor, well, accidents happen, and there *were* other dogs on the train, weren't there? Any little package he—I mean, the *other* dog—might have dropped off—well . . .

"Who's the bellyacher turned us in?" I sputtered, throwing a glance at the door across the way. "Shit! You'd think someone had died, the way you're looking at us!"

"And, what, Mrs. Parker, do you know about it?" asked the corpulent detective.

"If I knew where Woodrow had done the dastardly deed—"

"I don't think Woodrow's behavior is in question, Dottie," said Roger.

"Well, why the third degree?"

"Was there a robbery?" asked Ruth.

"When someone is murdered—" said the detective.

"*Murdered!*" we all choked out *sotto voce*, as if uttering the word loudly might prove the heinous deed a reality.

Our neighbor, the elegant lady who had been wearing the coveted hat, lay dead behind the closed door, explained Detective Gum.

"But, she was alive—" I started to say.

"And now she's dead," corrected Gum, giving me the hairy eyeball of scrutiny. There are many types of hairy eyeballs, from the romantic to the accusatory. This one was most unpleasant.

The breeze created from the open window of my room and drawn into the hallway sent a shiver through me, although I was hot under the collar—that is, I would have been if I'd been wearing a collar.

"But, she was alive when I saw her—"

"No one is disputing that fact, my dear," consoled Mr. Benchley.

"But she's the one who has—had—*The Hat*," I said.

"And of course," acknowledged Mr. Benchley, "that should make perfect sense to the detective, should the question ever arise."

"What is the question?" asked a confused-looking Detective Gum.

"I suppose that query will eventually present itself in the *New England Journal of Medicine* or the

Podunk Chamber of Commerce monthly newsletter, or from the lips of Gertrude Stein," said my friend.

"I don't know what you are talking about."

"If it's any comfort, sir," said Mr. Benchley, "few people do."

The obtuse dialogue was making my head swim. "Will you both please shut up! You're getting me confused!"

Everybody looked at everybody else with incredulity.

"Dottie, remember *why* you got sent to jail in Boston, now," said Heywood, like a stuffy old father. "You really can't go around telling policemen to shut up, you know!"

"That's not why I went to jail, and you know it! I went to jail because I started the demonstration and because the feds told the police that Ruth and I—I mean—"

The detective's eyes took on a bovine expression of revelation. "Now, I recognize the name! You were the one—with that other dame—"

"Who are you calling a *dame!*" burst out Ruth, pushing through to stand in front of her brawny husband and assuming a defiant pose before the policeman.

"You two were the terrorists from New York sent to bomb the courthouse square," said Gum.

"That's what *they* thought, but not why I was hauled into jail!"

"But your scheme to bomb—"

"This is getting out of hand," interrupted Heywood, sweeping his little wife back behind him with a gentle gesture of his arm. "Dottie, the detective, here, is not interested in your terrorist activities or your rap sheet."

"I'll decide that," said Gum. "I'll have to take you aside for questioning, ma'am."

"But that was just a rumor, that we were bombers, probably started by one of those celebrities who wanted to get me and Ruth out of the way so they could hog the limelight! Now that I think of it, it *was* a rat that started the talk. I wouldn't put it past that nasty Edna Millay—"

"Vincent hasn't the imagination to think up anything so diabolical, Dottie," said Ruth.

"That's what you think. That dame—"

"But, I wouldn't put it past Aleck to have made the call just for a joke on us—"

Heywood jumped in: "Detective, why do you think the ladies had anything to do with a murder?"

"There's been a wire received that terrorists intend to bomb this train."

"*Ohhh!*" screeched Ruth, and there followed additional yelps from the elderly woman with the cane

I'd seen boarding earlier, and who had appeared from the room next to the Hat Lady's and across from Mr. Benchley's.

"Oh, my God, what did I start?" said Heywood. And then he and Mr. Benchley tried to explain to Gum that the women had not planned to bomb the train, and that we were just overwrought from the events of the past several weeks.

"What the hell do you mean, *overwrought*?" objected Ruth. "We're furious over what's transpired!"

"Enough to kill, I'll bet?" asked Gum.

"*You betcha!*" said Ruth. And then realizing what she'd admitted to, added, "figuratively speaking, of course!" And then she turned to me, "Wait 'til I get my hands around Aleck Woollcott's throat!"

"He's too fat for anyone to get their hands around his throat, Ruth! A gun will do the trick, though; remind me to get a gun, " I said, before addressing the detective. "We are nonviolent protesters! We don't need bombs," I assured the detective, who didn't appear assured of anything I might have to say.

Roger jumped in with a logical thought, asking, "Why would anyone, especially a trainload of anarchists, want to bomb the train they were riding on?"

"But I'm not an anarchist!" I objected. "But, even if I were, which I'm not, Mr. Mellon is right. I wouldn't put a bomb on a train I was riding on."

This point struck home for a brief moment, and the resulting silence gave Roger an opportunity to throw around the weight of his name and position as well as a short biographical summary supporting his importance in the world of our nation's defense. He had been one of the biggest arms manufacturers during the War, when he'd made his fortune by holding several government weapons contracts at the time. This fact did not appear to hold any weight with Detective Gum, however. The War was nearly ten years in the past, and Mellon's companies today were simply manufacturing steel bolts for bridges. To be fair, he did vouch for my patriotism and good character, laying it on a little bit too thick, I'd say, to be convincing.

"Well," said Gum, "we've got a bomb on this train and a woman who's been bludgeoned to death."

"*Ouch!*" screeched Ruth as she clutched her mouth. A pathetic little mewing sounded from the old lady, who nearly slipped off her cane upon hearing the word *bludgeoned*. Then again, the idea of a bomb could have sunk the old girl, too. Mr. Benchley reached for her elbow to steady her.

"Excuse me, everyone," said Roger. "I need to check on my wife; she has not been well and she gets excitable—"

"Yes, all right, but if it would not be too upsetting and she can answer a few questions—"

"I will see if she is awake, Detective." And with that Roger reentered his drawing-room. He almost immediately stuck his head around the curve in the hall to say, "She's just getting dressed," before he rejoined us.

The famous socialist had joined our little pajama party, having overheard our discussion; he looked very serious and stated that the train must be searched.

"A search is being conducted," assured Gum, and with that there appeared a policeman from the bedroom of the deceased woman.

"I've found a package, addressed to the court-house on Center Street, sir," he said nervously to the detective, pointing into the room from whence he came. "I hear clicking noises."

And from whence I stood I could peer around the figures of the policemen and the doctor and into the room, where I glimpsed sticking out from under a bloodied sheet the foot of the dead woman, and an outstretched arm whose hand uncannily appeared to be pointing to a brown-paper-wrapped package the size of a shoebox protruding from under the bed.

"We'll have to evacuate the train immediately," ordered Gum to a conductor standing a little distance away.

"Wait, Detective!" said Roger with a nervous smile. "There may not be a lot of time. If you do that—well, you'll alarm the other passengers and there may be panic, you understand?"

"We can't very well throw the damn thing out a window!"

"No! Let me open it, see if I can defuse the bomb."

"That's too risky."

"I'm experienced with this sort of thing—at least let me try!"

"Where?"

Roger looked around. "It's too dark outside—men's lavatory, I should think—"

"What if you can't—"

"If I can't stop it, I'll be able to get it off the train fast, away from the tracks. The car ends right next to the bathroom. Have the conductor open the gate—on the wooded side of the tracks, far away from any houses, please, just in case. I need a penknife—anyone?"

Mr. Benchley offered his own handy tool, the Swiss army knife that has got us in and out of lots of jams, while Detective Gum ordered his man to follow and assist Roger in his mission. The conductor prepared the exit from the car.

The silence was unnerving. The policeman carefully carried the parcel from the room and handed it to Roger. No one spoke as he made his way slowly along the corridor to the lavatory and the conductor set about his duties. Those of us who'd gathered in the hall began walking to get off the train at the other end of the car. Detective Gum was about to awaken the Harvard boys, his fist ready for a knock on their door, when the officer reappeared with a big grin and his youth restored to say the bomb had been defused.

Roger came out of the lavatory, wiping his brow with one handkerchiefed hand while cradling the opened parcel in the other, the brown paper still clinging to the box, the interior wiring and components like the disemboweled guts of a strange machine. Applause greeted him, and the women discovered a new hero. "This package would never have exploded. It was not a real bomb, no explosives in it."

"But it was ticking," I said, a little numb from the idea that death could be just a door away, across a narrow hall. *And I had planned my suicide for today. Someone almost beat me to it!*

After a moment to contemplate that averted tragedy, there came accolades and back slapping from the men and adoring glances from the ladies.

Just think, I said solemnly to myself: *It might have all been over for me. No longer would I have had to decide between the razor blade or the sleeping pills, the window ledge or the shotgun.* I was angry, not for the missed chance to end my miserable life, but for the reason that I didn't want someone else deciding for me *when* I would leave this life! Anyway, I wasn't certain I wanted to leave. But it was an alternative. I was always a little curious about what I'd miss the day *after* my suicide.

I broke the spell. "Who was the dead woman in Bedroom Two?"

"We cannot give you that information," said Detective Gum. "The woman's family must be notified before that can be revealed."

"But, who could have killed her?" I said.

"Need I remind you that you, yourself, said you would kill for that hat—"

"Ruth!" shouted Heywood, and his wife bit her lip.

There followed a series of questions for the gang milling about in the hallway: Where was I, where was he, where was anybody at any time during the evening? Who saw whom? Who heard what? Who said that, and to whom? You were where? What time was that? You left your room? Stayed in all night? Who saw you there? Were you alone?

And then I had to explain about *The Hat*. The detective lifted his eyes toward Heaven as I briefly relayed a few details of the shopping trip with Jane, and how I loved the hat that had floated dreamily by on the head of a faceless woman, the veil draping her, a few hours earlier.

"If there was a hat, as you describe, it's not in the room," said Gum.

"No hat! Then perhaps it's a different woman I saw. But I could swear she entered this room. Yes;

I am certain it was She of The Hat. The porter saw her in; he might remember the hat."

"Maybe the killer took it."

"It was a lovely thing . . . " I mused. "A coincidence that the bomb you were warned about was a fake and found in the dead woman's room," I said. "That ticking sound probably woke her up. I'm not making a joke—it just struck me. Who discovered her?"

"The porter found her."

"She probably caught the fellow trying to plant the real bomb and he killed her," suggested Ruth.

"But, why was it planted in her room?" asked Mr. Benchley, mostly to himself. "Perhaps she had something to do with it?"

"Maybe she made the real bomb, or was going to *plant* the bomb, or maybe even she *found* the bomb! And then the bomber tried to get it back and he had to kill her!" said Ruth. She was on a roll: "And then, maybe someone came by, and he feared discovery, and never got to—I just lost my train of thought!"

"Could it have been—" I said, and then caught my tongue. All eyes turned questioningly toward me. "Well, you see, Woodrow was out in the corridor."

"Who? Woodrow?" said Gum, scanning the manifest. "There's no one on the train by that name."

"But of course there is—"

"Don't be an Airedale!" came a familiar, if annoying phrase, before appeared the glamorous Hermione, leaning into the crowded hall, supported by her husband. "Woodrow Wilson."

"But, he's—"

"Yes, dead," chimed in Mr. Benchley. "But not *that* one—*this* one," he said, patting Woodrow's head.

Gum rolled his eyes and shook his head. "The dog?"

"Yes," I said, "my dog."

"What does your dog have to do with anything?"

"Woodrow may have actually frightened off the killer. When I followed him—"

"You were following the—"

"Woodrow, yes. I mean, no! Woodrow was doing the following."

"And who was—"

"Woodrow—"

"—following?"

"Yes, who was the dog—"

"I don't know who he was."

"You don't know who *who* was?

"The fellow whom Woodrow was following."

"I don't get the joke," said Gum.

"There was nothing funny about it, Detective. After we heard the knocking the second time—" I said.

"You mean there was a first time?"

"Well, for there to be a second time, there would have to be a first time, of course," said Hermione.

"That's true," said Mr. Benchley. "There was knocking both the first and the second time."

"And you heard it, too?" asked the detective.

"Why, yes," said Mr. Benchley, "and I came to see what all the knocking was about, but Mrs. Parker yelled at me, so I went back to sleep."

"I heard the knocking, too," said the elderly woman, whose name we were to learn was Miss Meriwether, a longtime-retired teacher on her way to New York to visit her niece.

"All right, now let me get this straight: You heard knocking—"

"Twice," I nodded, as did Miss Meriwether.

"I was asleep," said Mr. Benchley. "I sleep soundly, you see, so I didn't—"

"I didn't hear anything," said the famous socialist.

"And you investigated the cause of the knocking, is that right?" the detective asked me.

"Yes, and the second time, Woodrow didn't follow me back into my room. Instead, he scratched on the door."

"And?"

"Well, when I got out of bed for the twentieth time to let him in, he was running down the hall, following the man."

"Ah! Now we're getting somewhere. And this man?"

"He looked frightened, I thought, as if Woodrow was going to bite him."

"Did he?"

"What? Bite him? Hell, no. Woodrow only bites on command, or when we are playing 'Hail me a cab, Woodrow!'"

"I see," said the detective, shaking his head as if to clear it, "but not really. Back up a bit and give me the details, please."

"Well, 'Hail me a cab, Woodrow!' is often the only way I can get a cab in the city. I give the command and Woodrow sets to motion—Mr. Benchley and Aleck Woollcott trained him to do it, isn't that right, Fred?—"

"Who's Fred?"

"Oh, that's Mr. Benchley. Sometimes I call him 'Fred.'"

"All right, never mind the names you call each other."

"*Fred*'s not so bad; you should hear some of the other names people call me," said Fred.

"Please answer the question," said Gum in a huff.

Mr. Benchley smiled, puffed up proudly, chuckled, and said, "It's a matter of distraction, you see: Woodrow does a little figure-eight run around the victim—I mean around the man trying to grab a taxi—nipping at one trouser cuff and then at the other." He made a swimming figure-eight with his hand in demonstration. "This allows Mrs. Parker to grab the taxi door and hop in before the victim—I mean, the mark—I mean the *fellow*—realizes that the cab is occupied."

"Oh, *wha-da clevva wittle doggie Wood-wow is!*" said Guess Who?

"It takes hours of training to achieve a precision performance," added Mr. Benchley, proud tutor to his star pupil.

"Would you like to see how he does it, Detective? If you'll stand right where you are, and Mr. Benchley will stand there, I'll give the command: *Woodrow! Fetch me a cab!*"

"*No!*" shouted an irritable Gum as Woodrow began corralling the men's feet and nipping at their trouser cuffs.

"There's a natural herding instinct in that pup," said Heywood, as the others moved back to make room for the maneuvering. "Unusual for his breed, don't you think, Detective Gum?"

"I *meant* continue telling me the details of what you saw this evening, Mrs. Parker, not the details of the education of your Airedale."

"Don't be an Airedale, Detective, he's a Boston terrier," corrected the maddening Hermione, who hooted encouragement: "What other tricks have you taught him, Dot?"

I could see that the detective was not amused, so I picked up my little devil and decided to be more helpful, although I really had nothing more to tell that might prove useful.

"Let's get back on track, all right? From the beginning, please."

"I heard tapping sounds, like someone knocking on a door, not my door necessarily, but *a* door, nonetheless."

"And then?"

"Woodrow growled and I knew he wouldn't be satisfied that nothing was wrong until I opened the door and let him see for himself that nothing was wrong."

"And then?"

"I got back into bed and fell back to sleep—"

Mr. Benchley cut in. "Back up a minute: Was that when I peeked out my door?"

"No, that was the second time."

"Wait. I thought you said—" said Mr. Benchley, "that Woodrow was scratching at your door. Wouldn't that make three times?"

"No. There were *two* incidents of knocking and *one* incident of scratching. It was after the second time—or was it the first—now I'm getting confused— that I noticed the woman's bedroom door was ajar."

My friend scratched his head, the others sighed, and Detective Gum lost it. *"Everyone just shut up!"* The steam released, he said, "You, Mrs. Parker. What did you see?"

"Well, the door to her room was open, just slightly ajar. I thought she must have been peeking out, too, to see what all the fuss was about. I thought for a moment about pulling the door shut, and then realized it was not my door to close. Do you think she was lying there, dead, all that time?"

The order of events was sorted out, and after giving a description of the fellow whom Woodrow had pursued, I was asked to be available to the Detective and the police at our arrival in New York City to identify the apparent killer from the disembarking passengers. Then we were told to return to our respective rooms.

"I hear my husband was a hero tonight!" said Hermione, gazing up lustily at her husband.

What a catch—rich and a hero! I wondered if he

was any good in bed, too. I suppose rich *and* a hero might just be enough for some women.

"Detective, keep this quiet, please," said Roger. I don't want it getting around town—out to the press or anything. It'll just make our lives hell, and my wife, here—"

"As you wish, sir!" said Gum, with overdone admiration just short of clicking his heels and saluting the millionaire. *All right, he did save the day, I suppose.*

"I will instruct my men to keep this evening's events confidential. But, we will be in touch concerning particulars about the construction of the bomb if it becomes necessary to do so, you understand?"

On a train filled with reporters, and columnists like Heywood Broun among them, how was this story to remain untold? Funny, but Roger didn't even look over at Heywood, who was standing right next to him, when he made his request. False modesty? Half-a-dozen people, from the conductor to the engineer to little old Mrs. Meriwether, had seen him in action. Did he really expect that no one would retell the exciting episode of murder and terrorism on a train, if only to bask in the bystander's glory of having been witness to the event?

Within half an hour the train was again moving at a fast clip toward New York City, after a thorough but unfruitful search of the cars for the suspected murderer. It was assumed that, at the time that the body of the woman in Bedroom Two was discovered by the porter, and the train had been stopped a few miles north of Westport, the culprit must have fled from the train.

Mr. Benchley and I were more than a bit shaken by the events of the evening and having experienced the high drama of the failure to stay the anarchists' executions, so we dressed and packed our night bags and joined the equally strung-out Brouns in their compartment for the last hour of our journey.

———◆———

The porter brought us coffee, which we improved upon with the contents from Mr. Benchley's hip flask.

Mr. Benchley said: "The murderer must be part of a band of conspirators, because someone had to have sent the wire to this train from elsewhere."

"Perhaps, but why that kind of distraction?" asked Ruth. "The murderer merely brought attention to the crime sooner than was necessary. The woman's body might not have been found until the train reached New York, or not until after the bomb had gone off at Grand Central as planned. Someone was trying to stop the crime!"

"It might not be that obvious. The train had to be stopped on some pretext," said Heywood.

"—so that the murderer could hop off!" said Mr. Benchley.

"*Before* we pulled into Grand Central. Get off the train where he could find shelter in the woods around Westport or thereabouts," nodded Heywood.

"Any closer to a big town boasting a large police force would have increased his odds of getting caught," said Mr. Benchley.

"And considering this train has a cargo of what the politicians are calling 'bomb-throwing *arnycists*,' how else to stop a train heading into Manhattan but with the knowledge that a bomb was on board ready to take down Grand Central Terminal and kill God-knows-how-many people? With what better threat do you stop a train in its tracks?" said Ruth.

"A herd of cattle? A gander of geese? A brace of pheasant? A klatch of coffee?"

"That's enough, Mr. Benchley."

"I don't feel comfortable about pointing a finger at the Italian man Woodrow followed. The fellow may have just been taking a stroll through the cars. Perhaps he couldn't sleep. There could be a dozen reasons why he was passing through the hall at that time. Why, we've just come from protesting the unjust death sentences of a couple of men who were tried and convicted on circumstantial evidence. I won't be party to another anarchist witch-hunt."

"Well, the point is that the culprit probably bolted from the train when it was stopped," said Mr. Benchley, "if that's any comfort."

The Midnight Owl entered the tunnel on Upper Park Avenue in Manhattan, signaling our imminent arrival at Grand Central.

Bartolomeo Vanzetti and Nicola Sacco

Chapter Four

I was escorted off the train by Detective Gum, with Mr. Benchley close behind and the Brouns fending for themselves and seeing to our luggage, the purpose being for me to stand watch alongside the one ramp that led up to the concourse, the other exits having been closed off from the stream of departing passengers for our review. New York City policemen, several with bomb-sniffing German shepherds, were awaiting the train's arrival, having been wired ahead of the crime committed and the possibility of a real bomb on board the train.

The crowd ascending the ramp was a heterogeneous mix of the cultural and economic classes befitting a city as diverse as New York. But, too, in this crowd the majority of people possessed a political bent that under ordinary circumstances would not have been so obvious.

Many of the socialists bore the carelessly dressed air of the Bohemian. Whether this was an intentional affectation, I cannot say for certain except, perhaps, they were expressing their disdain for our consumer society. They looked hungry, feral, and reckless. The deliberate costuming coupled with a predatory gaze to some diminishing point far off in the distance gave these characters an air of martyrdom, a die-for-the-cause aspect. These poorly recompensed, underfed labor organizers and activists were soldiers always marching purposefully toward the next battleground.

As for the anarchists, most were blessed with the dark, soulful faces right out of Caravaggio masterpieces, their dark, arched brows and long thin noses refined through centuries of Italian ancestry. These were mostly immigrants, some laborers, whose fathers had dug the subway tunnels or built the great hand-hewed Croton Dam in Westchester County—men who knew the backbreaking work of the pickaxe. They walked by me in their Sunday suits, shiny and frayed with age and wear, with dignity. They were cleanly shaven, moustaches groomed, collars gleaming, shoes buffed to a shine even though the polish brought attention to the cracks across the toe leather or to the tilt of worn heels. These men set their brows with a look of determination, too, but just as the cracks along their shiny leather boots gave evidence of their poverty, so did their feelings of last night's defeat shine through their eyes.

One doesn't distinguish the anarchist from the socialist from the capitalist so easily while watching passersby on the street. But this train was packed with the politically charged, coming from an event that was politically charged. They moved like separate schools of fish, the anarchists, the socialists, and a sprinkling of the devil-may-care capitalists weaving their way through the hoi polloi, flashing their Brooks Brothers linen suits and Hattie Carnegie accessories to the disgust or envy of their fellow man. And those capitalists included the Roger Mellons, who, with an entourage that greeted them as they stepped from the car, were shielded as they were whisked away up the ramp. Hermione was blowing me a kiss off her lavender-gloved little hand, and braying, like a Cockney Music Hall chorine across her audience, "See you a week from Friday, Dot!" before turning to pose for the newspaper photographers who were shooting in great puffs and flashes for the society pages. As the passengers filed through, I felt not unlike a general reviewing his haggard troops.

And then I saw the Italian man who was the alleged suspect, hat low over his brow and clutching his small valise as he approached inconspicuously toward the ramp. His eyes cut to the left, caught mine, and then quickly darted away. In that split-second of visual contact much had been discussed between us. Had he held my gaze a moment or two longer I would have believed he was a criminal. But, for some reason, in just that short glance, I knew he was not guilty of any crime. A decision had been made; whether for good or for bad I was not to know for some time.

Detective Gum, alert and scrutinizing, had to be distracted, so I turned to look behind us, standing on my toes, as if I had at last recognized the fellow I had sought to identify walking up the ramp. I quickly dropped my purse, and as Gum bent down to retrieve it, I conspired with Mr. Benchley, who nodded and then moved around us to depart in the flow of ascending passengers.

"It's been grand, Mrs. Parker, but I have to be on my way. Late, I'm late, for a very important date—the Brouns will see you home. *Ta-ta!*"

Jeez! I said under my breath. *Ta-ta? Did he really say ta-ta?*

And when Gum asked me to repeat what I had said, I answered, "—that fellow! The one passed us in the straw boater."

"Which one? There are dozens of men with those hats."

"Exactly!"

The flow of people was thinning, and as the last of the stragglers cleared the platform I turned to Gum and said, "I suppose he got off the train when it stopped in Westport or thereabouts."

Before the detective could reply, our attention was drawn toward the dogs coming out from the Pullman cars, their police officers at the ends of taut leashes. No bomb had been found, the police lieutenant was told, and then through the chain of command informed Gum, just as the rubber-bagged corpse of the dead woman in Bedroom Two was carried out on a stretcher. The Coroner addressed the lieutenant with his findings: "Bludgeoned."

As if we didn't know.

———◆———

When Woodrow and I arrived home and I checked at the front desk for messages, atop the score of sheets was one from Mr. Benchley asking me to come to his rooms across the street immediately.

I was anxious to find out if he had spoken with the Italian man I had sent him to follow, and why in Heaven's name he was going around saying *ta-ta*. So I fed and watered Woodrow and, leaving my valises unpacked by the door, departed from my rooms to traipse across the street to see what was so urgent it couldn't wait.

Mr. Benchley keeps rooms at the Royalton, the bachelor hotel directly across the street from the Algonquin Hotel, where I live and where I lunch with my famous friends. We have been dubbed the *Algonquin Round Table*. We call ourselves *The Vicious Circle*, a name I sort of thought up, because we often ruthlessly and generously toss vitriol around regarding lots of things that we encounter in our work, and that includes people. That's what we critics do when we can't find anything nice to say about a play on

Broadway that we've reviewed or a book that's just been published that really stinks, or an actor who should have chosen another profession. When we love something or someone, we of the Round Table like to shout it from the rooftops through Aleck Woollcott's column, or Frank Pierce Adams's, or Heywood Broun's, or Robert Benchley's, or, of course, my own bylines in various publications. And those brilliant people that we do love and admire have often become precious members of our little circle, like Harpo Marx and Helen Hayes and Irving Berlin and George S. Kaufman, Edna Ferber, Jascha Heifitz, and Tallulah Bankhead, and the wonderful acting couple, Alfred Lunt and Lynn Fontanne.

We've been meeting for lunch most days at one o'clock since 1919, and we have become more than just friends; we are family. And like members of any family, we have our disagreements, our petty fights, our nasty moments. But, at the end of the rants and the grudges and the day, we come together, because the truth is we love, admire, and depend on each other. Being summer, and all the theatres closed (meaning there is scant stuff to attend and review until the fall), we are scattered about—Aleck on his island on Lake Bomoseen in Vermont, wielding a croquet mallet while holding court over vacationing friends, mostly Round Tablers, and others traipsing about the Cote d'Azur at the hospitality of the Gerald Murphys, or, having survived tagging behind Hemmingway through the

Pamplona Bull Run, enjoying the relative tranquility of an English countryside summer.

While the Algonquin is a rather warm and cheerful place, in spite of its dignified wood-paneled Edwardian interior with its palms trees and plush furnishings, the lobby of the Royalton has the uninviting air of a Dickensian Workhouse. One expected to see Uriah Heep lurking about, and he was there, all right, slumped behind the desk when I entered through the lobby door. As I whisked past the ugly little man for the elevator, I cut him off before he could ask my business by saying that Mr. Benchley expected me. He made a small croaking sound, an ineffectual effort to halt my progress, and then, with a look of alarm, picked up the telephone, most likely calling up to the room to alert an unsuspecting Mr. Benchley of the imminent intrusion on his privacy.

So for this my friend had given up his perfectly fine rooms at the Gonk? I thought, as I went up in the elevator. Enforced discipline, it was!

A while back, Mr. Benchley had made his home-away-from-home in an apartment on Madison Avenue that he shared with Charles MacArthur, and later, at the Algonquin, as the need for a weekday residence had become a necessity during the time he headlined on Broadway in Irving Berlin's *Music Box Revue of 1924*. Taking the train after evening performances to return to the home he shared with his wife, Gertrude, and their small sons in Scarsdale proved exhausting.

His schedule was grueling and resulted in his being in a sad state of health for a time. So an apartment in Manhattan seemed the best solution. When he and Charlie gave up the apartment, Mr. Benchley took rooms at the Algonquin, even though the run of the show was over, because he became theatre editor of *Life* magazine, a position that required his reviewing the opening nights on Broadway for the rag—as many as a dozen plays or movies every week. But there was a problem: The Thanatopsis Literary and Inside Straight Club—an ongoing poker game of Round Tablers—met on Saturday nights in a room on the floor below. There were also the many after-luncheon and after-theatre cocktail-party shenanigans going on in my rooms, or in Tallulah's, or in any of the rooms of the Round Tablers who happened to be residing at the hotel.

My friend would sit down at his desk to work, crank a sheet of paper through the roller, fingers poised at the keys of his Royal and about to diligently write the review of the previous evening's play or that humorous piece for Harold Ross's *New Yorker*, when, as he searched the ceiling for the opening sentence, there would drop into his head the idea that he was missing something that was going on down in the lobby. *Wasn't Coward in town? Didn't Mrs. Parker say that F. Scott was stopping by for a drink today after a meeting with his editor, Max Perkins? Wonder what the stakes are in the game downstairs? Aleck said Swope was playing tonight . . . .*

Ten minutes, twenty would pass, maybe an hour without a key-stroke to mar the pristine white glare of the stationery. He had to start somewhere, so he'd type in *T-h-e*.

The! The perfect start! *T-h-e!* Such articles eventually lead to nouns and verbs with a spattering of adjectives here and there, and it's a good place to start!

Ten minutes later, after a flurry of activity that had him twisting and turning about the room like a whirling dervish—pouring a drink, arranging his sharpened pencils according to length across the desk—he would leap head-first into an ocean of contemplation on the philosophical insight of a Schopenhauer quote as the possible explanation he'd been looking for all these years to describe the astonishing success of *Abie's Irish Rose*. This play was considered by Mr. Benchley and other critics to be the greatest abomination ever to open on Broadway. Yes! That was it! Schopenhauer said it more than sixty years ago, the reason that damn show won't ever close: "All truth passes through three stages. First, it is ridiculed. Second, it is violently opposed. Third, it is accepted as being self-evident."

From the profound he would leap to the profane: *Why are those birds making such a racket out there? Don't forget to return the telephone call from George! What was the Christian name of the second Duke of Wellington?* Time to take a break, to clear the mind, to let those next good words take form.

So down to the lobby he would go to see whatever it was he might be missing. An hour later, if the gang didn't move on to a tour of the speaks, he'd determinedly return to his work, refreshed by drink and socialization. He'd sit at his desk, rub his hands together, look up toward the ceiling for inspiration, fingers hovering over the keys, and the Muses would mischievously lodge a splinter in his brain: *Charlie* [MacArthur] *and Sherry* [Robert Sherwood] *are meeting Bunny* [Edmund Wilson] *at Tony's* [Tony Soma's speakeasy]*!*

Swiftly typing *E-N-D*, Mr. Benchley had, for the present, completed the opening and closing words and was now free to gallivant about town for the rest of the evening.

One day, after our one-o'clock luncheon, Mr. Benchley took Frank Case, the Gonk's owner and manager, aside. "I'm giving up my rooms here, Frank."

"Oh, Bob, we'll miss you!"

"Oh, I don't know," smiled my friend. He laughed and kicked his foot in an *awww-shucks* kind of way. "I'm going to miss being here, but I've no recourse."

"Hollywood?"

"No more of that, no. I'm moving across the street to the Royalton."

"Bob, I don't understand," said Frank, his eyebrows raised like a tent, his mouth a horseshoe. He shifted from one foot to the other, probing Mr.

Benchley's face. "Is it our service that you don't like? Is it—"

"The service is great, Frank; that's not it."

"Well, what can I do to get you to stay?"

"I just can't get any work done here."

"Is there too much noise on your floor, the other residents perhaps? Well, I'll see to it—"

"No, no, no, Frank, it's not noisy."

"Privacy? Ah, I see," said Frank with a great sigh. "That can be dealt with. I will make sure that you are never disturbed when you are working! No one will be allowed to go up to your rooms—"

Mr. Benchley cut him off. "You may be able to keep them from coming up, but you can't keep me from going down." And so the move across the street.

Of course there were only a few yards' distance between the Gonk and the bachelor hotel, and that didn't really stop anyone, especially Mr. Benchley, from walking across the street.

The door to Mr. Benchley's room was open, as Uriah had indeed called up a warning.

"His name is Giusto," said Mr. Benchley, indicating the young Italian huddling in the corner of the couch. "In Italian that means *justice*."

I nodded, and wondered if the name given by the Italian was actually given him at birth or adopted with his cause.

"Did anyone see you take him from the station?" I asked.

"The kidnapping, you mean?" said Mr. Benchley, with raised eyebrows. "He came willingly enough, but then, it's not wise to wrestle with such a formidable figure as Heywood Broun," he added, "or Ruth Hale, for that matter. Perhaps the Mellons saw us, because they waved *ta-ta* as they climbed into one of their limousines."

"What's with this *ta-ta* crap, Fred?"

"You don't complain when Aleck bandies it about."

"Aleck is a pretentious—" I stopped in midsentence as my eye went to the new addition in the apartment: a tobacco-store Indian by the front door.

Upon entering, one is impressed—or should I say, smacked in the face?—with décor reminiscent of a French whorehouse of decidedly Victorian embellishments, so much so that a friend stole the beaded curtain from a Parisian Bordello for a housewarming gift to Mr. Benchley to complete the look. It brazenly hangs as a testament to bad taste between the living room and the bedroom alcove. But then, everyone had been bringing junk—I mean, *items*—to help furnish the little apartment. Mr. Benchley has simply chosen to enhance the nineteenth-century features — the dark woodwork and diamond-shaped casement windows — by draping everything in red. Red-velvet curtains keep out all daylight and exterior distractions, if not the bone-piercing assault of sirens from the fire station on 43rd Street, and the pigeons that torment his early mornings; red tablecloth, chairs, and rugs keep the theme flowing, and if you were in any doubt about the design period, three framed portraits of Queen Victoria hang between the windows to set you straight. Green student lamps brighten the space and keep the ambiance cozy rather than manic. Bookcases line the walls, floor to ceiling, with volumes bought for their titles alone — *Talks on Manure, In and Out with Maryanne, Keeping a Single Cow, Diseases of the Sweet Potato,* and, of course, my favorite treatise, *Perverse Pussy.* Once, when I opened a closet door in search of a corkscrew, there was revealed the true intellectual life of my friend: Stacked behind the mess of household items was a bookshelf filled with the works of the great philosophers and poets, and histories of the world, which he keeps hidden from the world at large.

And so, when word was out that Mr. Benchley had moved to an unfurnished apartment and was in need of the various necessities to fill a household, there began a competition of sorts among his friends to do just that — fill his apartment. These outlandish friends saw fit to provide only the outlandish. Forget the simple pot or pan, the toaster, the broom, the can opener, the odd lamp or side table. No! Instead, didn't

Sweet Old Bob ("S.O.B." as he was often called) need a stuffed fox terrier from the taxidermist's shop, bought for a song because it had seen better days and wasn't molting too badly? And as a companion piece, why not get the raccoon, too? It's not that tatty. Surely, Bob would appreciate a hitching post? Perhaps he would find inspiration from a bust of Sir Walter Raleigh? And who didn't need a flight of stairs leading to the ceiling? Upon entering for the first time, Noel Coward proclaimed it "Bob's little rose bower."

"I wanted things I could use," said my friend, weeping into his gin (he never cared for beer). "I didn't say that I was starting a whaling museum," he had said plaintively one night at Tony's. "I have a terrible premonition they are going to drag around a Pullman car and ask me to give it a home."

He got rid of most of the junk, but kept the cello and music stand brought by a friend to whom he'd confided that he "would like to learn to play the cello, someday." And although he has not touched the instrument since it entered the apartment three years ago, his cleaning lady keeps it dusted and at the ready.

Mr. Benchley bade me enter. "As I was saying, according to his passport, his name is Giusto Maggiorani—"

I followed his eyes as they moved to rest on the Italian who sat, hat in hand, on the blue sofa. The man looked at me with a wary-eyed expression, a look commonly worn by many newly arrived immigrants trying to fend for themselves in this strange new world of New York City. If dealing with the English language wasn't enough, there were plenty of other hazards to contend with, lots of shysters in the shadows ready to pounce. Most immigrants had family members or friends in America who sponsored them, a family to live with, people who had arrived years before and could ease the newly arrived toward assimilation into American society. But for all the reasons of his rather tentative appearance, I wondered if he was quite alone in this country. Considering how he was hustled into a cab by strangers, perhaps he thought we were white slavers who'd abducted him. When he opened his mouth to speak, out came a flood of words in Italian.

I smiled, and said the only pleasant Italian word I knew, other than the expletive I have been called on several occasions, but that is another story.

"Aqua?" I said, maintaining the smile and indicating with my hand a glass of water brought up to my lips.

"*Si, si! Per favore!*"

Mr. Benchley filed a glass with ice and spritzed the seltzer bottle handle. He handed the glass to the man, who thirstily gulped it down.

There was a knock at the door, and Mr. Benchley revealed our socialist friend from the train, explaining, "We shared a cab from the station. And to my surprise, he speaks fluent Italian."

"I see he is holding the bag," I said.

Our socialist friend sauntered in through the cluttered foyer and placed the grocery bag on the table. From it he extracted donuts and paper cups filled with coffee, which he handed around. Then, he sat down next to the young Italian, who took a bite of a donut. "He's already professed his innocence, Bob."

"Yes, and I believe him, but for no reason that is more than a feeling. But the fact is Mrs. Parker saw him right outside the room of the murdered woman, whose bedroom door was ajar—"

"We asked him on the way here in the cab, Bob. He doesn't deny that he entered the woman's room."

"But, why? If he didn't know her, *why* was he in her room?"

The socialist turned to the now-sated young man, who was wiping away donut crumbs from his mouth with his handkerchief while never taking his eyes from us.

In Italian he asked, "Giusto, you said that you never saw the murdered woman before, but why had you entered her bedroom?"

"*Mi ha chiesto di venire al suo compartimento.*"

"She asked him to come to her compartment. So, you knew the woman?"

"*No! Poverina. Mi ha parlato prima di salire sul treno.*"

"He said the poor dead woman spoke to him while he was waiting to board the train."

"*Essa ha pagato per il mio biglietto.*"

"She paid his fare."

The young man pulled a ten-dollar bill from his coat pocket to show us. He placed it in the palm of his interpreter, closed the fellow's fingers around the bill, and with a gesture of wiping his hands, spoke in Italian in the face of Mr. Benchley's and my blank expressions.

"He was just doing what she asked him to do. She gave him ten dollars and promised fifty more at delivery." The socialist pressed the money back into Giusto's hand.

"Yes, but what was it he was supposed to do?" asked Mr. Benchley, preparing gin-and-tonics as a coffee chaser.

After several questions and answers between them, our socialist friend turned to us. "She asked him to call at her room at three A.M. for a package he was to pick up from her and later to deliver after arriving in New York. When he arrived at her door, he found it open and she was lying there, dead."

"So, the package he was to get from her and deliver in New York contained a fake bomb?" I asked.

"Now," interrupted Mr. Benchley, "that makes

no sense at all! Why would anyone in their right mind accept a package that was ticking? An Italian? Looking like he's stepped right off the boat? Riding a streetcar through Manhattan with a ticking package? On the morning after the executions? Only a fool would be so stupid! Or an anarchist."

I had to laugh, although it was not really a laughing matter: People of all nationalities promised to be out on the streets in protest all over my city and in cities throughout the world if the executions were not stayed. And it was bad enough that these poor people were the victims of discrimination all over the country, accused of violent anarchistic ties, even when most were law abiding and hard working, yearning for better lives in the country that advertised streets paved with gold!

"Well, he is one."

"One what?" I asked.

"An anarchist."

"*Si! Io sono un anarchic.*"

"Yes, of course you are," I said sarcastically, knowing he didn't understand a word I was saying. I looked up at Mr. Benchley. "What have we gotten ourselves into?"

"You mean, what have *you* gotten us into, don't you, my dear Mrs. Parker? I was only following your instructions to follow him. I was doing *your* bidding."

"I never said to take him home!"

"That's spilt milk, and all that!"

"I no bomb, no hurt no one."

"Ah, he does understand!"

"Not much," said our socialist friend. "But he knows enough to deny violent activity. All who embrace anarchistic philosophy are accused of purporting violence. And you know that isn't always the case. Didn't we just come from the executions of two innocent men?"

"If you're going to begin an exegesis on the topic for my benefit—"

"I'm sorry; you're right. But he had no idea what the package looked like, or what was in it, or to whom he was to deliver it. He never got further than checking to see if the woman in Bedroom Two was still alive, and then when he heard you at your door he bolted."

"Should we consider espionage, here?" I said.

"I see what you're getting at: Why else choose a fellow at random, if what Giusto says is true, and I think it is. Why pay him to deliver a package? Would a spy trust a complete stranger for such a task? How can you know for sure that he is trustworthy, and will deliver the package?" said Mr. Benchley.

"A promise of fifty smackeroos upon delivery, don't forget. Maybe he was meant to be just a decoy," I said. "After all, there was that wire stating there was a bomb on the train, so maybe there was another bomb, yet to be delivered."

"Oh, so the intended courier could get through clean, while Giusto, here, was meant to be snagged."

"The package was wrapped, taped, and addressed, and yet wasn't even a real bomb. Surely it was a diversion, a decoy," I said.

"And yet, there is no reason to assume espionage had anything at all to do with the woman's murder," interjected our socialist friend.

"But, something she had—or knew—was important enough to kill for," said Mr. Benchley.

"And all we know for sure about the woman was that she sought out the services of this young man, knowing full well he did not really know his way around and could barely speak the language," I said. "The whole thing smells, if you ask me. Spy or not, she was up to no good, that's for sure."

"You've raised a good point: He can barely speak English," said Mr. Benchley, and with that our interpreter turned to ask the young Italian more questions.

"He says that when the woman approached him at South Station, she referred to a piece of paper, as if reading from it, and then handed it to him to read for himself," said the socialist.

"Does he still have her note?" I asked, and Giusto pulled a scrap of paper from his coat pocket to show me. "What does it say? I can't read Italian."

"Come to Bedroom Two in Car Seven at three A.M. to take a package for delivery at a New York address. Upon delivery you will be paid fifty dollars for your services."

"Well, the note suggests the woman knew she needed an Italian for the job and had anticipated a communication problem," I said.

"But the police didn't find anything other than some bomb components in her room, not a real bomb there or anywhere on the train. Giusto, here, hasn't anything on his person or in his suitcase to suggest he took anything else from the room."

"Perhaps he passed the package to someone on the train last night, after Woodrow and I saw him leaving the car?"

"It's possible," said Mr. Benchley, "but we searched him and he certainly hasn't fifty dollars, the promised payment, on him."

"Well, whoever killed her probably took the real bomb. Wherever it was to go we'll never know until it goes off, but it was worth it to someone to murder for it," I said.

"So, if this young man has been telling the truth, there are many possible scenarios: A delivery is still expected and the awaiting party is unaware of the murder of the woman on the train, or her accomplices killed her," said Mr. Benchley.

"Where there's one spy there are three more

lurking. I wouldn't be surprised if the news has already traveled around," said the socialist.

"Hey! Wait a minute!" I yelled, jumping up from my seat. "What if they think this young man actually picked up the package? Only the murderer would be sure of that, if he didn't find the package after murdering for it. What I mean is, wouldn't this young man be a target from both sides if anyone believes he successfully retrieved the package?"

"That's possible," agreed the socialist.

"*Whoa!*" jumped in Mr. Benchley. "We're making assumptions. We've scripted a little play with spies and espionage and two sides each ready to kill the other over obtaining government secrets or securing the plans for a new kind of weapon, when all that the woman probably wanted was for the fellow to pick up and deliver her dry cleaning!"

"You really know how to put a damper on things, Mr. Benchley!" I said, the wind sucked out of my sails. "You've no romance, Fred, not an inkling!"

"Who's 'Fred'?"

"It's what Mrs. Parker affectionately calls me when I've scolded her and taken her toys away. She thinks it'll soften me up. It usually does, you know," laughed my friend, before turning all serious once again: "Of course, there is still the possibility that the object of intended delivery was of some importance to someone. I suggest we wait and find out more about the dead woman and who comes to claim her body *and* belongings."

"Do you think we can find out from Sgt. Joe?" I said.

"Who's this 'Joe'?" asked our socialist friend.

"Joe Woollcott, Aleck Woollcott's cousin who's with the police force," explained Mr. Benchley. "He'll have details before the Department releases the information to the press."

"If we can find out a few facts about her and those interested in her death, we can find out what's been going on," I said.

"We'll, that's a good idea, if you want to get involved with all this stuff," said the socialist with a dismissive shake of his head as he rose to his feet. Giusto looked at him searchingly, seeking direction I suppose, but none was offered. "I've got to get downtown. Word has it there's a demonstration at Herald Square this noon, and I've got to check into a hotel to scribble down notes for my new book, and then off to a labor rally in Ohio before the weekend."

"You're just *leaving?*" I said, miffed at his sudden disregard of responsibility. *That's right,* I thought, *go write your next Pulitzer-Prize-winning exposé. Just leave this poor little anarchist in our care!* Our care? What on earth were we supposed to do with him? I started to voice my dismay: "But, stop! What about—?"

Mr. Benchley ignored my protest and shook the fellow's hand before seeing him out the door. Giusto looked from one to the other of us with wide-eyed wordless query, and was bidden to sit again as Mr. Benchley dialed the telephone. When he hung up the receiver, we left the Royalton and got Giusto into a cab for a ride down to Mulberry Street.

Stylish boaters

Chapter Five

The cab put us out amid the madness that is the Lower East Side, made worse by the noontime hour when it seemed the entire population of the city had decided to descend upon the few square blocks known as Little Italy. Chinatown was just across Canal Street, and the smells of roasting duck and exotic spices wafted drowsily on the still, hot air to mingle with the more immediate odors of garlic and tomato sauces and sausages frying and yeasty bread baking in the bakery down the street. Automobiles and trucks competed with the traffic of the horse-carts. The *hee-haw* of car horns sounded, the horse-drawn cartwheels creaked and horses' hooves clanked along the cobblestones, and vendors shouted in brash voices to be heard over the din. The iceman carried his delivery with huge iron tongs, and children, home from school, raced to retrieve the chips deliberately hacked off for their pleasure. The vegetable man hawked eggplant, onions, chard, and escarole fresh from Long Island farms. The junkman was making a deal with newlyweds for

the wares he'd bought from the son of the old woman
who had died over on Mott Street. The soda-man and
his teenaged son unloaded cases of White Rock for
the residents of the walk-ups, for the grocer, and for
the little restaurant in a storefront across the street.
There was the serious air of business being conducted,
but because of the residents' close proximity, a family
atmosphere persisted in a manner unheard of between
merchants and salesmen above 14th Street. I got the
immediate sense that here everyone knew everyone
else along the street; everybody knew everybody's
business, fortunes, and failures. This street combined
a little bit of Naples with its familiar flavors, a touch
of Palermo's music for the heart, and a great dose of
the spirit of America for inspiration.

Everyone was busy working and determinedly
moving about; the camaraderie among the players of
the street scene predominated, broken only by the
raising of angry voices among a couple of men in serious discussion at the door of the tailor shop. Children
ran about between the carts, automobiles, trucks,
and their elders. A bunch of boys tossed marbles at
the curb while little girls pushed baby prams con-
taining younger siblings, over whom they fussed like
tiny mothers. Adolescent girls in bright sundresses
lounged on stoops, riffling through movie magazines
and dreaming of a future in pictures and becoming the
romantic object of affection of Douglas Fairbanks.
Every so often their eyes would drift over to the strap-
ping gang of young men at the street-corner, a city

crew digging with shovel and pickaxe toward the water main, their sleeves rolled up to their elbows, forearm muscles tanned and speckled with sand and glistening from the sweat of their labors. Italian dialects and broken English and the accent of New Yorkers alternated in conversations as we walked out from under the relentless sun and into the dark entryway of the building, its street number matching the one scribbled on the scrap of paper that Giusto clutched in his hand.

Once over the threshold, the heat seemed to pervade with a vengeance, and as we accompanied Giusto up the stairs to the fifth-floor apartment, at each landing the air grew more stifling. The heat and our exertion saw us pathetically dragging ourselves across the floor tiles of the top-floor hallway. We dripped unpleasantly. My hair had frizzed and was damply matted to my skull in a most unattractive way—I could tell by the expression on Mr. Benchley's face when he recovered his breath and tossed a glance over at me, his moustache and eyebrows weeping.

"Next time, dry off when you get out of the bath," he puffed.

"Next time, I'll stay home in front of the fan with a good book."

The door opened before we could knock, and out flew a brown little black-haired boy with the bluest eyes imaginable, followed in close pursuit by two little heads of bouncing blonde banana curls and the pungent aroma of something burning. One of the girls dropped her ragdoll, which Mr. Benchley retrieved, and which she snatched out of his hand to race down the steps to catch up with her intended quarry. A tall, reed-thin man in his thirties brought up the rear of the passing parade, but instead of bolting through the open door, he reared back in surprise, flashed a great white grin, and flung his arms around young Giusto. He shouted over his shoulder within the apartment, and then turning back toward us upon the appearance of a very beautiful young woman, introduced himself as Lamberto Maggiorani and his wife, Lianella. She laughed with a brilliant smile, and indicated with extravagant sweeping gestures for us all to enter the apartment.

"Our Giusto is arriv-ed!" said Lamberto, heading for a bottle of wine on a sideboard, filling glasses and raising his glass to toast the young Italian's arrival in New York. "And tanks to 'is friends!" Then, remembering his manners, "Sit, please," he said, indicating the chairs that encircled a small dining table.

There was a brief exchange in Italian among the foursome, Lamberto shaking his head, Lianella leaving her dinner ministrations to lean, frowning, on the back of her husband's chair as Giusto spoke with a fervent fluidity. I got the drift of what was being said through their hand gestures and their occasional glances to smile at me and my friend during Giusto's compelling account of the past few hours. When the questions and answers had run their course, Giusto turned to me

and Mr. Benchley: "You very kind peoples for help
... me when come trouble."

"Yes," added Lamberto, "we are fortunate Giusto is safe, not wid police, arrested. He not do any
bad. Giusto is good boy," he said, playfully slapping
his brother's face with a soft palm and then squeezing
his cheek. Giusto blushed, but laughed at the show
of affection. "Si, Giusto, he is good broth'."

Mr. Benchley and I sat there mutely in the little
front room of the apartment, smiling benignly and
watching as the exchange continued, looking like we'd
been caught in a rainstorm without an umbrella. The
heat seemed to shimmer outside the opened windows.
A fan whirred on top of a cupboard, barely stirring
the air around the room, which held little more than
the table and chairs, a sink, the stove, a small icebox,
and a bathtub topped over with a sheet of plywood
covered in yellow oilcloth. At the moment the plywood was leaning on its side to accommodate the
laundry that was being hand-washed within. On the
small stove something was frying, and Lianella left
our little gathering and proceeded to scoop out and
strain the contents of the frying pan. Bare-handed,
she reached inside a bowl and pulled out some flour-
covered morsels and dumped them into the frying oil.
The sizzle sent tiny bouncing sprays of oil above the
pan. She set to work preparing sliced tomatoes with
other ingredients, and slid a loaf of crusty bread onto
a cutting board. And then I spotted the source of the
pungent burning smell that hit me when we entered.

Lianella had been roasting red peppers directly over the flame on the stove top, for now she began to peel away their charred skins.

A flash of color drew my eyes out the window to a bobbing clothesline, moving along a squeaky pulley, one of a dozen ropes cross-hatching through the air; sheets and shirts and towels and curtains waving and dangling like soggy flags of nations at a World Exposition, hung out to dry several stories deep over a courtyard. Music, peculiar to this humanity-swollen quarter of Manhattan, echoed within the canyon created by the neighboring tenements and poured in through the open windows: a woman's sing-song call to her neighbor across the way, the cry of a baby, the whine of a police siren, the barking of dogs, music from the radio, and children's screams of delight and dismay. No very tall buildings around to absorb the noise, no wide streets to disperse the racket of daily commerce. Here, people couldn't afford the quiet, staid conduct demanded of the Upper East Side mansions' residents, or the elegantly muted strains that wafted through the newly fashionable Central Park West community. Down here, life was an honest chore, a down-to-earth proclamation of hardship, the loud determination for survival, and the resounding belief that in America all could be accomplished through hard work and resolve. The heterogeneous mix of cultures and customs is what feeds innovation in our city, in our nation. The constant influx of new blood, like youthful aspirations, builds and strengthens us, and the influence of all the best we have to offer is celebrated; it's what makes New York and America so great.

I felt instantly at home in the little apartment with its unpretentious appointments. There had been an attempt to brighten the sad condition of the cracked and chipping plaster along walls that were in desperate need of paint and repair. A colorful poster, slightly beaten around its edges, from a production of *Carmen* at La Scala hung unframed on the wall. There were blue gingham curtains flanking the apartment's two windows and shorter ones wrapping around the sink and small work area. Above a narrow backless couch—probably doubling as a bed—the Virgin Mary looked on lovingly at the baby Jesus balanced on her arm, his face and demeanor that of a bald old man gazing up with pointed finger toward the Heaven He was soon to enter. A crucifix hung on a nail over the front door. Between the two windows a small braided cross made of dried palm leaves brought home from church last Palm Sunday was stuck in place atop a framed picture of Jesus holding His Sacred Heart, an image from my childhood that always frightened this Jewish girl ever since I first caught sight of it at the Blessed Academy, where my Christian stepmother insisted I attend school. Still, all in all, despite the religious images—or perhaps *because* of the religious conviction held by the couple—and the loving way they had tried to make a cheery home, I felt perfectly at home. Truth is, I envied them a little. In many ways, they had much more than I had. Sure, I had a

slew of brilliant and famous friends, was the toast of
any social scene, read my name and the witty things
I'd said in the daily columns, attended opening nights,
hung out in the pié-a-terres of the rich and famous,
was a best-selling poet, toured Europe with Hemmingway and the Fitzgeralds. Sure, I was the embodiment
of all the qualities the modern young graduate from
Vassar wished to emulate. But I lived alone in a small,
furnished two-room suite at the Algonquin Hotel, and
nobody, no man, that is, ever really loved me. Lamberto and Lianella were obviously in love, and poor
as they might be, they were together in their journey.
That is really something to be envied.

Soon appeared at the doorway to an adjoining
room an elderly man who buttoned the top button of
his shirt when he saw me, lifted the suspender that
hung at his side, and ran his fingers over his bald head
as if through the ghost of a full head of hair, proving
that old habits die hard. He smiled, and after Lamberto had introduced him as his father-in-law, Mario
Corelli, there began a series of hugs, kisses, back-slaps,
and face pinching and other affectionate assaults upon
the young Giusto.

The little boy who had run out from the grasps
of the two little blonde girls returned with an appeal
composed of English and Italian phrases for a penny
with which to buy a stick of Turkish taffy. He hung
on his mother's skirt, pleadingly, and after first trying
to discourage him, which didn't end his incessant appeal, she decided to ignore him as she went about her

business at the sink. Finally, with a jovial laugh and a sweep of his arm, Lamberto lifted him off his feet and presented him to his brother.

"*Questo e il tuo Zio Giusto, Enzo, guarda! Zio Giusto,* your uncle from Italy!"

After hugs and kisses between uncle and nephew, Lamberto slipped a coin from his vest-pocket and pressed it into the boy's hand. A slap to the child's rear-end (these people were not at all shy about physical contact, judging by all the slapping and patting and kissing and pinching they indulged in), and then instructions were shouted at the child as he sprang out from the apartment on his mission. The brothers smiled lovingly after him.

Now that we had delivered our wayward young Italian, Mr. Benchley and I thought it was time to depart. We stood to leave. But Lianella indicated that we should stay. Mr. Benchley and I began making our excuses, but the men joined in and were insistent that we remain for lunch. Lamberto said, "Pleez, we want you 'av meal wid us, simple, not fanzy, though."

"Oh, thank you, but, we don't want you to bother—" I said, taking in their poverty, thinking that they didn't need our big mouths to feed, too. But to decline would have meant insulting their hospitality. It was expected that we stay and break bread with them. It was their way of thanking us for delivering Giusto into their care. Lianella began setting the table while Lamberto refilled our glasses with the excellent wine. The pretty woman moved proudly about, her spine straight, putting the finishing touches on the meal, removing her apron to fold and then hang from a hook. Lamberto spoke about Giusto's near arrest as Lianella carried a huge bowl of what she had been frying to the table.

"My broth', Giusto, 'e is yong, and nev' should 'af take mony from lady stranger. I write 'im no talk wid stranger. Get on train, com' a New York and we get 'im job in bakery make pastries wid me."

"How long has it been since you've seen each other?" I asked.

"O-most nine year, I come 'ere. *Si*, nine year. Giusto just piccolo bambino," he replied, fussing over his brother, telling him to sit in one of the chairs at the table.

"*Ho ventuno anni.*"

"Yes, you twenty-won years old, now! You work in bakery, go night school, learn English, make nice life, marry *bella ragazza* . . . ."

"*Madonna!* One step at a time!" said Papa Corelli.

Lianella chuckled, placed the bowl of sliced tomato wedges covered with olive oil and seasoned with herbs on the table, and then carried over a huge crusty loaf of bread, which Papa sliced into great chunks. "From bakery," said Lamberto, patting the wonderfully yeasty loaf. "I bake."

As Lamberto continued to speak, from the ice-box Lianella carried to the table a wedge of cheese on a plate, and fresh mozzarella wrapped in layers of cheesecloth. She looked over her table, went to fetch a serving spoon, and then pulled over a wooden bench for her seat at the table. She urged us to dig in, and we gratefully did partake of the incredible fried squid, roasted red peppers salted and sprinkled with olive oil, the delectable summer-ripe tomato salad, into which we dunked ripped-off chunks of bread, and the golden, nutty parmesan cheese we cut from the block. The freshly made mozzarella literally melted in my mouth, and I piled a slab of it atop bread with a red-pepper topping. Heaven! It'd been a long time since I had eaten such a veritable feast of simple, yet intensely flavored foods. Suddenly, Italian food became my favorite kind, and would be for the rest of my life!

Lamberto, with the occasional comment from Lianella, told us that he came to the States soon after the War—Italy's economy was in shambles, there were political battles being waged, labor was struggling for better wages, and the bosses began taking benefits away in order to make bigger profits for themselves. Now the Black Shirts were terrorizing hard-working men and women. When he passed through Ellis Island and set foot in Manhattan, he knew no one here from the Old Country, and although he was helped early on by acquaintances he made within the Italian community, he had to take the only work he could find, that of a ditch digger. "I work pic-shov! Ten, fourteen hours day. Break-back work, kill even strong man." After enduring three years of hardship—at low wages—he took work in a factory six days a week for the paltry sum of nine dollars a week. "Get sick, or don't work Sunday, you get fire-ed." Then a year at the fish market down on Fulton, where he met Mr. Castelli, who owned a little restaurant on Mulberry Street. Castelli liked to go and buy the fish for his restaurant himself; it was odd, of course, that he didn't let the chef do it. But, he was a Sicilian, the son of a squid fisherman, and he knew best what fish he wanted served. Lamberto and Mr. Castelli soon discovered they were both natives of Agrigento. They even had friends in common. This forged an instant bond, and Castelli proceeded to make it his business to help Lamberto advance successfully in his new country. A man in his forties, he had no children of his own. He had no wife, for the woman he loved would not leave Italy with him as her father had objected to the marriage, calling Bernardo Castelli a dreamer who would be the ruin of his daughter should she go on this misadventure to the barbaric country across the sea! That Bernardo Castelli proved himself a success—he did, after fifteen years in America, have his very own restaurant in New York City—would have made little difference to the father of his beloved. The old man had died soon after Bernardo's departure, but not before wedding his daughter to the village tailor. So in many ways the young man and the older restaurateur helped each other. They adopted one another as friend, son, mentor, and confidant. America had been good to Bernardo; he'd made a success of his venture in the New World. And Bernardo Castelli was as good as his word, happy to share his good fortune by helping a fellow country- man make his own. As Lamberto had trained as a baker in Italy, and although there were few jobs and many bakers on both continents, Bernardo decided to expand his restaurant, and next door opened a bakery. This decision made Bernardo a wealthy man, for he contracted his bread to restaurants around the city. Lamberto was in charge and earning a good living. "In two, three year, I buy house in Long-a Island near sea. I miss sea. So I buy house by sea in Long-a Island." And then, from out of left field, he said, "Vanzetti and Sacco dead, now, you hear?"

"Yes," said Mr. Benchley, nodding grimly.

And as if he held some sense of guilt for his rising success while watching compatriots struggling, Lamberto said, "I send for Giusto. In Italia, it very bad. Mussolini, who long time 'go say he want to help poor worker, turn back on dem, *come si dice?* Sell out? He sell out to rich men own factories, take mony to make himself power, *power-ful*! He lead *i fasci di combattimento—polizia*—like police—beat, put in jail, kill labor and *socialista* and communists. We call dem *fascista*."

"Forgive me," I interrupted—they had just fed me a most incredible feast, and I sensed these were gentle people, whatever their political beliefs. "Giusto told us he is an anarchist—"

"*Si*, yes, he believe in worker be pay enoof to feed family, live good after hard work all day. Who don't tink dat? Me, I agree, but America system has been good for me and Lianella. But many *amici—friends*—they not so much success-a-ful. Dey only can work to make richer da rich man, da big capitalist! But, we no Dago Red, like some. No!"

Giusto watched the intense volley of words back and forth across the table with wide-eyed interest, if confusion. His hair was very dark, almost black, and in spite of the heat he'd hardly broken a sweat. It was then that I saw how very good-looking the young man was—spare, his features chiseled into fine angularity. Age and experience would try their best to ruin him, but I doubted they'd succeed, for he was just the type to benefit from their influences, his face becoming more richly etched, less the boy and more the man, handsome instead of sweet.

"So, you agree with the socialists and the communists—the 'Reds'—to a certain degree, about Labor, anyway?" asked Mr. Benchley.

"It is so, yes," nodded Lamberto, and I could see he was choosing his words carefully by the way his arched brows raised and quivered and the fire that flashed in his brown eyes when he had found his way. "But in America, we free to speak da prop-o-ganda, no? We have right to say we want or not want. Is de American way, no? I am for dis. I believe. Socialists and da communists, dey want to make union, committee—offish—"

"*Offic-i-als*," corrected Lianella.

"*Si*, yes, *offic-i-als*," repeated her husband. "No *offic-i-al*, no *union* should tell me or worker what to do. Corr-upt!" he said, rolling his *r*'s. "Like Mussolini, he start good man, help worker, and den, he all power. He make corr-upt!"

"*Ahhh*, yes, corruption," nodded Mr. Benchley. "Complete power corrupts completely."

"Dat is so. Dat what happen when men dey organize, make *offic-i-als* in charge."

Lianella cut in: "We do not make bombs, no! No violent—*vi-o-lence*. We *pacifico*—pacifists. We do not believe in war. Rich men, powerful men make war to make profit on poor worker, take land, more land, more power . . . ."

Lianella blushed, pushing damp tendrils of hair from her forehead, and looked shyly down at her plate. I admired her fervent little speech, her heartfelt convictions, and the few, very convincing words she'd chosen to make her point. We all sat quietly for a moment. The silence must have been too much for her to bear; embarrassed by her outburst, unsure of what her guests must have been thinking, she leaped from her chair and proceeded to clear the table. I stood to help her, but her gentle hand on my shoulder told me to stay.

"*Cara*," said Lamberto, "*café?*"

"*Si, si*," she said, and carried out the task.

Lamberto said, "When Giusto working, maka da mony, maybe he feel diff-er-rent. Maybe he don't. We see," he ended, with the singularly Italian pull of the face and lift of a shoulder. Mr. Benchley and I understood him to say, "Only time will tell."

Papa Corelli spoke now in pretty good English and with a confidential whisper: "I went to Union Square last night to wait with others, my friends, to hear the fate of the men. Must be four, five thousand people there. The police, they with machine guns on the roof of building on the east side, and after midnight, the people in the office of the Red newspaper—"

"*The Daily Worker?* They have their offices on the Square," said Mr. Benchley.

"Yes, yes, *The Daily Worker*. A man put a big sign out window say, *Sacco murdered!* And all the people, all thousands—the words took breath away! People cry and moan together, and when the new sign they show, *Vanzetti murdered!* it got real bad, the people crying. All the people—the Reds, the socialists, the Italians—all the good American people of all parties, they mourn."

In a few minutes we were sipping espresso and devouring luscious pastries from La Luna Bakery down the street, baked by Lamberto at dawn this morning.

Right off the boat and eager to see the streets paved with gold

Looking toward a better future

Little Italy

The neighborhood

A room with a view

"Pic-shov" laborers laying down streetcar tracks

Anarchists on the march, 1914

Aftermath of anarchist bombing of Wall Street

Wall Street bombing

Fat Cat Capitalist

The Red Scare

COMING OUT OF THE SMOKE.
—Kirby in the New York *World*.

Labor

Copyrighted 1919 by The Philadelphia Inquirer Company
PUT THEM OUT AND KEEP THEM OUT
—Morgan in the Philadelphia Inquirer

Suspicion

Sacco's & Vanzetti's New York funeral

Martyred

Chapter Six

After leaving the Maggioranis' apartment, I took a chance that Loretta, my hairdresser, could fit me in for a wash and set at La Belle Coiffure that afternoon. The shop was just a few blocks away from the Algonquin on Madison Avenue. Mr. Benchley dropped me off and then sailed on in the taxi to his offices at *Life*. We planned to meet up again for cocktails before dinner.

As I approached the salon I spied a familiar sight, only, I couldn't for the life of me place where I'd seen it before. I stopped in my tracks to stare, and then it dawned on me: *the beret*. In a city where the usual summer attire gracing the head of the cosmopolitan male is a straw boater, a beret, albeit of linen fabric, lent an air of the continental. And that it was perched at a rakish angle atop a rather tall fellow of some distinction standing at the entrance to a haberdasher's made him stand out in the crowd of pedestrians moving at a brisk New York clip. I recognized the man. He was a fellow passenger on the Midnight Owl. Small world, isn't it?

It was too hot to linger on the street, so I buzzed in through the door and begged the receptionist to see about a wash and set with Loretta, if she was free. I took a seat and picked up a magazine. The fans were spinning currents of cool air from the refrigerated-air conditioner, to my great relief. I was thinking that next week I would go out to Aleck's island on Lake Bomoseen in Vermont, if I could convince Mr. Benchley or any one of our friends to join me in hiring a car. Three or four days on Neshobe Island are about all the rest I can bear, but the thought of remaining in the city in the summer was even less inviting. I was flipping through a movie magazine when I was beckoned by a wave of *Shalimar* and a familiar drawl that brought a smile to my face. I looked up to see a welcome sight, my dear friend, Tallulah Bankhead, standing before me in a wrapper, her nails dripping red paint.

"Lamb returned from the slaughter?" she asked.

"It certainly wasn't a picnic."

"I see you haven't lost your head to the damn executioner. Are you here to do something about it? The hair, I mean. You look like Nazimova."

"Thanks! That bad, huh? Well, if Loretta can take me—"

"She's just finishing up with someone. You'd never guess who is getting her black roots bleached."

"Not *Twenty Questions*, not now."

"But you're good at games. Oh, all right, I'm impatient to tell you, anyway. Hermione Mellon. Right off the boat from England."

"I met her on the train home from Boston," I said.

"Well, she's a peppy thing, ain't she?"

"If that's the right word for it—"

"She's just enthusiastic.

"Is that why she can't shut up?"

"Really, Dottie, you are a viper, you know that? But it's true, she is a chatty thing. It can't have been easy, though, the emotional and physical toll of a breakdown. That's what I heard, anyway. In a sanatorium for years. The memory loss . . . . Imagine not remembering your childhood?"

"A pleasure."

"Somehow the doctors put her all back together again!"

"Yes, like Humpty Dumpty would have wished," I replied, thinking that Tallulah was being just a little too nice. In ordinary circumstances someone like Hermione Mellon would have sent her reeling dizzily out of the room for a breath of fresh air.

"The manicurist, the masseuse, and your hairdresser, Loretta, have been giving her the works for more than three hours."

"I could give her the works in under thirty seconds, but I'd need brass knuckles."

"The whole damn place is running around fixing her up."

"Did she come undone?"

"They sent a boy out to fetch her coffee and petit-fours. While her mask hardened I stole a couple. Who knew when I'd have a chance to eat again?"

"I don't get it. What's all the fuss about? A little nervous breakdown, for cry'noutloud, and everybody treats you like royalty."

"I figure by the way Loretta ordered me to go wait in the corner—after she'd made me put the cakes back—that she thinks Hermione, being rich, will send her other rich clientele. If that's going to be the case, she'll raise the price of a finger-wave to two dollars!"

"Why is she coming to our little beauty shop instead of some highfalutin' establishment? Doesn't she have a lady's maid or something?"

"She likes it here; I heard her tell Loretta. It's 'less pretentious.'"

"Than what?"

"I think she said Henri's—that salon on Fifth? That's what I heard—'less pretentious'—and oh!—she invited me to her summer home on Long Island this weekend," drawled on my friend, like an antebellum heroine without the hoopskirt and corkscrew curls. "They say it's grand!" she gushed. "Can you believe

Roger built her a mansion on the North Shore? They say it's a palace, and he named it *Last Call*, ain't that a laugh? They say it's bigger than Swope's place," she finished, figuratively batting her eyes coyly behind a fluttering lace-trimmed fan.

"*They* say, do they?"

"They certainly do!"

"I didn't know you knew the Mellons."

"Well, I didn't know them, just heard the usual talk about them. But now that I've met Hermione, I can see she is quite a—uh—nice girl—if a little chatty."

"When you get to know her you'll want to rip her heart out," I said.

"Don't you like her?"

"Gee, did I say that? Does a dog like fleas?"

"That's too bad. You really ought to give the gal a chance."

"Don't be an Airedale—I really don't give a shit."

"Funny, I heard Hermione use that slang. It must be all the rage in England. '*Don't be an Airedale!*' *Soooo* clever!"

"Oh, all the rage, God help me!"

"You are . . . irritable, Dottie!"

"I don't suffer fools."

"You met her husband?"

"Yes, I met him a few years ago, at a dinner party as a matter of fact, long before he married Hermione. Bit of a bore."

"What's he like now, I wonder?"

"Married," I said, knowing full well what Tallulah was getting at.

"Silly, just wanted to know if he was as—how to describe her?"

"Idiotic?"

"No!"

"Imbecilic?"

"Dottie!"

"Moronic? As asinine as his wife? How could anyone know; he rarely has a chance to speak. Why do you think he stutters?"

"That so?"

"They had a drawing-room in my Pullman on my return from Boston. They invited me and Bobby in for a nightcap."

"On the train? The Mellons? Those rich people rubbing elbows with the plebes?"

"Thank you very much, Tallulah, for including me among the rabble who stormed the Bastille!"

"Oh, darling, I didn't mean you and Bobby! No, I mean, I would have thought they'd have had a motorcar meet them at port."

"Yes, that's right, I said as much, but Roger said the car broke down on its way up from New York and the chauffeur was having it repaired in some garage in Connecticut."

That's when the object of gossip appeared, looking refreshed and glamorous, her blonde hair a shade lighter than when we'd met on the train. I moved to where she couldn't see me hiding in the little lounging area, separated by a wall of lattice, as she breezed by on her way out of the door.

And then Tallulah's hairdresser, followed by mine, peeked around the partition to beckon us for the usual ministrations. We agreed to catch up at luncheon tomorrow.

———•———

Mr. Benchley drove onto the long driveway of Last Call to a wave of orchestral music; we could hear the party before we could see the house from the drive. And let me say that after three hours in the car with my friends, I was ready to trade them in for new ones. Perhaps, after a mint julep and swim in the pool, I might reconsider.

Mr. Benchley's straining tenor was a sad substitute for the absence of a car radio, I discovered, after we and Tallulah and Edmund Wilson had set off in the snazzy yellow Mercedes Benz Sports Touring car on loan to Mr. Benchley by the owner of the Mercedes dealership on the East Side, whom he'd befriended to each man's advantage. Actually, they had an arrangement. Loaning such a beauty for an outing to the Island, for a weekend at the Morgans' or the Swopes', to be admired as it glided up the driveway, might ignite a flame of envy in a rich partygoer and result in a sale for the dealership on Monday morning. Mr. Benchley kept a stash of the man's business cards handy to be doled out to the rich and needy. So we were off in style with our friends.

Bunny Wilson, for whom we felt sorry, had been hanging around the Gonk with no particular place to go, as most of the gang had scattered out of the city for the duration of the heatwave. Some were cooling off in the Adirondacks or, as ordered by Aleck, on his Island in Vermont. Frank Case, the Gonk's owner and manager, begged that we take Bunny away someplace as he had been brooding and sleeping on one of the lobby sofas. The lobby was cooled by refrigerated air, and Bunny's apartment was stifling hot, he'd been complaining. It wouldn't have been so bad but that the writer and critic insisted on sleeping until noon, sprawled and snoring on a sofa just a few feet away from the front desk. This was a sight and sound not quite in keeping with the character of the residence that Frank wished to maintain. Had Bunny Wilson chosen a couch farther away, say in the corner, or the one near the Oak Room, the management might have been more tolerant. After all, the Algonquin did cater to *artists*, didn't it? (To *me*, more specifically, was what Frank really meant.)

And so, in our open touring car, Bunny slept most of the way in the seat next to Mr. Benchley, who drove while singing through the entire score of *The Desert Song*. (His rendition of the soldiers' wives singing "Why Did We Marry Soldiers?" was warbled in a creepy falsetto that smacked of latent depravity, if you really want to know.) Then there ensued an argument when Tallulah, in the backseat with me, began spewing forth a dirge-like interpretation of "Stout Hearted Men," which she was sure was from *The Desert Song*, only we all insisted it was from *The Student Prince*, which led to Mr. Benchley's whining that she'd upset the whole lineup leading into his big finale. Undeterred and determined, she kept on singing—if that's what you'd call it. It sounded more like a sluggish ship's horn blasting on a foggy night in the North Atlantic, bringing to mind the *Titanic* and the coming death of innocence. All of this sent Woodrow into a disturbing series of whines and howls, which in turn evoked a most unpleasant reminder of my brother Harold's earliest violin recital when he was twelve. Woodrow had provided, since we had crossed the Queensboro Bridge, an even tempo of yips and yaps, a metronome for Mr. Benchley to keep his "rhythmic integrity"—at least that's what he said to the dog during his three-minute intermission between the musical acts. By the time we had reached Long Island, both man and dog were well into the second-act score of *Thoroughly*

Modern Millie. Tallulah had settled in to hum the bass section.

The sun was setting; the sky was as brashly painted as the cheeks of a Parisian whore when we turned onto the winding driveway of Last Call, the Mellons' estate, poised grandly on a peninsula jutting out into the sound. So it was with my great relief that the brassy notes of a big orchestra playing the hit song, "The Muscat Ramble," greeted our arrival and put a death blow to what promised to be a bowdlerization of the Gershwin Brothers' musical, *Oh Kay!*

Tallulah was raring to go, and after shaking Bunny awake, we made our way along the car-lined driveway toward the floodlit entrance of the mansion.

All I can say to describe the fabulous monstrosity into which we entered was that, should the Hippodrome burn to the ground, the grand entry hall of Last Call offered enough space to house a three-ring circus. The semicircular hall's ceiling was vaulted and soared some thirty or more feet in the air, atop which sat, like a sultan's hat, a *duomo*, the likes of which one might see during a Roman tour of sixteenth-century churches. Half a dozen crystal chandeliers floated down from the heights where a *trompe l'oeil* masterpiece depicting Neptune and his undersea kingdom promised a stiff neck if you wanted to take it all in. This explained why several youngsters were flat on their backs staring up at the sight. Then again, perhaps they were just passed out from too much fun. The blues and aqua greens washed down pale along the walls like sea-foam to the marble floor, which was polished to a high sheen and brought to mind the wet sands of blushing Bermuda beaches.   What the heck, it was gorgeous, for all its ostentation. Museum quality all around, starting from the carved-wood busty mermaid balustrades grounding the floating twin stairways that curved up to the second landing and arriving at a depiction of the harpoon-clutching god himself, whose bearded head appeared dead center at the apex. Of course, this was all meant to be taken seriously, but anyone with a modicum of humor would see it for what it was: *New Money gone awry*. Oh, well, *a little bad taste is like a nice dash of paprika*, I always say.

The stairs were littered with guests leaning, lounging, and generally posing for the visual benefit of others who were leaning, lounging, and posing in similar attire. The women were drifting about in a variety of soft, sheer, and sleeveless pastel-colored frocks and close-fitting bejeweled or embroidered caps; the men were attired in summer flannels or linen suits with silk shirts peeking out from under their coats. We were met by butlers and footmen directing the flow of guests about the house and waiters offering champagne in crystal flutes and presenting delectable canapés on silver trays.

Walking to the left, we followed the source of "The Varsity Drag," passing through a long room—a sort of solarium or drawing-room filled with flowers and potted trees and exotics and lined with French doors that opened onto an expansive stone patio.

I have to admit that when arriving at such places, at such high-flying gatherings, I never really know what to expect, and that sparks the air I breathe. So, as we hurried toward the source of the music, toward the beating heart of the party beyond the doors, suddenly, and as eagerly as that proverbial moth first glimpsing that seductive flame, I felt a thrill of excitement rush through me and, like that foolish moth, forgot to consider the dangers.

Hundreds of elaborately gilded and fringed Chinese lanterns shone red and yellow as they hung in a line against the darkening sky before disappearing into the inky oblivion of water beyond the stonewalled jetty shaped like an arrowhead pointing to Connecticut across the Sound. Long banquet tables and smaller groupings were set with cloth and dinner service for the first dinner of the night. The usual custom of these affairs was to serve a sit-down supper again at midnight, the hour marking the arrival of the theatre people driving out after final curtains on Broadway. There was no point in figuring out how many guests the Mellons had invited. There might be hundreds, and perhaps many more would wander through after making an appearance at the Morgans', a couple miles down the road.

This was not just a dinky jazz band tootling away, but a full-sized orchestra hired to fit the bill, with a dozen men in the string section alone, a wall of brass pumping out mellow notes, and woodwinds providing the necessary details. A warm baritone voice was crooning through the microphone, "I'll See You in My Dreams." On the dance floor the flappers, having finished with the "Drag," gave way to the fox-trotting couples. As they strolled off, their chatter and giggles floated into the night like fireflies seeking new haunts along cool lawns in lush shadows.

"Where's Tallulah?" I asked Mr. Benchley, who had my arm and was leading me toward the bar for the hard liquor.

"On the search for stout-hearten men, I should think. Scotch on the rocks?"

"Make mine a julep, please, and I suppose that means that Bunny—"

"What about the boy?"

"Oh, never mind, I've spotted him. He's got Woodrow, a surefire method for attracting the babes," I said, belting down the remains of the champagne. I grabbed a bacon-wrapped scallop from off a passing *hors d'oeuvres* tray, and then made a beeline for the buffet table for a plate of crab-cakes and a couple of Little Necks on the half-shell. Mr. Benchley reappeared at my side to warn he'd spotted our hosts. I asked how we might avoid them altogether; I was not really in the mood for the chatter of halfwits. But, I knew that eventually Hermione would sniff me out— caught hiding behind a pillar or palm, or holding my breath under the waterline of a wharf piling. It really was better to get the chore over with so she might move on to setting her claws into the arriving movie star, her director, and their respective spouses. Gossip had it that these refugees from Hollywood were having affairs with each other. At the thought, I tried to calculate how many possible combinations there really could be, if one didn't set rigid standards about such things. I'd arrived at a figure of eight, when another thought popped into my mind. I was about to turn to Mr. Benchley to ask if such a thing were physically possible—as he would surely know—to increase the final number to twelve combinations, when there she stood before me, Hermione Mellon, and Mr. Benchley nowhere in sight! I cursed the man under my breath and into my glass, the sprig of mint catching between my upper lip and teeth, before turning a leafy smile on my hostess.

"Dot, honey!" brayed Hermione. "Why, there's something in your—that's it; I love chewing mint, too. Cleans the breath. So glad you could come."

"Delighted," I drawled out exaggeratedly, like I meant it. "Some digs you got here, by the way."

Roger put his foot in, thinking I had paid them a compliment: "Dorothy," he began, taking my hand in greeting, "this house took three years to build, you know. I always believed that Hermione would get well and come to live here. I built this house with that faith."

And three-hundred-thousand dollars!

Let me give you a little tour of our humble home," he said, taking my arm and steering me toward the grand staircases. "All the marble is imported from a quarry in Italy; the mahogany, Honduran; the tile—"

I would have asked him to send me a price list, but that would have been crass. I was pretty sure he would eventually tell me how much the whole damn thing cost, so I would just have to endure the docent tour. After all, I was drinking his liquor and planned on eating my fair share of the filet mignon, so I allowed him to drone on as he guided me from room to room along the east wing and then on to the wonders of the west. And a generous little tourist I was, *oohing* and *aahing* about the specially fitted sunken tubs and solid-gold fixtures in the eighteen full bathrooms attached to the fifteen suites and five cottages, and god-remembers-how-many square miles of inlaid starburst-patterned parquet flooring, costing god-remembers-how-much, that were installed using seven kinds of hardwoods, as well as the controlled humidifying heating system, and the ninety-seven Venetian glass mirrors on the walls all over the house. All the while I was waiting for Hermione to close the floodgates against the boring host with her signature "Don't be an Airedale" remark. Alas, she remained mum.

And then I was led into a long room, a gallery that held the art collection, and I sighed. Here were gathered some fifty or more masterpieces of impres-

sionist art—several Monets, two Cézannes, one spectacular Manet river landscape, a Van Gogh, a Renoir,
and a delightful Corot, along with a smattering of
Renaissance masters—a Titian, a Rembrandt, a Da
Vinci silverpoint sketch, a Durer, and a Michelangelo
study! I wanted to linger in this room, but after a
prideful smile and a few boastful words about the ac-
cumulated value of the collection, Roger steered me
out of the room by the elbow to continue on the tour
for another excruciating ten minutes of viewing the
accoutrements here, and the appurtenances there. My
eyes were crossing by the time we landed in the suite
of rooms that comprised Roger's and Hermione's bedroom. It smelled warm and citrusy of her perfume.

Their bed was a huge round affair, covered with
plump gold-satin bedding and draped from the ceiling
with gauzy and shimmering gold netting. Except for
the gallery, I had nearly bored myself to sleep with my
mantra of accolades, and upon seeing the oversized
bed, wanted nothing more than to crash-land on King
Midas's inviting monstrosity, which I figured was so
full of goose down that I could sink into an abyss of
feathers and never be seen or heard from again. But,
alas, the tour was not yet over, for I was led into a
sitting-room alcove off the bedroom. I half-listened
as Roger pointed to the large portrait of a blonde
woman sitting on a blue-velvet sofa, very Bouguereau
in its romantic style, and painted by a very competent
hand around the turn of the century. On either side
of the beautiful woman stood girls in their early teens,

Hermione, I was told, and her sister, Penelope, who had died. The portrait hung above one of the three-thousand or so fireplaces that heated the joint.

A maid entered the bedroom, linens draped over an elbow, carrying a grand bowl of gardenias, which she placed on a table. She walked into the extravagant bathroom, and then out again without the towels. I followed her progress across the thick powder-blue carpet in the bedroom to Hermione's dressing table, atop which was a shambles of dozens of elaborate perfume bottles arranged like a city skyline of skyscrapers. There was the hypnotizing sparkle of diamond and gold and ruby jewelry, flung about like so much junk beside discarded tissues bearing cosmetic fingerprints, cotton balls, lipstick tubes. The powder puff's snowfall-like dusting cushioned the vivid ice of diamonds.

Finally, we trotted down one of the curving stair-cases, I with a feeling of lightness at my imminent release. I would have slid down the banister like a sick child being told she was well enough to go out and play but for the fact that people were standing on the stairs, leaning against the railing, like Dresden figurines resting upon display shelves. I was headed for the bar when I was stopped by Hermione and introduced to a young man.

"Roger, honey, I'm sure Dot wants you to take her on a tour of the wine cellars, but maybe later. Right now, I have to fulfill a promise I made to Johnny, here, to introduce him to our Dorothy, don't you know."

Roger, in the fashion of his hairline, receded back a bit to make way for the introduction. He appeared chuffed and mumbled something before turning to another mark, a poor fellow alone at the bar, so he could finish his tour of the cellars.

It was not long after he'd taken my hand that I recognized this "John" as one of the many youthful "refugees" born high up on the Social Register. Like many I've come across, he was currently on the prowl for adventure, looking for a good time to be had away from the stuffy drawing-rooms, dusty from all that flaking old money just lying about on their parents' tasteful estates that dotted the waterfront. These sons and daughters of statesmen, bankers, and industrialists, these young Brahmins of American Society were just itching to shed the hairshirts worn by past generations and touted as a privilege of their class. They just couldn't strip-down fast enough and escape their stone palaces for adventures to be found in the garrets of artists, writers, and people of The Theatre—the lowly society of riffraff snubbed by their staid parents. Golly! There was jazz in the clubs of Harlem, sassy musical revues aplenty in Greenwich Village, the new abstract art to see hanging on the walls of galleries and in the salons about town. And there was booze to be had and cocaine to make things all light and gay. No girdles, no corsets, no barriers, no rules, no holds barred!

The new sensibility insists on honesty; be honest and say what you really think, and the more shocking, the more self-liberating! Even if you sound rude, you are being honest, aren't you? True to yourself? Same thing with sex. Why try to deny *sex*? *Sex* is everywhere. *Sex*, and all that Freud said about it, has to be discussed out in the open, and you have to be ready for a fast rejoinder about this or that conquest, because that's all anyone ever talks about. *Sex*. Even when you don't want to hear about the dalliances of others the conversation is always in progress and hard to get away from. Virginity is deemed a burden and a modern taboo.

So I danced with this fellow, John (a possible future senator from New York State if he ever returned to the fold, or a professional polo player if he didn't), to a couple of peppy tunes.

"Hermione looks pretty good, considering," commented young John, as he pushed me around the dance floor like he was dealing an old deck of cards around a poker table.

"Considering what?"

"I expected an old lady, from what I heard tell. The old maid Roger married over in Africa. I'm surprised she isn't an old lady, and with her pretty blonde hair, she looks like a movie star. I think she's dazzling, don't you?"

"She's a dazzler, all right."

"And now, after all these years, Roger's come back to live here in the States, and his wife is a beaut!"

"What are you? Twenty, twenty-one?"

He hesitated, nodded, and then came clean: "Nineteen . . . next December."

I wanted to put an end to being pushed about by this little bulldozer, but the music didn't end and nobody cut in.

"Mother says they stayed in Europe these past three years because Hermione was ill. She never got over the death of her parents, they say, and her twin sister who drowned when she was just a little kid."

"She looks pretty healthy to me."

"I hear she has spells, headaches and stuff. But the big secret is that she was in a sanatorium with an alienist."

I thought about it. It's why Hermione seems so loopy, why she rattles on no end. It has to be a cover-up for her mental limitations. If so, I am sorry if I was mean to the poor thing, with my little innuendos and impatient barbs.

"This house is the bees' knees, ain't it? Got a games room with a pool table and a basketball court—"

"Well, build a fortune like Roger Mellon's and you, too, can have your very own games room and court."

"Father refuses to put in a basketball court."

"Then I misspoke. You already have a fortune like Roger Mellon's."

"Well, it's mostly Hermione's money, now, you know; Mother said."

"'S that so? Well, when two fortunes collide—"

"Father said Mellon Industries is sinking. Stock's been sliding this past year, with Roger out of the country and Hermione ill, and all. No big munitions contracts. No war, no money, says Mother. Father had a friend who was on the board, you know? No, this was built with Hermione's money."

"All in the family, I guess . . . . Listen, Johnny, my dogs are killing me."

"I'll walk with you."

I took off my shoes and we walked on the cool lawn, the night air fragrant with the smell of camellias and the tang of the sea.

I asked the kid, "So, you must be going off to college soon?"

"Monday, I'm afraid. Yale." Said like a doctor informing his patient he'd be dead within a day.

"You don't sound too thrilled about roaming the halls of academe."

"I want to sail around the world, first, before they tie me down with school and all," said Johnny, an adolescent whine bleeding through his voice. "Father says there is plenty of time *after* my degree."

"What kind of business would you like to go into?"

"We Harringtons don't work. So I think it's silly, having to go to school. Why? If I don't ever need to work . . .?"

"What will you do with yourself if you don't work? What are your interests, other than sailing?"

"I like industry. I'd like to have thousands of men working in some kind of factory I own, with me running the show, so to speak," he said, frowning in all seriousness while sorting out his thoughts. "Father says there will be another war. I like guns and stuff— like Roger Mellon—so maybe if there is another war, I'll open a factory and make them and have more money, only, I won't lose my shirt or have to depend on a girl to keep me afloat."

Oh, crap, a little capitalist—or was this a budding fascist?

"Might go into politics . . . ." He was now puffing up from the possibilities he was presenting himself. Didn't I just say to myself a few minutes ago that here was a future senator? "Yes, I might do that, go to Congress, run for political office . . . ."

"What are your politics?"

"Oh, I don't know—this and that, I suppose. Repeal the Nineteenth Amendment—"

"Surely, you jest! You don't want women—?"

"No, no! I mean Prohibition—which is that?"

"The *Eighteenth* Amend—"

"Yes, that's the one! Why, Father has the hardest time getting—"

Oh, my God! When I thought of all the boobs already serving in Washington, I felt it my duty as an American citizen to steer this budding one onto another course: "You play polo?"

"Yes, but I don't like it very much. Father says it is important to play."

"Why, in fresh hell?"

"Social connections, and all."

"You're a good-looking young boy; ever think about trying your hand as an actor?" *Lots of boobs in the Theatre,* I thought, and with family money he wouldn't have to worry about actually earning a living.

He was musing over the possibility when we arrived back where we'd started from—on the dance floor. Fortunately, Mr. Benchley appeared and fox-trotted me off to one of the dinner tables set for six where sat Tallulah, busily seducing a couple of "boys" who rented a house down the road. They had seen all the lights on here and decided to crash the party. (A month later, these same two fellows were to have their faces on the front pages of all the big dailies when they were arraigned for jewel robberies from the homes of the better North Shore families. For now, Tallulah was safe from their pilfering hands, if not their wandering ones, 'cause she wore only paste.)

Bunny arrived, Woodrow in tow, just as the waiter began to serve the first course. I suppose Bunny was exhausted from all the fawning, the petting, and the scratching behind the ears because he curled up to sleep under the table as we ate, my foot his pillow. So as Bunny snoozed, Woodrow Wilson jumped up into Bunny's chair, lapped out the Coquille Saint Jacque off the shell, turned his nose up at the salad, and ran off with a dinner roll.

"Why do I let you drag me to these things, Dorothy?" said Bunny, when I accidently kicked him in the head. He'd begun dribbling on my foot.

"Really, Bunny, come up here and sit in a chair like a grownup!"

He crawled up, using my knee as leverage, and claimed his seat, recently vacated by Woodrow.

"You had a very nice nap in the car to the musical accompaniment of Mr. Robert Benchley, baritone and sometime-contralto—"

"No, no, my dear," piped up Mr. Benchley, "not contralto, rather, boy soprano."

"Excuse me, Fred; I stand corrected. As I was saying, Bunny, you fortunately slept through the entire mind-numbing concert."

"Why, I never!" protested Mr. Benchley.

"And you, Edmund Wilson, Frank begged me to take you off his hands. You were turning his lobby into a college dormitory—only *not* so fresh-smelling."

"Now, see here, Dorothy Parker!" objected Bunny.

"That's good," chuckled Tallulah, "at least he remembers your name!"

"Well, in the spirit of good fellowship," said Mr. Benchley, casting off feigned hurt feelings, "on the return trip, I will sing not one single note—"

"I knew there was a God," I said, "and He is good—"

"—but instead will recite all 49 verses of Edgar Poe's, *The Raven*—"

"And once again, I become an atheist!"

"—and if you are very good children, I shall present to you my rendition of *The Wreck of the Hesperus*—"

"I'll be taking the train," I said.

"—accompanied with the sound effects of an ocean voyage—"

"What's that supposed to sound like? Confetti being tossed?" said Bunny, softening. At this, Mr. Benchley let loose the blood-curdling *caw-caw* of a seabird (I suppose it was meant as a preview of *his* idea of what an albatross sounded like). Those at other tables turned to look at us and laughed, and because

they were well sloshed on gallons of champagne—
the imported stuff—they thought Mr. Benchley very
clever indeed. Raising their glasses to toast him, and
with the infectious inanity of drunks, they began a
series of birdcalls that swept over the tables and out
into the night. In the near-distance I heard Roger
Mellon's voice boom out, "Goddamn seagulls stealing
the shrimp! Where's my shotgun?" This nonsense—
the birdcalls—went on for the rest of the evening.
Whenever anyone else was about to speak, they'd
start with, "*Caw-caw!* It's a real dandy! *Caw-caw!*"
Which proves that even *stupid* seems funny if you've
had enough to drink.

   After the orchestra played "Bye, Bye, Blackbird"
to the accompaniment of a hundred *tweets* and *caws*,
I walked off by myself and settled in an Adirondack
chair overlooking the beach and the dark waters beyond the quay. Woodrow lay in my lap, content with a
bellyful of tenderloin and potato salad. Mr. Benchley
was up on the terrace playing cards with some people
he'd met, Bunny had retired to the bungalow we were
sharing, and Tallulah was off in a sailboat with the boy
named John. Out in the distance, where the Sound
meets the Atlantic, I could see a lone ship neither ad-
vancing to shore nor retreating into that great ocean.
It was a good night for the rumrunners to smuggle
their cargo of liquor into the many coves that dotted
the shoreline.

   Headlights blazed harshly along the west side of
the house. Automobiles were recklessly maneuvering

around, tearing up the lawn and crushing the flower borders edging the driveway, so that headlights could illuminate the lawn for the croquet players who had set up wickets but were a little too drunk to find them in the dark.

It was nearly two in the morning and the orchestra was winding down for the night, playing mostly ballads as if to lull its audience to sleep. I closed my eyes when I heard the violins play the verse of "What'll I Do?"

Gone is the romance that was so divine,
'Tis broken and cannot be mended.
You must go your way and I must go mine.
But now that our love dreams have ended . . .

The melody, the sentiments, sent a painful longing through me — for a man, for a man who could love me.

What'll I do?
When you are far away
And I am blue,
What'll I do?

What'll I do?
When I am wond'ring who
Is kissing you,
What'll I do?

What'll I do with just a photograph
To tell my troubles to?
When I'm alone
With only dreams of you
That won't come true,
What'll I do?

Why had true love eluded me? Why did I always fall so hard? Did I expect too much from the man, and give too little in return? Why did it always seem like I was stumbling around in the dark, unable to find my way through love, when maybe all I had to do was open my eyes? Things were always so disappointing when I finally opened my eyes . . . .

Woodrow licked my hand, which made me smile.

By the time they were well into the waltz, "Always," I was so melancholy and full of self-doubt that I figured if I gave up writing poetry now, I might have a great career writing sappy song lyrics.

Just as I was considering a turn onto Tin Pan Alley, a girl on the beach, standing there alone, pulled my attention and my thoughts out from my own personal darkness.

She struck a pose, the girl in lavender-blue, a rather contrived stance with an arm thrown up as if reaching for a star; then with bent elbow she tented her shingle-trimmed head. Her legs were apart, with one knee bent, foot arched and toes flirting with the sand, thereby allowing the sheer fabric of her kerchief-edged skirt to pick up the breeze for just the right amount of playful fluttering.

Just a sliver of a girl gazing vacantly over the bay, not unlike the sliver of moon that hung in the sky this night. She, like that moon, would grow substantial someday, and I could imagine her rounded and mature body twenty years hence, as she might then stand considering the bay. If she grew to be wiser, I felt, her gaze would hold less vacancy.

Could there be something more, some compelling thought beyond the obvious that generated that seemingly calculated pose? Perhaps there floated a genuine yearning within her soul. Maybe she knew there was something more beyond the high-life she lived on Saturday nights, when she and the other girls, carried along by young swells toting monogrammed flasks in the hip pockets of their white flannels, would pile into Simonized roadsters to speed over the Queensboro Bridge, past the grim factories of Long Island City, until at last the road gave way to the sandy-edged open parkway and the salty promise of champagne revelries.

Eagerly, and without fear, these children were adept at crashing these celebrations of decadence, either claiming a mutual friendship with an acquaintance of the hostess or having once been, without question, a bona fide guest—the date of a Broadway star, perhaps, or more likely of a hoofer from the show at the Palace. No one really cared. The more the merrier. There was always an open door to the young and playful, whose antics only complemented the host's determination for a roaring good time to be had by all. The success of any party seemed to be measured by the number of plastered guests found passed out and strewn about the house and grounds at seven o'clock the morning after, or by the cost of repairs from cigarettes stamped out in the carpet. Yes, perhaps there was more to be had than just a good time, but the girl on the beach wouldn't be thinking about such things now—perhaps in five or ten years, when her laughter became a bit strident and her smile less quick to flash.

On Monday, the girl could charm and disarm or shock and appall those whom she wished to with stories of that Saturday night, that weekend on the Island when she danced with the boys on the roof of the cabana, or waded into the fountain to the music of Buddy Ray and the Downtown Boys blasting out a perky, "Ain't We Got Fun?" And when all this went out of fashion (as surely it would, for all things *au courante* become the tarnished fads of yesterday), the stories would remain to be told and retold again and again. There would be these memories in lonely years to come, when she was no longer a Bright Young Thing. She could reminisce, with embellishments if she so fancied, about these glory days to future generations so that they might know, and she might prove, that once upon a time she, too, had been young and carefree.

But the thoughts that were dancing around in this girl's head were merely the fancies of my own imagination. I really knew nothing more of what went on in her little brain than I understood of what was going on in mine! Whether she was expressing genuine yearning for self-discovery or had simply planted herself in a premeditated tableau designed to take away the breath of an admiring suitor was a mystery. She needn't have bothered to do anything at all to draw attention to herself, what with her slim and boyish figure. And, for all of the artifice applied with the defiant hand of youthful rebellion, the charm of her face remained in spite of her efforts to rouge her cheeks and darken her eyes. She possessed that contradiction most attractive to men—a combination of loose morals and childlike naïveté. When a lanky youth sidled up and awkwardly threw a bare arm around her shoulder, as if to tell her that *he* was the answer to her dreams, I imagined her wary assessment: *He'll do for tonight.*

I hadn't heard Mr. Benchley's approach, but when I looked over to the chair next to mine he was there, watching me watching the girl and her beau.

"Those kids think they're having fun, but they are disillusioned and don't know it," I said, seeing things a whole lot more clearly now.

"Unlike us grownups," replied my friend. "We're certainly disillusioned, too, my dear, but we *know* it."

"Is that why we're always so determined to have fun, Fred?"

We looked at each other, and we didn't need automobile headlights illuminating our thoughts to see the disillusionment that clung to us, that we just couldn't seem to shake from the War, from the execution, from so many things happening in the world in this year of 1927. And in spite of the great cleansing elixir of liquor and laughter, and without bothering with words, we arrived at a new, more profound understanding: *Having a good time isn't always that much fun, is it?*

Chapter Seven

We went in search of our hosts to bid them good-night, but we were told that Mr. and Mrs. Mellon had left for their apartment in Manhattan a little after midnight. Well, it was nearly three o'clock and, aside from a few diehards and insomniacs lounging on the plush furniture in the public rooms, the house was quiet, the overnight guests asleep in their rooms or in the family-sized bungalows assigned upon arrival. The lanterns still glowed along the grounds, illuminating the abandoned tables, which were a shambles with dirty dishes and wilted tablecloths drooping in the morning dew that clung to everything. A couple of waiters were stacking the remains of the night on trays and picking up from the pristine lawn the litter left by careless guests. Mr. Benchley and I walked across the grass toward a stand of birches, alongside which stood our two-bedroom cottage. As we entered the sitting room, the snores of Bunny Wilson drifted out through the door of the bedroom that Mr. Benchley would be sharing with Bunny for the next several hours.

"Sounds like a mastodon is snoozing in there," said Mr. Benchley in a resigned tone.

"You are *old*, but I had no idea you roamed the boulevards during the Stone Age."

"The Tertiary period, I believe . . . . "

"Smartypants."

"Perhaps a deckchair or hammock outside?" he said.

"You'll get eaten alive out there. I wouldn't recommend it."

"It's a matter of life and death!"

"How's that?" I asked, walking into the bathroom to check out the amenities.

"If I stay, and he keeps that racket up, I will surely kill the man."

"Sleep in here on the couch and stuff your ears with cottonballs, for God's sake. There's a jar of them here in the bathroom."

I closed my bedroom door against the noise, leaving it unlocked for when, or if, Tallulah returned. I turned on the bedside lamp and then crossed to open the windows, hoping for a breeze. The window screens made opaque the view. Woodrow took his usual place on my right side at the foot of the bed, as I stripped off my dress, got in, and reached over to shut the lamp. I was too tired even to be annoyed by the incessant barrage of chirping insects that always took getting used to when a City Girl slept in the country: crickets, frogs, moths beating themselves to death against the screens . . . .

I was lying there, trying to get comfortable, the sheets damp from seaside humidity that permeated everything it touched. A welcome breeze wafted in through the window and suddenly I shivered through my sweat. I drew the counterpane over me. I was listening to the racket of wildlife outside and thinking I should have grabbed a bunch of cottonballs from the bathroom to stuff in my ears, as I had suggested to Mr. Benchley, but was too tired to get up and fetch them. Drifting off, I was startled awake by the cooing of intimate laughter outside my window. *Tallulah had another think coming*, I thought, if she wanted to have a fling in here tonight!

But it wasn't Tallulah; the female's voice was too feminine, too high-pitched to be the Broadway star's.

"Get a goddamn room!" I shouted into the darkness, causing all God's creatures, great and small, to suddenly stop their racket. Woodrow's head popped up to look at his mad mistress. It was quiet for a long moment and I lay very still. And then, human noises— giggles and scurrying through the bushes surrounding the bungalow—could be heard as the lovers skulked away like skunks through the underbrush.

I was beginning to doze off again when I heard voices—men speaking in raised whispers—close by. My first thought was that Mr. Benchley had confronted our Bunny. My vision focused on the view out of the screened window. With the interior light off, the opaque effect of the screen melted away to present a new clarity, and there were revealed figures of people standing silhouetted against the dim light from the big house. Bushes rustled, there was grunting, and the crush of pebbles underfoot suggested a sexual encounter. I threw off the covers and knelt down to peer out the window to better see what was going on. After a moment or two, I heard a short cry and more rustling noises in the dark, but I saw no one, now. Well, I thought, if they weren't lovers, then it must have been a couple of drunks tripping over tree roots and wildlife while trying to find their bungalow in the dark.

Woodrow wasn't alarmed: He knew about sex and what it sounded like, and as for drunks stumbling about at all hours, well, he lived with me, after all, so he just laid there on the bed, on his back, legs up in the air and looking shamelessly comfortable. I fell back into bed and awoke with the sun and the smell of frying bacon drifting in through the window.

———————◆———————

"This is the forest primeval. The murmuring pines and the hemlocks—"

"Oh, for cryin'outloud, Bob!" whined Bunny.

"*—Bearded with moss, and in garments green, indistinct in the twilight,*

Stand like Druids of eld, with voices sad and prophetic—"

"Haven't we heard enough of 'Robert's recitation of all the poems he had to memorize in High School'?" I said.

"When I asked Teacher why I had to put these 'odes' to memory," said Mr. Benchley, interrupting himself, "Teacher said that, like memorizing my multiplication tables, they would come in handy one day, and they have for times like these. Now, where was I?"

Bunny moaned and with resignation said, "Pick it up at, *Where is the thatch-roofed village, the home of Acadian farmers—*"

"Yes, that's it! Thanks for the cue, Bunny: *Where is the thatched-roofed village—the home of—*"

What was the point of fighting it, Bunny's expression seemed to say when he turned around to look at me from the passenger seat of the car. He rolled his eyes upon glancing at the sleeping Tallulah, and then offered me a cigarette from his case.

"*Men whose lives glided on like rivers that water the woodlands—*"

We'd endured an hour of recital and thought that the program had come to an end with Longfellow's *The Wreck of the Hesperus*. We soon discovered that Mr. Benchley could be as longwinded as Longfellow himself, when he began his dramatic recitation of the first two cantos of part one of *Evangeline*. Happily, he hadn't put to memory the eight remaining cantos, and when he had finally run out of steam, Mr. Benchley noticed that the car was running out of gas. We drove off the highway past a peeling and punched-out billboard on which remained the depiction of huge, disembodied lips setting off a toothy smile, advertising the "expert dentistry" of Dr. Heckleman, D.D.S. Where the paper had peeled away it left gaps in what was once a perfect smile. And it looked like the work of a bunch of kids out one night with a can of black paint, a brush, and mischief in their hearts that took out a couple more teeth as well. It was funny, as most vandalism is not.

Mr. Benchley stopped at a railroad crossing and then continued on, following the dusty side road that ran parallel to the railroad track. On the other side of the road there wasn't much more than the occasional wood-framed house gone to seed—mostly ramshackle little buildings, with paint worn down to rotting gray clapboards, given over to hardware supplies, a variety store, a locksmith, and a seedy luncheonette. The landscape was bare and sandy with patches of grass struggling to hold onto the earth. Our car kicked up dust and obscured the road behind us like a past we wanted to forget.

A crosshatch pattern of telephone poles lining the tracks up ahead looked like the grim remains of foliage-ridden trees after a fire. And sitting defiantly in this sad little world was a little pink house that came into view as we rounded the bend, all the more vibrant in this spitefully gray place, its ultimate destiny doomed.

It was a little bakery done up in rosy paint and with flowered curtains that brightened the windows, its sign reading, Jenny's Cakes and Pies. Someone, probably Jenny, had tried to grow flowers in the windowboxes, but this attempt at beautification was beaten to dust by the merciless sun and the fetid smell of tar pitch that had settled on the place. Here, it seemed that all of the rich soil that once supported lush meadows and woods had been stripped away with the carving out of the rails and of the highway, the staking of the billboards, and the ground-driven poles on which were strung the electric, telephone, and telegraph wires that connected our thoughts, our voices, and our future. Nothing vital was left from the past; it had all been shoved aside and then trucked away to fill in the wetlands to the east where flower gardens mattered.

A kid with a stick rolled a rusty barrel hoop along the side of the road, his old hound following and nosing at the debris. An ancient and miserable picket fence leaned arthritically; a rusty tin can was stuck on one of the pickets like a mottled wart on the place, a final, painful rebuke.

This decayed junction was a testament to oxidation, for beneath the rusted-out metal roof of a garage was a rusty old red gasoline pump. In the bay of the filling station was an old car, a relic from earlier in the century, encrusted at its joints and propped up on blocks. Above it all was a pitted and faded metal sign, its worn red letters telling us we had arrived at WILSON'S GARAGE. As we pulled in and stopped in front of an incongruously bright and shiny new blue gas pump, I glimpsed the eager face of a young woman peeking out through the curtains of a room on the second floor of the shack. The desperate look of the girl stirred in me the image of a small trapped creature ready to forfeit a leg to save itself.

A young man in stained overalls squeezed lubricant from an oilcan along the hinges of the old heap's passenger door. He looked over at us, his demeanor as devoid of enthusiasm as the surrounding landscape. But then, with rising, if measured, interest he put down the can, wiped his hands on a rag, which he tucked in his hip pocket, and sauntered out toward our car, coolly appraising the graceful lines of molded metal. *Funny*, I thought, *how easy it is for those who struggle and know they can never afford such luxury to turn a critically envious eye on things of beauty and extravagance.*

As if by rote he said in a voice as colorless as his countenance, "Would you like to try our super-ethyl, leaded Blue Streak blend with a higher octane for superior performance and extended mileage than any other brand?"

"Will it shine my shoes and curl my hair?" I asked.

"Are you Mr. Wilson, the proprietor?" asked Mr. Benchley. He and Bunny stepped out of the car and walked around the front fender, watching intently as the fellow opened the hood to check the oil.

"Yeah, I'm Wilson," replied the man, nonchalantly. He was trying to hide his interest in the automobile, although his eyes and his body couldn't lie.

"Bunny's a Wilson, too," said Mr. Benchley.

"Hah?"

"Me, too, I'm a Wilson," said Bunny Wilson, peering over the man's shoulder and into the mysterious maze of mechanics.

"Uh-huh."

"He's a Wilson, too," said Mr. Benchley, pointing to Woodrow, whose leash he had taken so that I would be free to walk over to the bakery. "No relation to Bunny, though."

"You named your dog, there, Wilson?"

"His name is Woodrow Wilson."

"Like the president?"

"No relation, though," said Bunny.

The gas station owner looked over our party clothes, the men's shirts and ties in sorry, slept-in condition, and Tallulah's and my now-limp dresses that we'd donned the night before. "You from the city?"

"Heading back there, yeah."

"Why ain't I surprised?"

Bunny walked around the car, kicking tires, while Mr. Benchley checked his teeth while repositioning the sideview mirror, both men pretending they actually knew something about cars. They didn't, of course, but it was necessary to keep up the masculine front—observing and nodding as the proprietor, Mr. Wilson, filled the water tank, washed the windscreen, and pumped the gasoline.

Tallulah, awake and hungry, walked into the bakery with me for a sugary snack. After making our purchase of half-a-dozen donuts, we walked back out into the sun and grabbed a few bottles of Coca Cola out of the refrigerated cooler alongside the garage door, while the canine "Wilson" lapped up water dribbling out of the hose used for filling the car's radiator. The writer "Wilson" paid the mechanic "Wilson" for his services. Family reunion over, we set off back toward the highway.

An hour later, Mr. Benchley pulled the Mercedes into a space in front of the Algonquin, and we all eagerly got out of the car. The doorman stood poised to be handed my little overnight case by Mr. Benchley, who stood in front of the open trunk, staring down stupidly. I was about to ask my friend if he'd forgotten to throw in my little bag, for I could picture it still standing at the side of the drive, where I'd placed it, ready to be put in.

"Everybody back in the car," said Mr. Benchley, closing the trunk. It was an order, and not a request, because he opened the door for me and Tallulah to reenter, and then repeated the order to Bunny with an officious impatience that was out of character with the man I knew. And because his behavior was peculiar, we did as we were told. Even Tallulah's braying objections held no power, so she refrained from escalating them with four-letter words. But that didn't stop me:

"Shit!" I said, "You forgot the bag!"

"I didn't forget it."

"I don't understand," I said, as he pulled away from the curb with a jolt, turning uptown at Fifth Avenue.

"Neither do I," was his reply.

"Where are you taking us?" asked Tallulah. She dabbed a bit of *Shalimar* under her arms, as the bath she was longing for appeared to have been delayed for further adventures.

"To see Joe Woollcott, up at the police station."

"Sergeant Joe? You mean, Aleck's cousin?" asked Bunny.

"What did you do, ya damn fool, run a light, and you have to turn yourself in?" I said with a chuckle.

"I didn't do anything! I don't know anything about it!"

"What didn't you do?" And what *don't* you know?" I asked, getting nervous.

"I didn't kill anybody and I have no idea why a dead man's body is stuffed in the trunk of this car."

Chapter Eight

What can I say about Sgt. Joe Woollcott? Everything that Aleck is, Joe is not. Aleck is flamboyant; Joe is reserved. Aleck adores glitzy attire; Joe lives in NYPD blue. Aleck speaks with affected, florid audaciousness; Joe is all straight talk. Aleck is at home in a theatre; Joe prefers Yankee Stadium. The only things they have in common are their identical reflections when they look in the mirror, their great love of food, and their maternal connection: Their mothers were sisters.

It just so happened that Sgt. Joe had been on duty Sunday morning and was just punching out to go to his home in the Bronx where his wife and five children were awaiting him for the start of their Sunday dinner of meat and potatoes when Mr. Benchley pulled up in front of the precinct house.

"Joe," called out Mr. Benchley from the driver's seat of the Mercedes, getting Joe's attention as he exited the station house. "Hypothetical question."

Sgt. Joe walked over to the curb, eyes running over the length of the car with lustful yearning. "Benchley? Oh, hello, Mrs. Parker, everybody..." he said, touching the visor of his cap. And then, with a sudden realization of why we were parked outside the police station, "Oh, no, let me say right off the bat: We don't yet know the identity of the woman who was murdered on your train the other day."

"Why did he call it *your train?*" asked Tallulah, looking at me.

Mr. Benchley would not be distracted from his mission with queries about a dead woman when he had a dead man on his hands: "Joe, suppose you just drove home from a weekend by the shore—"

"No such luck. Been on duty all weekend. Nice machine you have here, Benchley...."

"Like it? It's the new Mercedes Benz 630K Sports Touring car," answered my friend, opening the glove compartment and removing a business card, which he handed to Joe. "Forty-four-hundred pounds of steel is this baby! Got a supercharged six-cylinder 6240-cc engine, *and* with a hundred-forty horsepower, by golly, it's the fastest touring car on earth, Joe. But, as I had started to say, suppose you drove home with your friends from a weekend by the seashore, and—"

"You took a job as a car salesman? It's steady work, steadier than show business, that's for sure, if you're good at it. And you got a wife and a couple of kids to support . . . . Well," said Joe, looking at the car longingly and pocketing the business card, "I can dream, I guess. Is that where you've been, the seashore? We've been trying to find you."

"That so? Well, I'm here, now. But, back to my point, Joe: Let's just say you just drove this car back home—"

"Too rich for me, Bobby. I sure could use a couple days by the shore, though," said Joe, "but the old Ford will have to do until I get a promotion. I thought I'd take a drive out to Rockaway next week. The wife and kids would like—"

"Yes, well, as I was saying, let's say you drove home—"

"Don't waste the sales pitch on me, Bobby—"

"I'm not trying to sell you—"

"I couldn't afford this beauty even if I *was* in the market for new car. Nice paint job, though."

"Twenty-one coats, you know."

"Horsepower?"

"I told you! A hundred and forty—runs one-hundred-five miles per hour on the open road—"

"Nice wood-finished interior."

"Burl wood is standard; it's a Benz, after all."

"Radio's optional, Joe," said Tallulah. "And believe me, *you have to have a radio.*"

"Radios are too distracting, cause too many accidents," said Mr. Benchley.

"Yes, Bobby, but—" groaned Tallulah.

"Would they throw one into the deal at the list price?"

"I'm *not* trying to sell you a car, Joe," said Mr. Benchley. He looked on the verge of tears. "I'm trying to say that I discovered that there's more than just Mrs. Parker's overnight case in the trunk of this car."

"Okay, you're not trying to sell me a car, sure, I get it! Smooth sales pitch. Lots of room in the trunk, huh? Well, we don't go on any big, long trips, just day trips to Coney Island for the rides and a swim—bring along a few sandwiches, towels, and a beach umbrella," considered Joe.

Mr. Benchley shook his head and groaned. "What I was getting at, Joe—although I was presenting the whole account as a hypothetical, you see—" Mr. Benchley was pretty much talking to himself, now, babbling and chuckling and looking for help from the heavens as Joe was off and running somewhere else.

"Just practicing, you mean? You seem to know what you're talking about, all righty! Well, thanks for letting me know that you're back in town, Benchley. I'll call you at the dealership. Better yet, can you stop back in here tomorrow morning before work, to save time?"

"That's just it, Joe: I don't think it'll keep until morning, it's so darn hot. And I have to return the car, see?"

The men looked at each other, confused, as well they should be, and Bunny and Tallulah were no help at all, making jokes and laughing, so I decided to fix things: "For cryin'outloud, Joe, there's a dead body in the trunk of this car."

Well, that put things straight, and ended Mr. Benchley's hypothetical approach, although it took a bit of explaining to Joe that he had not actually given up his career as drama critic and his editorship of *Life* magazine in favor of selling automobiles. But, at least Mr. Benchley was not in jeopardy of being considered an accessory after the murder of the man in the trunk. For indeed, a crime of murder had been committed against the fellow, who stared up blindly from his resting place in the trunk of the car. Not only did the crack on his skull indicate foul play, but he hadn't crawled into the car's trunk by himself, so somebody had to have put him there. But it wasn't so much that we had been chauffeuring around a dead man all morning—or the embarrassment the discovery of the body might have caused Mr. Benchley at the automobile dealership—after all, he always returned the loaned vehicle swept, washed, and Simonized. And it wasn't the first time we'd discovered a dead body— we've been stumbling over them in all the best places over the past few years, so it was not exactly a shock that one had popped up in the trunk of the Mercedes.

It was the fact that the murdered man was instantly identifiable to me.

"I know this man," I said, and everybody turned to look at me, mouths hanging open like hooked fish.

"Elaborate, please," said Mr. Benchley.

"What do you know about this?" said Joe, frowning with pseudo-officiousness. After all, he was a police officer and no longer a potential Mercedes customer.

"I know nothing about it whatsoever, Joe Woollcott!" I was very good at "indignant."

"But, you just said—"

"He's the man who's been following me."

"Is that so?"

"Yes, that is so."

"And why has he been following you, Mrs. Parker, for your autograph?"

"Obviously not for his health, Joe," said Mr. Benchley, offering his hip flask all around, while we all lit up cigarettes.

"He's the man I saw on the train talking with our socialist friend, and then I saw him lurking a couple doors down from my hairdresser's salon, yesterday, and—"

"Lurking?" said Mr. Benchley, "and you didn't tell me? Why, he might have murdered you—"

Tallulah snorted.

I glanced at her with a sneer. "All right, he wasn't lurking, that's too sinister; he was just *looking* in the window of a haberdasher's shop on Madison. And he didn't murder me, but got murdered instead, as we can see. I recognize the beret he's clutching in his hand, and he's wearing the same gabardine suit and tie."

"I don't remember seeing him at the party last night," said Bunny.

"How could you?" snapped Tallulah, "When you didn't have your tongue down the throat of that little chorine you were romancing, you had your tongue down the spout of a cognac bottle. But, *I* remember him."

Bunny didn't make a rejoinder; he knew not to mess with Tallulah when she was irritable. We all awaited her explanation, because she took advantage of a dramatic pause to milk suspense. Finally: "I saw him when I arrived at our bungalow last night."

"Oh?" I said, "Arrived? Last night? You slinked in at dawn, after waking the dead with your foghorn lamentation of 'Swanee.'"

"All right, 'Miss Music Critic'—you've no ear for music, you know that?—all right, I *did* get in at dawn. We were watching the sunrise over the bay after our sail."

"*We* meaning you and that adolescent—"

"He said he was twenty-one—"

"Me-*ow!*" said Bunny. "Look out, Bobby, a pussy fight!

"Never liked pussies, Bunny, I'm a dog man," cut in Mr. Benchley, pointing at us women, in a "confidential" aside we all could hear.

"You certainly are a dog!" I turned on him, before turning back to Tallulah.

"Prefer dogs, myself," nodded Bunny, "ever since I was a boy and our pet raccoon dragged in Pickles."

"Every boy should have a dog," concurred Mr. Benchley.

"Like my friend Woodrow Wilson over there," said Bunny, turning to look at my pup, who was napping under the auto's chassis and out of the sun. "A kindred spirit, right down to our names. Look at him, lying there calmly, taking everything in his stride. Yes, every boy should have a dog . . . ."

"Why, a dog teaches a boy fidelity," said Mr. Benchley.

"Yes, he does . . . ."

"Perseverance—"

"Absolutely!"

"—and to turn around three times before lying down."

I looked at Tallulah. "And the more I know of men," I said to her, "the more I appreciate dogs."

Tallulah and I retracted our claws. We were both

out of sorts from the heat, the car ride, and the ordeal of two hours of recitations by an idiot.

"So what was it all about, Miss Bankhead? Where exactly did you see this fellow?" prodded Sgt. Joe, trying to steer us back to the object of discussion: the dead man in the trunk.

"He was sitting on one of those benches at the edge of the little strip of woods between the house and the guest bungalows."

"What house? Where?" asked Joe.

After a brief summary of our visit to the Mellons' Long Island estate, and a recap of the musical entertainment on our way there and the oratory highlights on our way back to town, all provided for our listening pleasure by Mr. Benchley, and after my recommendation that Joe absolutely must choose the optional radio installation when purchasing a car, Joe said, "All right! I get the picture! He was alive when you saw him this morning."

"Yes," said Tallulah. "He was sitting on the bench with a woman."

"A woman!"

"Watching the rising dawn, I suppose?" I asked.

"What woman? Do you know who she was?" asked Joe.

"Couldn't see her face, or his either, for that matter. They were locked in an . . . intimate embrace."

"How do you know, then, that the man you saw with the dame was this guy?"

"Well, the light-colored suit showed up in the dark woods."

"So, we know he was alive at dawn," said Joe, "and if we can find the woman, she will be able to tell us who this guy is. What else do you remember about the scene?"

I interrupted Joe: "What was *she* wearing, the woman?"

"Uhhh, let's see . . . a dress, not an evening gown, though."

"So, if she was a guest, she must have changed out of her finery," said Mr. Benchley. "That means she probably was staying the night, either in one of the other bungalows or in one of the bedrooms in the main house."

"Indeed," said Tallulah, throwing it off, tired of the questions, hung over from too much champagne (and God knows what else she had imbibed or inhaled), needing a cool shower, and just plain cranky.

"You must *think*, Lulla!" said Bunny, all altruistic and regaining his dignified sobriety. This was silly Bunny Wilson reverting to socially conscious Edmund Wilson, honorable young-man-of-letters. "What did you notice about her when you slithered back from your romantic assignation on the bay?"

(Oh, and I forgot to add, *pompous ass.*)

"Shut up, you silly virgin," erupted Tallulah.

"Alley cat!"

"Well, it's true, don't deny it! You're no tom cat, you ridiculous little sot! We all know you've been carrying around that same rubber in your pocket, never been used, same one you arrived with back in 'nineteen!"

"Now, now, kids!" broke in Mr. Benchley, playing Father. "None of this sex-talk around the dinner table, or we'll lock you in your rooms and draw the shades!"

"Keep out of this, you."

"If you insist, Lulla,"

"Well, that's a lie!" said Bunny, blushing. With his already-fiery coloring he now resembled a radish: red, puckered, and with wisps of reddish hair where the roots would be.

"It *is* the same rubber! And I have it from the horse's mouth that *it is so!*"

"Which horse?"

"That horse over there," she said, pointing at Little Me.

"Thanks a lot," I said, "I'm a horse, huh?" I got ready for a defensive retort but couldn't think of a thing to strike back with. It's hard to deny the truth when you're feeling hot and testy.

"It is *not* the same one—"

"*Ohhhh!* The first one disintegrated, did it? Had to be replaced? What happened, you play with it too much, rubbed it like a rabbit's foot so you'd get lucky some night? Ain't that why they call you 'Bunny?'"

"Why, you—"

"Go ahead, say it!"

"What the hell is going on here!" bellowed the usually soft-spoken sergeant, sounding oddly as if the Big Man—his cousin, Aleck—had suddenly appeared on the scene. And just in time, too, because Tallulah raised a fist and was about to throw a punch square into Mr. Benchley's head when Bunny, who'd seen it coming, ducked behind the car salesman.

"All right, you two!" said Sgt. Joe. "Now, you kids shake hands and make up, or I'll run you both in! Now, let's get back to the matter at hand. Mrs. Parker, you say this fellow was following you. Now why would he be following you?"

"How the hell would I know?"

"Mr. Benchley, you'll have to leave this car with me, so our crime scene men can look things over; the body must be removed."

"My friend at the dealership would appreciate that—"

"There may be evidence here." Joe told us to stay put, saying he was going back into the station-house to alert his chief to the situation.

"*What* are you doing, Mrs. Parker!"

"Well, he's lying on my overnight case and there's a bag of potato chips in there that I wanted—" I said after Joe had left. I nudged at the shoulder of the corpse, which was folded in a fetal position and wedging in my overnight case. But, I didn't see the familiar blue leather.

"Well, I don't see the harm, but I doubt you'd want to eat the chips now," said Mr. Benchley.

"I suppose not." I said, and then, rolling the fellow on his side, I said, "For God's sake, Fred, where the hell is my overnight case?"

Mr. Benchley looked at me and then flipped the fellow onto his other side. "How should I know? I thought the butler threw it in."

I remembered, suddenly, some confusion, and that the butler was called away to the main house by the housekeeper, but had instructed one of the Mellons' footmen to load up the luggage of the departing guests. At the time, Mr. Benchley had been saying his goodbyes to a Broadway producer friend, and had assumed the bag was in the trunk as we drove out.

"What are you doing, Dottie?" asked Tallulah, as I gingerly went through the pockets of the dead man's coat jacket.

"Mrs. Parker, you shouldn't be doing that," said Mr. Benchley as I struggled to reach for the fellow's wallet. He helped me shift the body, which was rigid. "Nice suit," he said. "Custom cut, Savile Row, H. Huntsman & Sons, London . . . where Noel Coward gets his clothes." He rubbed the fabric of the lapel between his thumb and index fingers. "Quality."

"Passport," I said, handing it over to my friend before continuing my search into the dead man's right trouser pocket. I winced, made a little whooshing noise, and Tallulah caught my eye as I looked up with a frown.

"He is—*was*—a big boy," I said, and then my thoughts returned to the task at hand—I mean the reason for my search: "Hotel-room key."

"Bunny, write this down, will you?" said Mr. Benchley while looking through the passport. "His name was Charlie Fanshaw: Capital *F-e-a-t-h-e-r-s-t-o-n-h-a-u-g-h*. Fanshaw."

"Feather-ston-hauff? What kind of a name is that?"

"Pronounced *Fanshaw*."

"Too many letters, old sport."

"That's how the Brits pronounce it."

"But—"

"Like *Maudlin* College: *M-a-g-d-a-l-e-n-e*."

"Magdalene, like in Mary, lady of the night? What's in that flask?" asked Tallulah.

"I was born in *Wuster*, Massachusetts: *W-o-r-c-e-s-t-e-r*—"

"All right, you crazy anglophile, look at this," I said.

"—And I have a friend named *Sin-Jin*: *S-a-i-n-t J-o-h-n*. Oh, and there comes *Sarjent* Joe Woollcott, spelled *s-e-r-g-e-a-n-t*. Tell me *that* makes sense, Mrs. Parker!"

Sgt. Joe was coming out of the station with three other officers. I grabbed the passport out of Mr. Benchley's hand and replaced it in the inside jacket pocket from where I had taken it. I palmed the key because I had no time to tuck it back into his pants; the officers had arrived by my side.

"You shifted the body?" asked Joe.

"To get my case, but I don't see it in there."

Joe threw a face, sighed, and said, "You can't tamper with evidence, Mrs. Parker, you know that!"

Something in my face must have given me away: "All right, hand it over. What'd you find that you shouldn't have taken?"

I handed over the room key—twenty-two-twenty-nine, which I recognized as a key from the new Sherry-Netherland.

"Joe, if you haven't yet identified the woman who was murdered on the Midnight Owl, has anyone even inquired about a missing person matching her description?"

"No, no one has inquired."

"What about her things—her hat, jewelry, luggage?"

"Whatever she had has been put into evidence. Coroner's report should be in on Monday—that's tomorrow morning."

"Could you—?"

"Mrs. Parker, you're gonna have my job—"

"I don't need to see it, just tell me what they found?"

"Call me in the morning."

Mr. Benchley was issued a receipt for the car, which would be returned to the dealership after the trunk had been checked over for prints and any other evidence. As we hopped into a cab, our destination Tony Soma's speakeasy, Mr. Benchley leaned out of the window.

"You know, Joe, considering the circumstances, the dead body in the trunk, and all, you might be able to pick this beauty up for a song," said Mr. Benchley, car salesman.

———◆———

Bunny wanted nothing more than to resume his place on the sofa in the lobby of the Algonquin, and Tallulah wanted a bath, so we dropped them off at home.

Mr. Benchley asked the cabbie to drive us to Tony Soma's, but I asked that we be taken further north to the new Sherry-Netherland, the apartment hotel on the corner of 60th Street at Fifth Avenue.

"Now, Mrs. Parker, what kind of trouble are you planning to get us into?"

"You saw the insignia on the hotel key that I found in the dead man's pocket. It's the Sherry's logo."

"It's distressing hearing you refer to the poor fellow as 'the dead man,' don'tchathink? I mean, he had a name—"

"A ridiculous one, if you ask me. All right, I shall call him Feather-ston-*hauff*."

"Fanshaw!"

"All right, Fanshaw! Gee, you're a pill. We need to search his rooms before the police get here," I said, hopping out of the cab. I looked up at the incredible feat of engineering that allowed thirty-eight stories to soar above the avenue. This was "the tallest apartment hotel in the world," boasted the ice-cream-and-candy king, Louis Sherry, when he opened the doors for business a few months ago. The neo-Romanesque and Renaissance building towered over its travertine marble base and was topped with an elaborate Gothic minaret.

Woodrow led the way into the gilded, chandeliered lobby, which was pretentiously modeled after the Vatican Library—vaulted ceilings, guarding griffins, and all.

"*Jeez*," I said, "give a tycoon a little bit of money and this is how he spends it."

"Don't you like it, Mrs. Parker?"

"It's magnificent," I replied, as we got on the elevator. The operator let us out on the twenty-second floor.

"You can put your Swiss Army knife away; the door is open," I told Mr. Benchley. A chambermaid had parked a cart outside the opened door of room twenty-two-twenty-nine.

"I see, but how do we get in past her?"

"Watch this," I said, and then shook Woodrow's leash to get his attention.

"Ready, set, go!"

Woodrow broke into a run around the cart and into the room, appearing to be leading me in through the door, but, like driving a horse-drawn chaise, I was at the reins. I feigned frustration at the behavior of my little devil just as the maid came out from the bathroom, and Woodrow and I landed on the bed, the former licking my face.

"Now, Woodrow, what would our Mr. *Fanshaw* say if he saw us bouncing around on the bed?" I looked up into the face of the laughing maid. "After this nice lady over here went to the trouble of changing the sheets and all? By the way, have you seen Mr. *Fanshaw*?"

She looked at me blankly. "There's a Mr. Feath-erstone-*haw* or something like that in these rooms, but—"

"It's pronounced *Fanshaw*, dear. I know, I had the same problem when we first met, and being married to a man with a name like that is not easy, believe me, trying to explain all the time that it's because he's British that the name is spelled so ridiculously! I should have married a Smith or a Jones! Have you met him yet?"

"Ahhh, no," she said, a little flustered, and before she could finish, in walked Mr. Benchley.

"Oh, hello, darling!"

"*Dear*..." he replied for want of something to say. I wasn't sure if he had caught on to what I was doing.

"Did you send that cable to Bobby, Charles?"

"Yes, uh, just sent it out, *dear*."

"You need to make that phone call, now, don't you?"

"Yes," he agreed, walking over to the telephone. He glanced over at the maid, who took the hint and left the room, pulling the door closed behind her.

I said with pride as I rustled Woodrow's little tummy—he was lying on the bed and enjoying all the attention—"Goes to show that people see what they want to see. Pretend you belong here, people assume you belong here."

Mr. Benchley went directly to the closet, which was empty, while I caught sight of two valises that were under the bed and appeared not to have been unpacked.

Mr. Benchley lifted the valises onto the bed and unbuckled the straps. Inside one was a suit—jacket, vest, trousers—evening clothes, and a variety of shirts, ties, underclothes, a pair of patent dress-shoes, several casual flannels, and a sporty jacket. Evening suits and shirtfronts were folded within paper to keep the garments' shape and press. Studs, white ties, and various other formal accessories were boxed, as were the patent dress-shoes. An opera scarf was folded over the flattened silk top-hat. *Funny*, I thought; none of the clothing appeared the least worn. It was as if the articles had been bought new, or at the very least, pressed and packed, but they had not been removed from the luggage. The dress-suit bore the name of a swanky British men's clothier, according to Mr. Benchley. And yet, all of the times I had seen the now-deceased Mr. Featherstonhaugh, he'd been wearing the fawn-colored gabardine, and the royal-blue beret atop his head. The fact that he hadn't unpacked his bags meant he hadn't stayed in the room very much—or perhaps he had unpacked and repacked them because he was planning to check out of the hotel soon . . . ?

An attaché case was filled with catalogues, news clippings, and envelopes, and a folder, like a dossier. In it were handwritten and typewritten notes and a couple of photos of rather poor quality. A large manila envelope contained several letters of introduction and a London bank's line of credit, along with travel receipts that offered new understanding, especially the document that attested that Featherstonhaugh was a licensed private investigator. From all the various items it became clear that the murdered man had been hired to follow a Mrs. Joan Trombley, and the detective had traveled from London to South Hampton on the boat train and then to Boston on the very same ship, the *Victoria*, that brought the Mellons and Giusto to the United States. *There was the connection.*

A photograph fell out from among the loose papers in the folder. A rather short dumpling of a man, looking ill-at-ease in the morning suit he wore, stood beside a taller, rather attractive woman holding a bouquet. A wedding photo? On closer inspection, the woman had very dark hair tumbling around her shoulders, but the pose was so animated, her chin raised, head thrown back, mouth opened in laughter, that it was hard to discern her features. I handed the picture to Mr. Benchley for inspection while I shuffled through the other photographs, mostly exterior shots of houses and landscapes and people wearing tweeds, with elderly gentry types, a few in hunting clothes, holding guns and dangling dead rabbits and birds from straps in group shots. Typically English, I surmised, from the wattle-and-dab Tudor structures and the sign above a pub depicting a man dangling by his neck from a rope and the words, *The Hangman.*

The waste-bin had been emptied by the maid, so there was nothing else to tell us what he was up to, or whether he had found his Joan Trombley, and whether in fact she was the woman murdered in Bedroom Two. But, who had murdered *him*, and why?

If there were papers or other valuable clues to be found in the hotel vault, they were unattainable unless you had a police warrant.

"The man was interested in fine jewelry," said Mr. Benchley. "Look at these," he said, handing me a couple of sales catalogues from Van Cleef & Arpels and Cartier's, listing various ornaments by name and description and to whom they were sold and on what dates, including carat weights in diamonds, sapphires, emeralds, rubies, and other rare gemstones.

"Jewel thief?"

"Appears so."

In the drawer of a bedside table were scraps of paper—one a sad little drawing of a bird on the wing from a three-quarter profile. It was all angles and points and not at all lifelike, rather an abstract of a bird, and not very good. There was a big circle where an eye would be.

"Let's get out of here; the hair on the back of my neck is rising. I sense discovery by the boys in blue."

But, Mr. Benchley was again studying the wedding photo when the telephone rang. We looked at each other, nodded mutual agreement, and then he picked up the receiver of the ultramodern, stream-lined, cream-colored-Bakelite telephone.

"Yes?" I put my ear close to the receiver.

"Charles?" came a halting, masculine voice through the line. "Charles?" repeated the voice, "It's Freddie."

"Yes, 'course it is," responded Mr. Benchley in an impeccable British accent.

"Are you all right? You sound rather chuffed."

"Fine, just fine. Bit of a cold, is all."

"Well, what do you say, man? I received your wire; didn't you receive mine?"

"Yes, of course, Henry."

"What? This is Fre—someone is in the room with you?"

"Yes."

"I see. No wonder you sound so . . . odd."

There was a long silence on the other end, and I could almost hear the thoughts tumbling noisily around in "Freddie's" brain.

"Where are you calling from?" asked Mr. Bench-ley, attempting to keep the caller's suspicions at bay through a casually tossed off query.

"From the lobby," came the reply. "For heaven's sake, Charles, when you didn't show up—I'm coming up to your room."

I didn't have to tell my friend that the police would be arriving at any moment to search the dead man's room.

"No. Go into the restaurant, get a table in a quiet corner, and order three glasses of orange juice. I'll be right down." And with that, Mr. Benchley put down the receiver.

We left the room, pulling the door closed behind us.

"Freddie" was sitting at a table away from the center of the room, out of earshot of other Sunday afternoon diners. I recognized him immediately from the wedding photograph we had found among the papers in Featherstonhaugh's briefcase. Mr. Benchley noted the three glasses of orange juice set before him on the table. Freddie looked confused and anxious as he searched the faces of people entering the dining room in groups of two and four, and as we approached the table, he impatiently peered around us, hoping Featherstonhaugh would appear.

"Freddie?" asked Mr. Benchley, as he pulled up a chair from an adjoining table to make a third seat at the table-for-two. He saw me seated, much to the chagrin of the man, who was annoyed at the interruption of his appointment. And when my friend introduced us, producing his flask to pour a shot of gin in each of our glasses, the gentleman began to rise from his seat, a frightened look on his face.

"We're here because Mr. Fanshaw is unable to join us, I'm afraid."

"What is going on here?" he asked, eyes wide and looking as if he were ready to bolt. "Where's Charles?"

"He couldn't come down to meet you."

He looked from one to the other of us with a frown that melted into sad resignation. "Charles? But—I just spoke with—he wired me. He said he'd found her; I was to sail on the next ship."

"I see," said Mr. Benchley. "And he asked you to come here because he *found her*." A statement, not a question.

"Joan. My wife."

Freddie obviously didn't like what he read in our expressions when he'd said, "my wife," because before we could even tell him of our suspicions, he assumed she had fallen to mortal injury.

His voice broke. "Is she—?"

"We don't know. You see, last week a woman was murdered. Her name has not been disclosed as yet."

"But, you think—? For some reason you are convinced the woman was my wife, Joan."

His body stiffened and I thought he was about to keel over, for he gripped the sides of the table, as if to anchor himself.

"Not for sure, no," replied Mr. Benchley.

"But, still, you wouldn't be telling me this if—
Oh, I should have guessed from his wire telling me to
come to the States immediately that there was something more than the fact that he had finally caught
up with her," he said quietly. "I suppose I knew all
along on the voyage over here that there was more
to it. I just didn't want to believe anything—*horrible*
could have happened! But, don't tell me Charles had
anything to do with her death!"

"We don't know; it seems unlikely," said Mr.
Benchley.

"We are not telling you that the dead woman *is*
your wife. We just want to know why you were searching for her, why you sent Charles Fanshaw to find her,
all the way across the sea."

"Did he ask you, the police, to break the news
to me? Charles? I'm sure he wasn't responsible for
her death. I'd not hold him accountable, so—"

"Mr. uh . . . ."

"Trombley."

"Mr. Trombley," I started, "there is more to
tell."

Freddie began to rise from his chair.

I covered Freddie Trombley's nervous hand grip-
ping the corner of the table with my own, and Mr.
Benchley gently pressed his shoulder for him to sit.

"I'm sorry to tell you that we have some very bad news: Charles Fanshaw is dead."

In telling about Charles Featherstonhaugh's death, we made sure to eliminate the harsher details of his trip in the trunk of a car, and then corrected the assumption that Mr. Benchley was somehow a police officer, saying that he was "in the vicinity" at the time of the murders.

How much can the man take? I thought as the tears began to stream down his reddened cheeks.

"It may be coincidence that Charles Fanshaw was murdered soon after a woman passenger on the Midnight Owl train from Boston was killed. And, remember for now, that woman may not have been your wife, Joan," I said.

"But, if that were so, if it wasn't she, he wouldn't have cabled me to come on the next available ship!" He sunk back down in despair.

"It is possible the murdered woman is some-one else. Someone he may have chanced upon, and then, gaining the knowledge of a conspiracy—there are some suggestions that the dead woman may have been part of a conspiracy to explode a bomb in New York City as part of an anarchist protest to the execu-tions of Sacco and Vanzetti," said Mr. Benchley. "That seems to be the more likely reason for *his* murder—to prevent him from going to the authorities."

"Now, the only way you can find out whether

this woman was your wife is by identifying her body," said Mr. Benchley.

"May I be so bold as to ask, was your wife sympathetic to the anarchists' cause?" I said. "Is that why you were trying to find her—to stop her?"

"*Joan?*" said Freddie Trombley with a gasp of utter amazement. "An anarchist? A political sympathizer!" And then, breaking down into peels of near-hysterical laughter, causing the conversation to abruptly stop at the nearest table as its occupants turned to stare for a long moment, Freddie choked out between breaths, "Joan didn't care a rat's ass about anything to do with politics. The only political philosophy *she* ever had was purely capitalistic!" He shifted from mindless laughter to a sneering, biting attack as he hissed out, "That nasty little piece of work! That money-grubbing *cow!*"

Suddenly, he leaned back in his chair, a lump of saggy flesh, like something had sucked out all the bones from his body and just left him there, spent.

"She's dead! I know it!" The man was stunned, I realized, by the shock of it all and probably by his own unusual and unchecked passionate display of rancor. Mr. Benchley moved the glass of gin-laced juice closer to the man, who then belted down the liquid. Mr. Benchley refilled the glass with another straight shot of gin, which the fellow downed in one sobbing gulp.

"I hated her—*no!* I loved her; I never wanted her to die. But she got what she deserved!"

I wasn't sure what the man was saying: He loved her; he loved her not? "No, no, that's not true! I wanted her to come home to me," he moaned. "I wanted her to forget that fellow she ran off with! How did it happen?"

Mr. Benchley went over the events on the train, minus the Giusto factor, replacing the word *bludgeoned* as the cause of death with *crowned*.

After regaining a modicum of composure, I asked if his wife had any distinctive scars or birthmarks that might help identify her.

"What do you mean? Oh, well, she was a brunette, blue eyes—I can identify her."

"Well, you see, she suffered some head trauma—"

"Oh, my God!"

There was no easy way of saying any of it, but what had to be said needed delicacy so that the man need not suffer the mental "bludgeoning" of learning that his wife's face was battered beyond recognition. And yet he had to understand that identifying her body had to be done through other means.

"A scar on her right leg from surgery after an automobile accident a dozen years ago. She'd also broken her arm then. And she had a birthmark on her breast—like a little quarter-moon. Oh, my God!"

After another round of grief, he looked up, sniffled, and sat erect in his chair. Now he was ready to tell us a little bit about why he'd sought the help of his cousin, Charles, a detective, to follow his wife to the United States. But, he couldn't tell us whom she ran off with because he didn't know.

———————

Mr. Benchley and I settled in at a checker-clothed table for refreshment and private talk about what we'd found in the dead man's pants, and in his room at the Sherry. We ordered bowls of spaghetti as well as G-and-Ts, as it was almost dinnertime and we'd not eaten anything more than the donuts we'd gotten from the bakery in the village where we stopped for gasoline on the way home from Last Call. Woodrow was brought steak bones and a plate of meatballs by a waiter who was particularly fond of my little mutt.

Mr. Featherstonhaugh was the topic of our discussion. "Look, what if Fanshaw was in cahoots with Joan Trombley? Maybe they were planning a jewel heist?"

Mr. Benchley put down his fork, leaned back in his chair, and narrowed his eyes. "Heist? Where did you pick up the term, 'heist'? You been hanging around with the Damon Runyon crowd?"

"I heard Ross use the word once to describe what the boys did to him at poker one night."

"Well, that would imply a band of thieves, would it not?"

"How the hell would I know? I just thought it meant stealing."

"All right, my dear," said Mr. Benchley with a chuckle. "Perhaps he wasn't planning a burglary as a cat thief; maybe he had been nasty Joan's lover all along, and together they were part of a gang or a syndicate, even. Those jewelry sales sheets we found weren't meant for the eyes of the general public, you know. Maybe he had an inside man at those concerns."

"'Inside man'? Where'd you pick that up?"

"Damon Runyan."

"Others, huh? You think, maybe his confederates killed him?" A thought hit me. "My God, do you think there was a robbery last night at the Mellons', and it had yet to be discovered when we left? He was at Last Call, and I'll bet there were millions of dollars in hot rocks all over the place. You should have seen the ice scattered all over Hermione's dressing table."

"Hot rocks? Ice?"

"Damon Runyon."

"I'm sure it is a point that the police will be investigating as soon as they find those papers in his room."

"Let's call Roger and Hermione and ask about it."

"I'm sure the police are already at the house, as that was the last place Fanshaw was seen—by Tallulah, in fact—before someone tried to make his narrow bed in my trunk."

"But there has got to be a connection to the Mellons, considering that he came over on the same ship, took the same train—shit!"

"What is it?"

"He wasn't following me. Fanshaw was following the Mellons. He was probably planning on robbing them!"

"It fits . . . ."

"And his partner, or partners, *done him in*."

My friend shook his head indicating dismay, stuck his fork upright in a meatball, and said: "Your language is appalling, Mrs. Parker. *Done him in*, my word! I've got to introduce you to a better class of people who speak the King's English."

"Cut the crap, Fred," I said, grabbing the fork and biting into one of his meatballs. "*Done him in* is a perfectly good term to express murder."

"You're right; it was probably his partners in crime who *knocked him off*."

That fact agreed, we ordered another round and plowed through our spaghetti for the next few minutes.

"So, what do we do now?" I asked, sated, and wiping the tomato sauce off my chin.

Mr. Benchley gave me the *look*, the wide-eyed, *oh-no-not-that-again!* look. "We do nothing. *Not a thing.* We mind our own business."

"But they *made* it our business when they put Mr. Fanshaw to rest in your Mercedes."

"Not *my* Mercedes, a loaned automobile, remember?"

"If you want to be picky about it, yes. But—"

"No *buts* about it! I won't be sticking my nose in crime this time."

"All right, y'old bag, if that's how you feel."

"It is how I feel," he said, pushing back his chair to stand and grabbing the check off the table. He reached into his trouser pocket for cash to pay the bill, and came up instead with the small wedding photograph of Freddie Trombley and his wife, which he'd pocketed at the hotel room of the mysterious Mr. Featherstonhaugh.

"Why, look what you took, you old heel!" I said, grabbing the picture.

"I didn't realize—I mean, I meant to return it for the police to find."

"Now look what you've done! How are you going to explain stealing evidence?" I stared at the image of the woman, and there was a fleeting glimmer of recognition, like when you have the name of an acquaintance on the tip of your tongue before it escapes your grasping memory. It is at times like these that I awaken at three in the morning with the name ringing in my ears . . . .

"I got it!" I said.

"Whatchagot?"

"The woman in the photo—she reminds me of Katherine Cornell."

"I don't see it," he said. "We'll have to return the picture."

"Whaddayamean, *we?*" I say we just forget about it. We know who the woman in the photo is. Joan Trombley."

"I suppose it's of little importance, anyway."

———◆———

As we emerged from Tony's, dusk had begun to cloak the city. As we walked, the slanting sunlight bounced along the lower-story windows of the buildings. The overflowing trashcans, the litter at the curb, and the scarred surfaces of the sidewalks were vividly rendered in the intense light. It felt even hotter than it had at noontime. The coming of dusk did not cool the pavement; it would be another torrid night in the city when rich and poor alike would sweat it out in the dark. Some would drag their mattresses out onto fire escapes, and those unfortunates who lived five to a room in the tenements, in the windowless railroad flats, might venture, from desperation and exhaustion, up to the flat, tarred roofs with the prayer of catching a breeze and a few hours of untortured sleep. It was not much better on the rooftops—people had been known to succumb from the heat rising from off the sun-baked tar.

We'd decided to try to forget all the problems of the past few days. Freddie Trombley would identify the body of the murdered woman, and so it was out of our hands. It was time to get back into a routine. In a couple of weeks the Broadway theatres would reopen with the cooler weather, so there would be opening nights to attend and reviews to write and lots of parties to enjoy. All of our friends would return to town, and my apartment would be open for cocktails every day at five o'clock.

To help along that feeling of getting back to normal, we decided to pop in for a visit with our friends and fellow Round Tablers, Harold Ross and Jane Grant. Their home was just a few avenues over at 412 West 47th Street, in the house they had bought and shared with Alexander Woollcott.

The sun was sinking fast into the Hudson River when we arrived at number 412, and an uncharacteristically disheveled Jane answered the bell.

We entered through the foyer into the parlor, where we could see into the dining room beyond. Woodrow wouldn't pass over the threshold; he looked like he was about to drop an offering on the hall rug. Perhaps it was the noise, a cacophony of squeals and an odor that even a dog who usually likes to explore dead things would cower away from. I picked him up, and he shivered in my arms.

"*Don't* go in there!" Jane said, "You might step on something and hurt yourself."

It was a real obstacle course of debris—*her* dining room, where the ravages of the Thanatopsis Literary and Inside Straight Club were strewn over every surface. There were islands of trash on the carpet—a medley of overflowing ashtrays, empty cigarette and cigar wrappers, and chunks of unidentifiable foodstuffs—Friday night's bologna sandwiches, chips, olive pits, and shriveled pickles. Smudgy-looking drinking glasses, crumpled napkins, newspapers, peanut shells, waxed-paper bags, and empty bottles of scotch lay among playing cards, slips of scrap paper, and sleeve protectors. Worse was the smell! What *was* that awful smell?

Jane's appearance was not one the outside world had ever seen. This otherwise-chic number was padding around in galoshes and wore a frazzled, wild-eyed look. Her hair and face were dripping sweat, her house dress hung damply from her shoulders and was stained with something that looked like mustard but might have been egg-yolk, and you could tell she was angry.

"Holy mackerel! I started, pulling a face. "That smell—"

"How'd you guess? It *is* a dead mackerel, yes!"

"Why is it lying on the floor—there are flies all over it."

"Harpo left it here. He said he caught it in Lake Bomoseen last Monday, and had the nerve to ask me to fry it up on Friday night. I told him to throw it out or stick it in the icebox."

"But it . . . it reeks! What fresh hell! Didn't he put it on ice—?" I said, gagging.

"Not in the icebox! It didn't smell *that* bad on Friday night."

Mr. Benchley corrected her gently, "Jane, dear," gingerly touching her shoulder. She looked about to sink to the floor from heat prostration at the gesture, and taking her elbow instead, for support, he said: "There are no mackerel in Lake Bomoseen, and from here I can smell it is a trout."

"If you wish to remain in this house, Bobby, you'd better—"

"What is all that callywogging?" I asked, because since we'd entered there had sounded a constant yowling, not unlike the cries of an infant, coming from the back of the house, and now Woodrow Wilson was shaking, violently.

"What is 'callywogging,' Mrs. Parker, may I ask?"

"That noise! The screaming like angels boiled alive in oil."

"No such word as 'callywogging.'"

"There is now; I just made it up."

"The neighborhood cats are trying to break in through the garden door," said Jane. "They smell the fish."

"Why not get rid of it?"

"I told Harpo I refused to cook the fish—it was seven days old and it smelled. I went away on Friday night and returned an hour ago, and this is what I find! It wasn't in the Frigidaire, and he hadn't put it out in the garbage. I couldn't find it—he forgot where he'd put it—and then he went upstairs to see Aleck, and—"

"Aleck is back?" he asked.

"This morning, and you know how he hates to leave that island of his; he's really out of sorts. He just had the nerve to telephone me to insist I stop the callywogging! I told him to get out his shotgun and do it himself, or better yet, send that 'clown' Harpo back down here to clear away that mackerel!"

"Trout, Jane, *trout*."

Jane glared. Mr. Benchley, miraculously dry under his collar, made amends. "I shall deal with this, don't you worry, Janie my girl!" With that he maneuvered a path through the obstacle course and disappeared through the kitchen door, returning with a broom and shovel with which he scooped up the fish to a flurry of flies and popped it in a paper bag lying handily on the dining room table. He then set aside the broom and shovel and proceeded through the foyer to the upper level of the house, bag in tote, flies on the wing. Within seconds came the shouts of Alexander Woollcott cursing Mr. Benchley and his offering, and then Harpo's voice loudly arguing that the fish was indeed a mackerel, not a trout, as Mr. Benchley kept insisting, until the crash of glass and metal silenced the house. Even the cats stopped their callywogging.

Footsteps on the stairs—and then reappeared Mr. Benchley, holding the fragrant bag at arm's length, followed by his buzzing air support, and behind him a repentant-looking Marx Brother, rubbing his crown where the glass-and-metal object had struck. Mr. Benchley held open the front door for Harpo to pass through and handed him the bag before shutting the door on the culprit, the fish, and the flies. The callywogging had ceased. Through the parlor window we watched as a dozen cats arrived en masse to greet Harpo, having bounded from the back of the house to the front to follow our friend along the sidewalk in a frenzied feline entourage. As a couple of the cats tried to climb his trouser legs, Harpo placed the bagged fish in the letterbox of the brownstone that housed the offices of the DAR and walked up to the corner, alone.

"I don't understand why he brought the fish," I said, following Jane around the house after she dragged in the garbage barrel from off the back porch to the dining room. She'd not been able to open the back door earlier to fetch it, because of the cats threatening to rush in. She started dumping the trash from off the table, sideboard, and floor into the big metal can, making grunting noises of disgust with every toss. Two table fans were adjusted to draw out toward the windows the odor of tobacco butts, stale whiskey, and male sweat—after all, there had been, for the past thirty-six hours, eight sweaty men gathered around that table, eating, drinking, smoking, cursing, and farting; add to that the stink of rotting fish and it was a lethal blend. It nearly knocked me out cold, sent Woodrow into shock and Jane to consult an alien-ist in the morning, and turned Mr. Benchley into an even-more-annoying grammarian. It would take some doing to clear the air.

"There is no point in wondering why Harpo brought in the *trout*," said Mr. Benchley. "Why does Harpo do anything? There is no rhyme or reason that anyone other than Harpo could explain."

"He claimed he was carrying the fish instead of a gun—defense against muggers, or some such nonsense."

"It's an 'evil eye' that's for protection, not a mackerel," I said.

"A *trout!* If you were a mugger, would you go after a man carrying that fish?"

"Certainly not," I agreed.

"I think he had planned to leave it hidden up-stairs in Aleck's place, just to cause him grief when he arrived home from Vermont—" said Jane.

"Welcome-home gift? Like stocking up the icebox with milk and eggs?" I said.

"—but Aleck arrived home earlier than he expected and before he could put it there. It took me some time to find that mackerel—"

Mr. Benchley sighed; it was useless.

"—hidden in the breakfront. Wait until I get my hands on Ross's neck."

We bid Jane good-bye and left her to the remaining cleanup, and the simmering in a saucepan of sugar, lemon juice, and cinnamon in an attempt to fumigate the house. No point in dropping in to see Aleck when he was out of sorts and as Ross was due to walk in through the door at any moment, returning from his *New Yorker* offices, we wished to avoid Jane's confrontation.

"It's back to the Gonk!" she said, knowing fullwell that the prospect of returning the weekend poker games to the hotel would be difficult at best. A couple of years back, Frank Case had politely asked the men to properly tip the waiters—who spent their night shifts scurrying up and down the elevator responding to constant room-service demands. He asked the boys to can their trash and to use the ashtrays, because the hotel could not afford to replace carpets riddled with cigarette burns. Aleck, the unofficial leader of the club, took offense, called Frank all sorts of lovely names, and then pulled the game from the hotel. But he managed to wangle having the games in Jane's dining room, because, he claimed, his section of the house was too small to accommodate the crowd. The winning play by Aleck was to suggest to Jane that she could keep an eye on her husband's losses, reminding her that, just a few years back, Ross had lost twenty-five-thousand dollars of the couple's startup money for their new venture into magazine publishing at a "friendly" poker game.

"Back to the Gonk!" hissed Jane, "and if they can't worm their way back in there, they can go to hell! It couldn't be hotter than New York in the summer."

———◆———

Although the city had been granted a reprieve from the direct assault of a cruel sun for a few desperate hours, the darkness did not lend much relief. No breeze swept through from the rivers hugging the island of Manhattan, and the humid air clung heavily upon its residents. The curbside trash was ripe and sour; the odor of unwashed streets rose from the broiled pavement. It had not rained much while we were away in Boston, I heard tell, and this child of the city would have been content with another night along the seashore.

As we approached our respective homes on West 44th Street, I noticed a familiar figure in front of the Royalton. The fellow was pacing, nervous hands in and out of jacket pockets, lighting a cigarette. With frowning impatience he anxiously looked at his wrist watch and then up and down the street.

"Lamberto!" I said, in greeting, and quickly wiped the smile off my face upon seeing his obvious distress.

"Pleece forgive I come to you."

"That's all right," said Mr. Benchley, leading the Italian into the lobby of his hotel and toward the elevator, past the bug-eyed, disapproving gaze of Uriah Heep behind the desk. "There is more tolerance and hospitality at your residence, Mrs. Parker," he said to me later. "That nasty little mole should have got used to me and our assortment of friends by now. He should've offered Lamberto to sit comfortably in the lobby while he awaited my return."

Once settled into the "red den," as I liked to call my friend's flat, and after much ogling at the extreme décor, Lamberto put down his glass of ginger ale and told us why he had come uptown to see us.

"Giusto, he cut with a knife. Stab-bed!"

"But, *who, why?*" I screeched. "Is he all right?"

"*When* did this happen?" asked Mr. Benchley. "*How? Where* did this occur?"

"For God's sake, Fred, give the man a chance. You sound like you're teaching a journalism class." We shut up long enough for Lamberto to answer all of our queries.

"I take Giusto from house to show bakery. Lots

people, street crowded. Children run around open fire hydrant, big group people listen to Leonardo Mosta-celli—he *communista*, speak-a on corner. I think he behind me, Giusto. I turn for find Giusto, I see him fall and people scream."

I choked out, "Is he—"

"No-no! He be okay. Cut shoulder, only, miss back."

"Where is he now, what hospital?"

"Oh, no hospit-al, no! He be deport!"

"But, he needs to be seen by a doctor, Lamberto," said Mr. Benchley.

"*Si, si.* I take to Signora Natali, she fix him up. She nurse, clean, put stitch. He rest, sleep. But I worry sum-bodie try kill Giusto."

We all remained quiet for a long moment, each of us thinking, looking at one another in turn. Lamberto searched our faces to see if we agreed with his suspicions that the stabbing was not just an accident or a random act of street violence by an impassioned listener of the speech, but rather a deliberate and premeditated hit on his brother. I could tell that Mr. Benchley didn't want to alarm Lamberto and his family that the chances were good that there was a connection with the murdered woman on the train; but *not* to alert them to the danger would be putting the family at risk. Someone had murdered once—the woman who came up to Giusto and offered him employment was dead. It made sense that Giusto might know something about the murder; or perhaps just the fact that he had had contact with the woman was enough for the killer to want him out of the way. Why, though? He was the perfect fall-guy to take a murder rap.

"We led the culprit to him," I said, and Lamberto seemed to struggle with the strange word. "The person, the *culprit*, who killed the woman on the train must have followed us here and then down to your home. The killer knew she had hired Giusto to make a delivery and was afraid your brother would to go to the police with information."

"He would not go to police, no!"

"But, your brother was with me and Mr. Benchley, and that was enough to make the murderer wonder—wonder if Giusto confided in us, wonder if he would go to the police because he knew something that might lead them to the identity of the killer. You see, my bedroom on the train was directly across from the dead woman's."

"And mine was located next to Mrs. Parker's room."

"And I believe that I have been followed these past few days," I said, "and the person following me—" I didn't voice my belief that the person I thought might have been following me was now dead and had been recently removed from the trunk of Mr. Benchley's borrowed Mercedes.

Mr. Benchley interrupted: "Mrs. Parker! Will you please fill Lamberto's glass with more soda and ice?"

I got the point. I would not be making things better for the man by updating the list of bodies. As a matter of fact, it would only make Lamberto pack up his family, close down the bakery, and head west just to get away from us, the harbingers of death. Thank goodness Giusto wasn't on the list of victims!

I filled the glass and handed it to Lamberto. I was about to speak when Mr. Benchley flipped through his address book and then picked up the telephone receiver.

"Forty-four-hundred pounds of steel is this baby! Got a supercharged six-cylinder 6240-cc engine, and with a hundred-forty horsepower, by golly, it's the fastest touring car on earth!"

Chapter Nine

It was not until noon the following day, an hour before the one o'clock luncheon with my trusty little band of friends, that I learned the exact course of events after Mr. Benchley had dialed the telephone number scribbled in his little address book. He appeared at my door with coffee and several of the morning editions. He was awaiting a return telephone call from Sgt. Joe, for news and answers to our many questions about the dead woman in Bedroom Two.

"I thought it particularly clever of Zeppo and Chico to procure a hearse," said Mr. Benchley, with a certain amount of pride in his voice at having pulled off the ruse. "And then, after Harpo came into the apartment wearing the toy stethoscope he borrowed from the five-and-dime to proclaim Giusto was dead of his wounds—" He chuckled at the absurdity of Harpo in a white butcher's coat mimicking a doctor's lab-coat. "And then Zeppo, collar turned 'round, giving last rites in pig-Latin over the corpse! The amazing thing is the neighbors believed it! In their passionate grief they didn't notice the details."

"I suppose we see only that which we wish to see," I agreed.

"The callywogging widows obviously drowned out the nonsense Zeppo was trying to sell, that's for sure!"

"You've adopted my new word!"

"Absurd as it is, it fills the bill."

"Well, now, all is right in the world, or almost. The assassin will think Giusto's dead and no longer a threat to his identity. And only our little gang knows that he and his family are in hiding up on Aleck's Neshobe Island," I said. "Now, did Frank get a mention of the stabbing death in the paper for the morning editions?"

"It was in the *World*, and should be in all the others by the afternoon editions."

Mr. Benchley left me to my own devices to drop in at his publisher's office. At one o'clock, Woodrow and I took the elevator down from my rooms and walked into the Rose Room, the small dining room just off the lobby.

Aleck was back once again, after nearly two months away at his tiny retreat, and holding court as the figurehead of our club. Our waiter, Luigi, was serving up Aleck's soup, which became fair game when Aleck was called to the telephone. Harpo helped himself to a couple of spoonfuls of the tomato bisque, made a face, and then cut into the cutlet on his own plate. Bunny and Tallulah had had enough of us, I suppose, as they had not appeared at table. (Actually, Tallulah had a first-reading rehearsal for a play set to open in October, and Bunny had a meeting with his publisher.) But Frank was there. Frank Pierce Adams, who wrote for the *New York World*, was best known to his friends as "FPA." He was the highest-paid columnist in the country and the man who gave me my start. "He raised me from a couplet," I always say, because when I was just starting out, he published several of my verses in his Samuel Pepys–styled column, "The Conning Tower." In his daily column he informed his readers of the goings-on around Manhattan, retelling each day his particular journey through New York City. As he related the clever quips tossed about at our daily luncheons, and tidbits about the plays he and many of us reviewed in the evenings, our gang of friends was often mentioned. Frank was dubbed "the comma-hunter of Park Row," for he was a fierce and exacting grammarian of the printed word, if not always of the spoken. Frank could be sophisticated and yet, at times, gritty. He was versed in classical literature and drama but had a penchant for the low comedy of Vaudeville; usually sharp, he could often be dense enough to frustrate. He was nobody's fool, and the Big Man, Aleck, had at times deferred to Frank as I'd never see him do to anyone else in the world.

Heywood Broun joined us, Ruth out shopping

with the children, getting them wardrobed for the school session about to start in a couple of weeks. Ross and Jane sat down, followed by George Kaufman, who wanted to see both Aleck and Harpo to discuss a croquet match on Central Park's Sheep Meadow next Sunday.

Aleck returned to the table: "Little Acky's back!" he announced, slapping Harpo's scavenging hand away from the croutons intended for his tomato bisque. He signaled Luigi to bring him a fresh bowl of soup and then took his place just as Mr. Benchley appeared.

My friend looked very excited, very animated with breaking news. He stood next to my chair as he announced: "Newsflash, everybody!" He was beaming. "I just got word that after five miserably successful years, the scourge of Broadway, *Abie's Irish Rose,* is closing; the stage door will be locked against the cast and crew! The lobby doors shuttered! To put it gently, they are getting the hell out of town next week!"

"I don't believe it," said Frank. "Publicity stunt."

"Lord help us, don't say that Frank," he said, sinking down into the chair next to mine. Woodrow rested his head on Mr. Benchley's knee and flashed soulful eyes of sympathy at him.

"It's been my most fervent campaign to shut them down, forever, through my column at *Life.* That's it, you know—they couldn't take the pressure from the stranglehold I've had on them."

In May 1922, *Abie's Irish Rose,* by Ann Nichols, opened on Broadway. The next morning Mr. Benchley had to reconsider his assessment of a play that had opened the evening before, *The Rotters,* which he claimed was "just about the worst show of the season," to bring the offending *Abie's* to the forefront.

One of his duties as theatre editor at *Life* was to list all the plays on the boards in a section called *The Confidential Guide* and briefly comment on each show. His first entry under *Abie's* title was, "Something awful," and he expected *Abie's* to close any day. A week later, the show was still running, so Mr. Benchley wrote, "Among the season's worst." And thus began five years of weekly commentary:

All right if you never went beyond the fourth grade.

People laugh at this every night, which proves why a democracy can never be a success.

Where do people come from who keep this going? You don't see them out in the daytime.

Eighty-ton fun!

In another two or three years, we'll have this show driven out of town. Closing soon. (Only fooling!)

"No more striving for a clever putdown each week; no more frustration at the birthday celebration each year!" he said with glee.

"You can *say* all you like, Bobby, but seeing is believing."

"You, Ross, are just trying to ruin my day. You hate to see anyone happy!"

Aleck dismissed the conversation with a flick of his wrist before picking up his soup spoon. "By the way, Cousin Joe just telephoned, Bob, and he asked to talk to you about some car you were trying to sell him. I told him you had yet to arrive for luncheon, and that I would relay his request for you to stop at the stationhouse this afternoon, or to telephone, to discuss the particulars. Why he could not leave a message for you at the desk is beyond me—unless it has to do with the dead body that you and Dottie transported over the state line."

"I'll call him right back," said Mr. Benchley, setting down his linen napkin to make for the telephone.

"We didn't cross any lines," I said, and everybody laughed. "At least, not any state ones."

"Isn't there some law against that," asked Harpo, "transporting dead bodies across state lines?"

"I don't know," said Jane, "but there should be one against transporting dead fish across state lines!"

"No," intercepted Chico Marx, who'd just arrived and wedged a chair in between me and Ross. "It's *women* you can't transport across state lines. I should know."

"You mean, *under-aged* women, don't you, Chico?" corrected Frank.

"Under-aged, over-aged, middle-aged, barrel-aged—they told me I can't do it anymore."

"Who's 'they'?" asked Ross. "The police?"

"No!" yelled an indignant Harpo. "The women told him!"

"That's right," nodded Chico. "They don't like the way I drive. So now I let the women transport *me* across the state line. If they get in trouble with the law," he threw up his hands and shrugged his shoulders, "it's not my problem, see?"

"Clearly," chuckled Frank.

"I keep telling Chico he should take a lesson from me," said Harpo. "I am not in the *transportation* business, and he should not be in the transportation business, either. You want women? You *chase* them across the state line. That way there's no transporting; they get there on their own steam. And by the time they get there, they're too exhausted to file a complaint. Do you want the rest of that carrot, Dottie?"

I looked at Harpo with suspicion. "What do you want with a half-eaten carrot? There are a dozen in the pickle dish."

"I got me a horse outside. She likes carrots."

"What are you doing with a horse, anyway?" asked George Kaufman, who instantly regretted asking and literally stiffened his spine to brace himself for an off-color reply.

"I asked him the same question," said Chico.

"You've got money, now, you can buy yourself a car, I told him, you don't need a horse to get around town, and you know what he answers me?"

We waited while Harpo gathered in one hand the entire contents of the pickle dish—carrots, radishes, celery, and several slippery pickle slices—and stuffed them in his coat pockets. Then he considered the empty oval dish, picked it up, checked the reverse side for the stamp, "Wedgewood," and forced it inside of his trouser belt, buttoning his coat over the bulge. He strutted about, patting his "full belly" should the management look suspiciously in his direction when it was time to leave the hotel. He looked at me expectantly, trying to shame me, and I finally relinquished the half-eaten root from my plate.

"Tell them what you told me," ordered Chico. "Tell them what you said about the horse!"

Shyly, Harpo demurred, and then broke out with, "We just met! It was Kismet! I turned a corner and there she was, as pretty as can be. I took off my sunglasses; she flipped off her blinders. I love the way she coquettishly tosses her head," said Harpo, batting his eyelids while a goofy grin played stupidly over his face. Of course he wasn't wearing his curly wig, he wore it only on stage, but he was ridiculous all the same. "Her name is Maggie."

"Who?" asked Aleck.

"His *horse*," said Chico.

"Shush! Don't you call her that!"

"Well, what is she? Your donkey?"

"My Lipizzaner!"

"What! Before the third date?" I said.

"Here, give her a popover," said Heywood, tossing a biscuit for Harpo to catch. "That will get you to third base."

"We're almost there; I got her a suite on the third floor."

We watched as Harpo made his way through the long lobby, only to come face-to-face with a mounted police officer, *sans cheval*, walking right at him. The sight of the two men told the real story: Harpo began unloading the vegetables from his pockets and placing them into the pickle dish, which he handed to the police officer to hold. Then he pointed in our direction, and when the policeman craned his neck to see where he'd pointed, Harpo flew into the elevator just as the operator was closing the gate. The policeman whirled completely around, scratched his head, and then walked out of the hotel cradling the filled pickle dish.

Mr. Benchley returned to our table with news. "Where's Harpo?

"Got a horse in the third he had to see about," replied Aleck. "What's the update?"

"Well, Freddie Trombley could not identify the corpse as that of his dead wife, Joan. He didn't need to see the woman's face, because he knew at once it wasn't she: This woman was completely gray-haired; his wife's a brunette. And Joe says that the identification found in the dead woman's bedroom was a made-up identity, because there is no person with that name at the address on her papers and passport, which stated she was a resident of Houndstooth-on-the-Heath, Surrey, England. No one can say for sure who she was or from whence she came. She was not on the ship's passenger manifest, although this woman, posing as one "Margo Hemmings," bought a one-way ticket on the Midnight Owl to New York City."

"So, we know nothing more than we did before," I said.

"Well, we know who she is *not*, and where she *didn't* come from."

"That's a lot of help."

"We do know that she was concealing her real identity. She was up to something, carrying a bomb, an innocent man her pawn in some crazy scheme. By the way, your overnight case was left in the driveway of Last Call. The Nassau County Police found it. They and our own NYPD are working together because the second murder was probably committed on the Island, but discovered in the back of my car here in the city. Also, because the murdered man was on the train at the time of the murder of this so-called Margo, the Bureau of Investigation is threatening to take over the cases because they ring of a bigger conspiracy. While they argue who's in charge, little will get done as they step on each others' gumshod toes."

I said, "So, let me get this straight: The two murdered people may or may not have been anarchists, or they may have been jewel thieves, but there is a possibility that they were lovers, murdered by a third member of a love triangle, am I right?"

"I haven't a clue."

"Oh, I'll bet the clues are all around us; we just can't see them through the red mackerels!"

"The term is 'red herrings,' my dear," corrected Aleck, and Mr. Benchley said, "Herrings, mackerels, something's fishy!"

Before the conversation could turn to fishing in Lake Bomoseen, I said: "I wonder if Freddie Trombley's story checks out, that he just arrived yesterday from England?"

"You're thinking he's been playing us along? That he might have murdered the couple?"

"He could have just called up to the room at the Sherry to see if the coast was clear before he went up to take evidence away of his relationship to the victims."

Mr. Benchley considered the possibility that the cuckolded husband had had his revenge. "Clever, if he did, and more clever to say the dead woman isn't his wife—gray hair and all. In that way his wife remains still missing, not dead."

I considered the motive. "So that he can be eliminated as a suspect in a murder! And Fanshaw's murder will appear to be tied to the chance discovery and ultimate silencing of a crime that had nothing to do with his tracking Trombley's wife."

"And this Italian fellow, just off the boat?" asked Aleck, "Why try to kill him?"

"Perhaps Giusto would recognize him, remember something that could point a finger at Trombley."

"I'll call Joe back and ask him if they've checked out Freddie's story, his movements over the past few weeks."

"Giusto has got to be kept out of this. I know he's safe, now," I said, "but the murderer knows who he is, and if anyone outside of our little group finds out where we're keeping him, he is liable to be targeted again, and his brother and his family hurt, too."

"Dottie," prefaced Aleck, "you've got to keep out of this thing."

I knew why Aleck was warning me to take care. The murdered man had been tailing my movements, and perhaps Mr. Benchley's, too. We had led the culprit down to Little Italy and the home of the Maggioranis. And whoever murdered Featherstonhaugh had obviously been following him, too. Lots of people following each other . . . .

Mr. Benchley picked up where he'd left off: "The various police departments combed the grounds at Last Call and found, in the hydrangea bushes lining the drive, a crumpled-up telegram addressed to our deceased Mr. Fanshaw."

"The date when that telegram was sent is important," I said. "What it said is even more important if it is to corroborate Freddie's story."

"Sorry, but I don't buy the lovers' triangle angle," said Frank. "Have the Mellons or their guests reported any burglaries during the party? Because the whole melodrama smacks of a burglary ring planning a jewel heist."

"I suspect you are probably right," nodded Mr. Benchley. "A string of very pricey pearls has gone missing, according to one of the guests. But according to Sgt. Joe, witnesses say the woman making the claim she'd been robbed had been seen stripped down to her skivvies and frolicking through the woods while spouting Hermia's lines from *A Midsummer Night's Dream* in the company of a very eager Lysander, an actor with the Royal Shakespeare Company."

"Hey," I said, an idea popping into my head. "Do you think the Mellons had anything to do with trying to claim insurance money by setting up a fake robbery? According to a kid I met at the party, Roger's business is failing."

"Don't you believe it," interrupted Frank. "Mellon Industries just bought up Amalgamated Coal and Gas!"

"Bilking an insurance company doesn't tie in with the murders, though," said Mr. Benchley. "Anyway, the Mellons took a personal inventory of their art collection and the family—uh—jewels and didn't find anything missing."

Chico was about to comment, but Aleck glared at him from behind thick spectacles: "One more joke about your 'nuts,' Chico, and I will feed them to the squirrels, my boy!"

"I've got to get out to Long Island more often," said Frank. "I've been missing all the fun!"

"Oh, and very important," resumed Mr. Benchley, "it appears to the coroner that our dear Fanshaw had been dead far longer than just the eight hours suspected before his discovery in the trunk. Tallulah had to have been wrong about seeing that fellow on a bench at the edge of the woods making love to a woman, because by that time he'd already been dead for at least eight hours."

"Whew! I imagine he smelled as bad as a mackerel in Jane's cupboard on a hot day," said Aleck.

"You mean a *trout*, of course," corrected Mr. Benchley.

"And I thought it was only your recitations that were stinking up the car," I said. "You may be my friend, but you slaughter the classics!"

"Too many critics!" said Mr. Benchley to a table full of critics. "As I was saying before I was so rudely reviewed, it suggests he was killed early during the evening of the party."

I said, "This ring of thieves is getting smaller."

"Hold on there," said Aleck. "What about the

bomb on the train? If you think it all has to do with jewel thieves, why the bomb on the train?"

"Sounds like a bunch of anarchists running amuck to me!" said Ross.

"Or, a very clever plan by thieves wanting the police to *think* the trouble is with anarchists running amuck," said Heywood. "Perhaps they were planning to burgle some of the train's more affluent riders of their valuables, and the plan went awry. Maybe they had their eyes on robbing the Mellons. After all, the Mellons were the only folks in our train car with valuables and then a few days later a man is killed on their Long Island estate?"

"That makes sense, you know," said Aleck, finished with his dessert, his coffee cup drained, and suddenly focused on the murderous puzzle set before him. "They botched up the job on the train and then tried to burgle them in their home."

"The thieves must have been after something very valuable—so valuable they'd kill each other for the prize," said Ross.

This was getting frustrating, listening to all the speculation about the crimes, and coming up with even more scenarios for the motive. Of course, understanding the motive could lead us to the culprit, but we were no further along in any kind of understanding at all. We were pretty much back to the beginning of our conversation. And so I repeated: "The two murdered people may or may not have been anarchists, or they may have been jewel thieves, but there is a possibility that they were lovers, murdered by a third member of a love triangle, am I right?"

"Frank, who are these people, the Mellons?" asked Aleck.

"Just your average rich folks. He was an ex-patriot living in Paris these past few years while his wife was being treated in a Swiss sanatorium for various ills.

"Roger Mellon made his fortune in munitions during the War. Then, while on safari in Africa, he met a British coffee baron with plantations all over Kenya. They got friendly. A couple of years later, Roger married the man's daughter, who'd been left the whole kit and caboodle after her parents were killed in a freak accident. Soon after the wedding she became ill. Mental problems, I heard."

"Was it the merging of two great fortunes that has people interested in them?" asked Aleck.

"Aside from his fame as an industrialist, and the fact that his wife—Hermione—has been a woman of mystery until now, well, yes, the biggest deal about the Mellons is that they are fabulously *rich*," said Frank, leaning back in his chair, bellowing smoke as he lit his cigar. He puffed like a trout out of water. "And that seems to be enough reason people find them attractive."

"I've never been a millionaire but I just know I'd be darling at it," I said.

Frank continued: "Rich people want to be rich with other rich people and do whatever it is rich people do; poor people want to be around rich people, hoping to collect the coins they shed along the way and that some of the golden fame and glory will rub off on them, if only by association."

"I didn't ask for a speech, Frank, keep it for your column," said Aleck.

"Want to know what I think?" said Ross.

"Not particularly, you addle-minded duck," said an acid-tongued Aleck, still angry that the poker game got booted out of the house on Ross's watch while he was away in Vermont. He would not be happy until they found other accommodations for the weekend card games. Anyway, he liked verbally abusing Ross. Ross abused right back. They'd been doing it to each other for years and they weren't about to stop now.

"Shut up, you overgrown cantaloupe; I wasn't asking you!" pitched back Ross.

"Fawn's behind—"

"Pin-head—"

"Prick face—"

"Lard ass—"

"Fart face—"

It could go on forever, with Chico and Frank joining in, much to the embarrassment of Heywood and George—especially George, who at such times shrank his six-feet-four frame down into his size twelves in an attempt to hide under the table. Actually standing up and leaving the table would have brought too much attention to himself.

Jane and I sat back in our chairs, waiting for the nonsense to pass, reflecting that even in a gathering of such brilliant personalities, men were still boys and would easily resort to adolescent tantrums. I figured they spent most of their time dreaming up new and better insults to throw at one another. Aleck, not to be outdone by the likes of high-school-dropout Ross, probably spent his free time scanning Shakespeare's play-scripts for nasty alliterations to pitch at the "illiterate." Where else could he have picked up, "I will knog your urinals about your knave's cockscomb!" or "You stale old mouse-eaten dry cheese!"

Aleck was now delving into his mental list of the Bard's insults, and Ross was still calling Aleck less-sophisticated names like "puke face" and "monkey balls," so I leaned in and offered Ross a couple of my own off-the-cuff inventions. He looked grateful for, "You scourge on nature, pox on humanity!," and thrilled when I tossed him, "You puss-oozing canker sore; you spittle on my spectacles!"

Mr. Benchley stood up among the name-calling idiots and tapped the side of his water glass with a fork. "Your attention, please!" he said with a laugh in his voice. "I have something more to add that I'm sure you'll be pleased to hear: '*Ode to a Grecian Urn,* by John Keats—seventeen-ninety-five to eighteen-twenty-one . . . ."

Everybody whined as he pressed on: *"Thou still unravish'd bride of quietness—Thou foster-child of Silence and slow Time!"*

He droned on as we rose en masse from the table, dropping dollar bills to pay for our luncheon fare and tips, and then left for our various destinations.

Mr. Benchley caught up with me and Woodrow as we strolled outside for our afternoon constitutional. Halfway down the block we spied a couple of familiar faces from the train in the compartment next to the Brouns'—the ukulele-playing Harvard boys—standing outside of the Harvard Club a few doors down from the Gonk. We stopped to speak with the young men, who recognized Woodrow from the train, but neither me nor Mr. Benchley. Knocked down a rung lower on the evolutionary ladder below the canine species, we introduced ourselves and explained that we had traveled on the Midnight Owl last week, returning from Boston.

"Benchley, did you say?" asked one of the dimwits. "Harvard grad, you say?"

"Class of '12, Delta Upsilon," said Mr. Benchley, rocking on his heels.

"Oh, yeah, I think I've heard about you," said one of the young men, "but you're dead—I mean, someone said you were dead."

Taken aback, and landing firmly on his soles, my friend said, "Well, you can put that rumor to rest and not the man."

"Sorry," said the other boy, "my friend here is a dolt."

"Noted."

"And I know who you are!"

"You do, do you!" Mr. Benchley turned to me. "You see, Mrs. Parker, I am fondly remembered along the halls of academe for my scholarship and contributions as president of the *Lampoon,* as well as the cup holder of the Obscure Secret Ritual Competition against the Skulls four years in a row."

"Is that so?" asked the kid. Getting nothing but a burning stare from my friend, the boy continued, "I remember seeing a cartoon of you with another fellow carrying a table down the steps of a house, captioned, 'We've come for the sideboard.'"

"We were carrying a *davenport,* and the caption reads: 'We've come for the davenport.'"

"You hadn't that little moustache, but the artist caught your peculiar nose perfectly. That's why I remember you."

"Well, Mrs. Parker, there you go: I am remembered for something, at least. Harvard has gone to the dogs—my apology, Woodrow! Remind me to withdraw my annual alumni donation."

"I didn't get what was funny about it," continued the boy.

"Well, you see, young man, it was a prank. We'd knock on the door of a house on Beacon Hill and tell the maid we'd come to pick up the davenport, and then we'd deliver the sofa to the house across the street."

"But—well, tell me, what was so funny about that?"

Mr. Benchley burned.

"You had to be there," I said.

Mr. Benchley bridled: "Listen here, young man. Let me be the judge of what's funny and what's not."

I couldn't resist: "I'll have you young whippersnappers know that Mr. Benchley is the drama editor and critic for *Life* magazine. When he said *Abie's Irish Rose* ain't funny, it closed!" I got down to business: "What I want to know is, did the police—or that detective—Gum, was his name—did he ask you and your friends any questions about what you may have seen or heard on the train when the woman in Bedroom Two was killed?"

"We were sleeping it off, I suppose," said the lanky kid. "Me and Boner and Sprat. Beaner, here, was gagging, I think."

"I was puking my guts out in the men's lavatory, back and forth for half the night," said Beaner. "Like

Bobo says, everybody was *plotzed*."

"Pie-eyed!"

"Pol-lut-ed!"

"Blot-to!"

"Blitzed!"

"Be-fud-dled!"

"Bombed!"

"Blasted!"

"Clobbered!"

"Crapped!"

"Young man, there's a lady present," interrupted Mr. Benchley.

"We beg your pardon."

"*Awww shit*, don't mention it!" I replied.

"Now that we know that you had imbibed enough to reel you off to oblivion—"

"Juiced!"

"Looped!"

"O-blit-er-at-ed!"

My friend sought an opening. "Yes, as boiled as an owl—"

"There's a new one!" screamed Bobo.

"As boiled as an owl—on the Midnight Owl! *Ha, ha, ha, ha!*" said Beaner, slapping his thighs.

Eyes rolling toward heaven, Mr. Benchley interjected "—and you didn't see anyone in the corridor, or hear anything unusual?"

"Well, no. No one was about, really, that time of the night; everybody was asleep, but me."

"That's right, we were snoozing," confirmed Bobo.

"Catching forty winks—"

"Boys!"

"Oh, yeah," said Beaner, "except for that one time when I was trying to get to the john in time and I passed the fellow in the hall."

"What did he look like?" I asked.

"Why, he's the famous one. Everybody knows who he is. The writer. Social stuff. You know—*whatsisname* . . . ?"

"Heywood Broun?"

"Who?"

There could have been only one other famous man—other than Heywood and Mr. Benchley—in our Pullman, so I suggested another name.

"That's right, the socialist, the muckraker," nodded Beaner.

"Where'd you see him?"

"At the door to the dead woman's room, but she wasn't dead, then, I don't think. I heard her voice through the door; I don't remember what she said. Then he walked back to his compartment."

"Did you tell Detective Gum about that?" asked Mr. Benchley.

"He didn't ask me, and I didn't see anything, really. I was back and forth to the john half the night. Why? Is it important?"

"It might be."

Woodrow was getting bored and began pulling toward the curb, lured by the delightful smells lurking there, and Mr. Benchley was getting testy—I could almost hear him thinking, *What's the matter with kids today?* I wanted to cross to the shady side of the street, so we moved as the fading contest of "wits" continued their game. "Loaded! . . . Snockered! . . . Soused! . . . Stewed! . . . Stiff!"

"You know what this means, don't you?" I asked.

"Oh, yes! I'll have to send my sons to Princeton!"

"He murdered the woman."

"That 'Beanie' fellow?"

"No! Our socialist friend!"

"Well, he must have had a very good reason."

"What, he didn't like her *hat*?"

"For going to her room."

"At two o'clock in the morning?"

"I've shown up at your door at two o'clock in the morning and haven't murdered you yet."

"I've always suspected someday you would strike me down!"

"Someday, perhaps, but you shouldn't jump to conclusions, it's a long way down, my dear."

"But that boy saw him at her bedroom door. He knew the woman!"

"So, what if he did?"

"Ah, I see where you're going. They met earlier, when I wasn't looking, and had arranged a late-night assignation."

"It has been known to happen . . . ."

"Then why didn't he say—"

"—anything to Detective Gum? Put yourself in his shoes: socialist, labor leader, ACLU lawyer, industry watchdog, activist, reformer, consumer protection advocate, a man about to write a scathing review in his next book about the judicial system, backroom politics, voting fraud, shady business practices in the banking industry, *and* police corruption."

"Yes, I see your point."

I was quietly pensive as we approached Fifth Avenue. "What you said a minute ago—that he must have had a good reason—"

"I didn't mean it how it sounded!"

"But, listen to this: Suppose he discovered she

was plotting a terrorist bombing, and they struggled and—"

"Bludgeoned, she was bludgeoned, not pushed aside, not slapped silly."

"A crime of passion," I said.

"Why else *bludgeon* a woman, if not out of passion?"

"Ah, *l'amore!*"

"When love turned to hate, when you despise . . . ."

"A crime of passion! It could not have been anything less! Do you think they had been lovers, and then she plotted a bomb, wanting to implicate him, and he found out—and then Fanshaw found out about the plot, so our socialist friend had to get rid of him, too?" I concluded.

"No. I think somebody else killed her."

"The only way to know for sure is to ask him what he was doing at her door that night."

"Not a good idea, Mrs. Parker. Just in case you are wildly on the mark. You see, he was the only person other than you and I who knew we had rescued Giusto from the scrutiny of the police. He was the only person other than you and I who knew Giusto was going to his brother's apartment downtown."

"So, there may be a connection," I said.

My head was swimming with possibilities and

no real answers. It needed clearing. All I knew was that, in just a few minutes' talk with the boys from Harvard, we'd added yet another suspect to the list.

It was too hot to drag Woodrow around town. I had a couple of errands to run, and a humorous piece to drop off at the *New Yorker* offices up the street, so we turned around and retraced our steps for home to leave Woodrow back at my apartment.

"Didn't he say he was heading off for Des Moines or East Podunk or someplace?" I asked.

"Our socialist friend?"

I nodded.

"I think he mentioned something about a labor rally out West, but he took a room at the Royalton the day we came back to town from Boston, and he may still be there."

"What! Why that makes me even more suspicious of him. I thought he was a thousand miles away. If he's been here, it means he could have stabbed Giusto, and he might have murdered Fanshaw, too!"

"All right, you may be onto something, although I doubt it."

"You think he is above reproach?"

"Yes, perhaps I do."

"Well?" I said, "What are we going to do about it?"

"We are doing nothing for the moment. First,

we have to find out if he had alibis for the times when Fanshaw was murdered and when Giusto was stabbed."

"All right, that's only fair, I suppose."

We had crossed back to the north side of the street where stood the Algonquin, and lingered under the hotel's canopy. Mr. Benchley checked his watch, and I could see his afternoon schedule flashing through his mind, before he turned to say, "You don't like the fellow much, do you?"

"Why do you say that? We agree on a lot of the same issues, and I have to admire the fact that he acts on his convictions."

"Nevertheless, you don't like the fellow."

I tried to find the words, because there was a measure of truth in what Mr. Benchley had observed about my feelings. "He just takes himself so seriously," I said. "Not that he shouldn't; the issues at stake *are* serious ones," I countered myself, unable to find balance. "Anyway, whether I like or dislike him isn't of any importance."

Mr. Benchley looked at me and I could see surprise in his eyes that he could not completely mask. When you are close to someone, you can read the flicker of an eye, the subtle nuance of a smile, the little leap of an eyebrow others might dismiss. I had failed to toss off the required *bon mot*, the one-line putdown, the succinct phrase required to define the fellow's faults.

Did I find him too passionate? Too earthy? Too rough? Perhaps, too brilliant? Did I feel he was looking down his nose at me, seeing me as simply a foolish and flighty sort, who, in her loneliness, had grabbed onto a cause célèbre like the Sacco and Vanzetti trials to justify her existence?

Was I just a fast-talking quipster who was fine to have around for a laugh or two at a speak or a party, but who at the end of the day neither lent real meaning to anyone's life nor affected anything for the better?

That thought stayed with me throughout the afternoon as I went about my business: Did he make me feel inferior? *Was* I inferior? Why did I feel self-conscious around him? I hadn't gotten the formal education most of my friends had received, and because I hadn't, or because I just had a thirst to absorb all I could about the world around me, I had become a sad autodidact, squirreling away in the back of my brain ideas and theories and facts and knowledge about everything and anything and everybody. In many ways, I was probably better educated than many of my contemporaries; but self-taught, I would never be as respected as the formally educated.

Before Mr. Benchley could continue his scrutiny of my thoughts and feelings, I was rescued by Jane and Ross, coming out of the Gonk. Ross had to get back to the *New Yorker* offices. Jane and I would follow, as I had copy to drop off and a check to pick up, and then we girls would do a little shopping.

———————

I needed a cool drink by the time we had completed our rounds and found ourselves on Madison Avenue, the Bond Street of America. I looked around and remembered a little luncheonette tucked in between a luggage store and a fashionable jewelry shop on the east side of the avenue, and suggested to Jane that we stop for a drink and a rest.

An egg cream. I want a chocolate egg cream, I thought, as we crossed the street, the hot pavement bleeding through the soles of my pumps, the exhaust fumes of passing motorcars and the pungent smell of burning rubber tires adding to my resolve to quench my thirst. A stiff wind flew up a side street, carrying along the usual sandy debris of grit and soot that pricked at my legs. My eyes were shielded by sunglasses and my hat strained at its hatpin to stay on.

"A chocolate egg cream," I said to the soda-jerk as I took a stool at the counter, Jane opting for a Coca Cola over plenty of ice. I watched as the man in the white uniform and paper boat hat pumped a stream of chocolate syrup into a tall glass and then added in a splash of milk. With a long soda spoon he mixed up the chocolate milk, and then, setting the glass on the soda fountain, he pulled down a lever and shot a blast of soda water into the mix while stirring it all into a rich froth.

The luncheonette was enjoying a healthy business as weary shoppers were looking for refreshments before moving on to the next specialty store on the avenue. We didn't want to bother with a table, just wanted the cold drinks, so we sat at the counter. Jane and I wanted to get home to strip off our stockings. I refused to gird my loins in such weather; the rubber would sweat and stick to my skin, leaving awful dents and creases and button indentations, but the stockings were a cruel necessity. In half an hour, I would be soaking in a cool tub of water with salts, the fan blowing noisily in the darkened bathroom . . . .

Refreshed from my foamy beverage, we gathered our packages and made for the door. I stood for a long moment in front of the big fan. As I moved out of the breeze to light a cigarette, I looked out from the storefront window, my eyes taking in the rear grounds of St. Patrick's Cathedral across the street. To my left stood the Ritz-Carlton, the luxury hotel where vichyssoise was first invented. There was one more stop I wanted to make before retreating into my fan-cooled lair.

We started down the avenue at a brisk pace, and then slowed as the heat took its toll. We arrived at Madame Charlotte's *Chapelier*, where a window dresser was adjusting a new display of the most delightful chapeaux of the coming autumn season. That meant "Summer Sale," we said in unison, suddenly revived as we eagerly entered the shop.

Madame Charlotte is a very clever young man of about thirty years who designs all the lovely angled affairs that grace the little shop. If my use of hyperbole gets out of hand when I describe these confections, remember that years ago I wrote copy for lingerie ads in *Vogue*. It is because of the gentleman's use of the fabrics and accoutrements that decorate these marvels, along with his attention to detail, the meticulous stitching, and the carefully measured and flattering proportions, which are beyond heavenly, that I so speak. This talented magician transforms the ordinary into the spectacular, and when you have donned one of these brilliant pieces of art you are assured of attention. After all, the Hat Lady from the train might have been one of the ugliest creatures on God's sweet earth for all I knew, but that hat gave her the grace, stature, and beauty of a queen.

That Madame Charlotte is a man was not generally known until about a year ago, when a patron overheard a conversation alluding to the fact and proceeded to spread the revelation along Park Avenue. Neither his manner nor his acquired breeding betrayed him, for he was content to play the role of manager at the shop. His shop-girls were convinced he was nothing but a gentleman—who, perhaps, favored other gentlemen more than the opposite sex, if that was his only fault. They assumed he was taking orders from the real power behind the scenes, a mature woman milliner. There was a brief denial, with the gentleman insisting that Charlotte was his great-aunt living in Paris, who sent her designs for production of the hats to the States. But a society columnist's investigation uncovered that lie when she found out that Madame Charlotte was in fact one Harvey Fish, a first-generation German Jew, born and raised in an Upper-East-Side tenement. The youngest of seven children, Fish had shown promise at an early age as a costumier, learning his craft from his Aunt Sadie, who sewed up flashy fare for chorus gals in Vaudeville shows.

As Jane looked over the selection of sale items, I answered the smiling saleswoman's query, "May I be of assistance, Madame?" with a "Yes, I wish to see Madame *himself*, please."

"Are you going to tell me what that was all about?" asked Jane as we left the shop, a hatbox dangling from her wrist. "You weren't at all interested in any of the hats!"

"I'd need a mortgage to buy one," I said with a laugh.

"But the white one—it suited you perfectly, Dottie, and it was only seven-fifty! So, what's up?"

I really wanted to keep Jane out of it, and didn't feel right about telling her too many of the details of the murders, besides what she'd heard at lunch. She'd been involved with me and Mr. Benchley in dangerous situations over the past few years while investigating crimes and it would have been rude not to keep her up to date on this one. I had a nagging feeling that if she knew too much, the knowledge might put her in jeopardy. But because so many people already knew what was going on—the news of the murders had hit the papers—it might be best to tell her a few of the facts that seemed benignly unimportant.

"The murdered woman—the woman on the Midnight Owl—I noticed her when she was walking toward her bedroom compartment because she was wearing a hat." Jane stopped dead in the stream of pedestrian traffic as we turned down 46th Street toward Fifth, and looked at me blankly. I elaborated: "She was wearing that gorgeous number with black veiling, the most wonderful expanse of organza unfolding from angled pleats at the crown, narrow at the forehead—with the stretched silk wings that widened at the sides?"

Still the blank stare.

"White egret feathers that swooped up from the band and then draped downward, forming an S as it brushed along the shoulder?"

"I didn't see it in there."

"The goddamn hat you said made me look like a shrunken chicken?"

"Oh, *that* hat! A thing of beauty," she said with a smile in recollection. "But not for you."

"Obviously not for me!"

"Oh! *That's* the hat your dead woman was wearing?"

"But it wasn't found in her room when they discovered her body, or anywhere on the train."

"So you think some crazed female killed her for the hat?" yelped Jane. "Why that's crazy!"

"Of course it is, and that's not a reason to kill," I said, and then, "although Ruth Hale thought I might've . . . ."

"Of course you wouldn't, the idea!" And then she looked at me long and hard.

"Oh, stop it, idiot child!" I said. "But you should have seen the brooch she had pinned over the veil. *That* would be something to kill for. It must have cost a mint!"

"Veiling? I don't remember—"

"Come to think of it, there was no veiling on the hat when it was in the shop. I think she wore a veil to disguise herself."

"What did you find out from 'La Madame Charlotte'?"

"Well, he told me that his creations are one of a kind, although he may produce one in black or navy and beige and white, if the colors suit the contours. Sometimes, it's only one. The black hat had been sold to a woman last June, around the time we were in there last, and he described her as rather tall with light-brown hair. The thing he noticed that made him remember her was that she wore sunglasses all the time she was in the shop trying on hats."

"She didn't want to be recognized, that's why."

"Yes, I think you're right—not there and not on the train."

"Incognito!" said Jane with a thrill in her voice, and I could tell she wanted to know all she could, and was hoping to play a part in another adventure in the world of crime. How could I deny her the pleasure?

"She paid cash for the hat, and when the sales-girl asked if she wanted the hat delivered and could she have her name and address, the woman declined, saying she wanted to take the hat with her."

"Ah-*ha!*" said Jane, the weariness from the afternoon of shopping replaced by the renewed excitement of the game. "She didn't want to let anyone know who she was!"

"I think you're right. But Madame Charlotte was in the shop at the time, and as the mysterious woman had an armload of packages, he opened the door for her on the way out, hailed her a cab, and saw her settled in. And as he stepped from the curb he heard her tell the cabbie the address of her destination, an address that he recognized as the prestigious new residence known as the Sherry-Netherland."

"Isn't that—?"

"Yes! Where Mr. Feather-whatever-you-call-'im—Fanshaw—had rooms."

"I will never understand the British," said Jane,

shaking her head. "Why they can't just change the spelling—"

"Yes, yes; that is not the point."

"So what do we do about it?"

"Nothing, Jane," I replied. "We are probably dealing with anarchists, the kind who make bombs—"

"Sounds like your average Broadway producer," said Jane with a giggle.

"—or thieves murdering a member of their burglary ring to increase their share of the cut. These people don't care whom they hurt."

"So who do you think killed those two anarchists?" said Jane, about to throw out a half-dozen barbs. "A socialist?"

"You may be onto something," I said, not telling her about my latest murder suspect.

———◆———

And wouldn't you know, he was sitting at the bar, our socialist friend; I saw him there as I entered my hotel, but I didn't want him to see me. I knew he was following me or waiting for me. Probably wanting to pick my brains about what I knew about the murders so far, and to commiserate about the death of poor Giusto!

The barkeep looked up and I shook my head. He read my silent message from across the room and stifled any words that might have been on his lips to tell the fellow of my arrival. I ducked into the waiting elevator and moved to the inside-corner blind spot so I wouldn't be seen, as the operator closed the gate and door. I told myself, as the car rose to my floor, that I was not being a coward, only cautious.

A cool bath, and then I spent the next few hours stretched out on my bed with the fan blowing over me, thinking. I do that on occasion: I just think. It is not usually the best thing I can do; often I think too much and I arrive at a place that is not so pleasant and can be difficult to get out of. But, lying there in the artificial breeze, in the darkened room after the cool bath, Woodrow on his back, allowing the breeze to cool his hot belly, I thought.

I thought about all the crazy events of the past several weeks—the frustration of my trips to Boston, especially during the previous two weeks, when working for a reversal of Sacco's and Vanzetti's sentence of death seemed like throwing shit against the tide, when even a stay of execution would have brought a smile to my face, and to all the others who believed in the injustice of the whole affair.

Who among those who had fought so hard for their freedom, for the men's lives, didn't feel responsibility for their own failure to succeed in the cause? Aside from Heywood, Ruth, and Mr. Benchley, my other friends did not have the same fevered determina-

tion to seek justice for the men. Not all of my friends
are politically minded, and those who are do not seem
to be very concerned with the plight of "the huddled
masses yearning to breathe free." Not to say they see
the new arrivals as "wretched refuse"; no, many of the
Round Tablers are first-generation children of immigrants. But none of them are Italian, and the Italians
have been arriving in greater numbers since the end
of the War. Like the Polish, the Germans, and the
Jews arriving decades before them, and suffering the
indignities of poverty as they crowded ten to a room
in the city's tenements, despairing of ever assimilating
into the New World society, the Italian immigrants
have become the new nationality to debase.

Is mine a delayed, inherited guilt? I used to
joke about the Irish, saying that my parents would "go
down to Ellis Island and bring them, still bleeding,
home to do the laundry." Of course, my father, Henry
Rothschild, was a Jew, and he was not of the famous
branch of the Rothschild line. No, he was from the
side of the family I like to call "of mud and flame,"
poor and self-made (and in the end, *un-made*, leaving
me nothing but alone after his death).

The Italians are viewed by the other rising
classes of last century's immigrants as the lowest of
the low, and unless you are a Caruso, it's a hard climb
to surmount a position above colored folk. And that
meant that Giusto was seen as an expendable pawn
in this murderous scheme: "just another wop" causing
trouble, an easy mark and a fall-guy, another Bartolo-

meo Vanzetti. A fishmonger, "pic-shov" laborer. The lowest sort with the nerve to want to be paid for his labors a decent wage to feed his family.

I directed my thoughts to recalling the hours leading up to the death of the woman in Bedroom Two. I reviewed the numerous passengers and eliminated the obviously innocent: the family with the young children, the elderly woman in Bedroom Four, next to the murdered woman, even the Harvard boys. Of course, beside me and Mr. Benchley, there was Ruth and Heywood, and the Mellons. So, in a carload of anarchists, socialists, communists, and syndicalists, there the guilt could lie.

In my mind's eye I watched the dramatis personae of the Midnight Owl murder pass the window of the Brouns' compartment door. I replayed the moment-by-moment movements of all of us throughout that night, searching for a clue, an insight, a trivial and ignored detail that might lead me toward identifying the murderer.

Too many wild theories, too many crazy motives! I realized that without uncovering the key elements of the case—the clues and evidence on which to build my own conclusions—the answers would amount to forming a baseless theory.

So, I had to let my mind pick through the few clues we had, search for others, eliminate the red herrings, and then, *and only then*, form a theory supported by evidence. To do otherwise was like trying to fit a square peg in a round hole.

Let the clues build the theory!

For the moment, everybody was suspect: the anarchists, the socialists, Freddie Trombley, the muckraker, the Harvard boys running amuck from too much drink. Even with names like Beaner and Bobo, they might not be so harmless; they may have tried to rape the woman, and perhaps accidently killed her. And the "little old lady" in Bedroom Four—she might have been wearing a good disguise. Someone staying in another Pullman car could be the culprit.

I would seek the evidence, the inconsistencies, and the details that were currently floating around aimlessly in my mind, waiting to be picked out and looked at with more scrutiny. That's how I'd get the square and round pegs to slide easily into their respective holes.

While deep in thought, I fell deep into sleep.

Funny, how the mind works. Buried things resurface—like discovering a photo you forgot you took with the Brownie, and then you open a drawer and there it is, the forgotten memory staring up at you. Such was the case when I awoke with a start. I'd connected two seemingly unimportant observations—clues!—and I wondered why I hadn't seen their relevance before, why had I not seen the obvious. I chided myself for stupidity, and forgave myself an instant later when I realized that my mind had been bogged down with so much mundane clutter that the smallest detail, being the most important of all the clues, had simply been buried under irrelevancies. It was like that junk-drawer everybody has in their home, a receptacle for stuff you don't have an assigned place for—rubber bands, string, the odd screw from your typewriter (which still works fine without it), a cup hook, ticket stubs, matchbooks, a few pennies, a Cracker Jack prize, and the occasional wing-nut that came from *somewhere*. While sleeping I had sifted through the debris and come up with a discarded gem!

I jumped out of bed, my energy renewed. *Yes! It's beginning to fit*, I thought, as I paced from the bedroom and back to the living room several times, Woodrow, at my heels, thinking my rapid movements and sudden high mood were all part of a game we were about to play.

The clues fit a theory, one I had not until now considered. Oh, it was a clever plan, and oh, I didn't like to think how the murderer might have gone unpunished. I'd lit a cigarette and was headed for the telephone when there was a rapping at my door, which triggered Woodrow's excited barking. I flung the door open to find Mr. Benchley, who held up an empty glass tumbler and asked, "Ice?"

Woodrow was all over him, but Mr. Benchley always came prepared with a treat for my pup, which he hurriedly retrieved from his coat pocket in order to get over the threshold unmolested. I was about to extended a hand toward the kitchenette, but he was there before I made the gesture.

"No ice at the Royalton, or in the bar down-stairs? You try the hotel kitchen?"

He cracked the tray open and then filled his glass and another one of mine with ice. Returning to the living room, he poured a couple of fingers of scotch and squirted a dash of seltzer into each glass and handed one to me.

He raised his glass and said, "Congrat-ulate me!"

"You get the Pulitzer?"

"That would be the day! No, my dear Mrs. Park-er, no! I have solved," and he drew a hand across the air as if to display a newspaper headline, "'The Case of the Murdered Woman in Bedroom Two.'"

"Oh, that," I said, "I solved that murder myself, Fred, and the headlines will not read 'The Case of the Murdered Woman in Bedroom Two' but rather 'Death Rides the Midnight Owl'—how's that sound?"

"What?" he said, pounding down the glass on the coffeetable. "You couldn't have!"

"What the hell do you mean by that?"

"Trying to steal my thunder, are you?"

"Thunder is nothing more than the gaseous rumblings of hot air between two cumulous majors!"

"Or a good description of Aleck and Ross ex-changing insults," he considered, before taking my comment personally. "But to think, Mrs. Parker, that you would reduce my keen insights to nothing more than the emissions of a flatulent colon is too much to bear! Why, I came here tonight to share with you the results of my efforts!"

"I thought you came here tonight because you ran out of ice! Or was it to brag?"

"Well, that goes without saying, my dear—wait! What do you mean by, *you* solved the case?"

"Well," I said, offering him a cigarette as I sat down on the sofa. I patted the cushion beside me and he and Woodrow sat side-by-side like the good boys they are. I patted Woodrow's head and Mr. Benchley's knee. "I went through my junk drawer," I explained.

"What does housecleaning have to do with it?

"My brain."

"Oh, well, of course, it is filled with—uh—junk. By the way, when I was snooping through your medicine cabinet the other day, I noticed it's in a state of disarray, you might want to tackle—"

"Figuratively speaking."

"Oh, very well, proceed," he replied, officiously.

"No. First tell *me* what *you* came up with."

"*Came up with?* I did not simply 'come up with' anything you may be comparing to a dashed-up meal of scrambled eggs and ham, and then calling it an omelet!"

"What? Eggs, ham, omelet? Fred, you've lost your mind."

"That goes without saying. But my methods were Sherlockian—"

"Were you playing Sibelius on your violin when you came up with your seven percent solution?"

"My banjo, actually; helps me think."

"Like your Harvard boys?"

"That institution has lowered its standards, if you ask me. That's why I've withdrawn my membership from the Harvard Club."

"You mean they threw you out when you didn't pay your yearly dues."

"Semantics! As I was saying, I recalled William Gillette's play, *Adventures of Sherlock Holmes*. From there I recalled the plot of a story where Moriarty distracts Holmes with false clues, leading him on a wild-goose-chase to a crime that does not take place, was never intended to take place, but rather was simply a decoy, all so that he, Moriarty, could pull off an even bigger crime."

"I see we are on the same page, then," I conceded, "because I changed my point of view when I realized that *what was shown was meant to obscure the truth!*"

"So there! You see! We're in agreement! We've solved 'The Case of the Murdered Woman in Bedroom Two!'"

"No, we've solved 'Death Rides the Midnight Owl!'"

"All right, we'll flip for it," he said, pulling a coin from his vest pocket. "Whoever wins gets his or her title on the cover of the book! Heads, it's mine; tails it's yours."

Joe Kennedy—Rumrunner

John Reed, buried in Kremlin

Harvard's finest

Chapter Ten

So now we had to gather all of the clues and put each to the test to prove our hypotheses before we pointed a finger at anyone. We were already closing in and needed to confirm a few facts. Just a couple of stops along the way, a telephone call or two would do the trick. We were interrupted in our strategic planning by a telephone call from Tallulah, gushing about the fact that Hermione and Roger Mellon decided to be angels for the play she was about to star in. It was their first venture into the world of backing a theatrical production, and they threw a big chunk of money into the venture once they read in the papers that she was going to be in the play.

"So now you're the little darling of the millionaire Mellons," I said, after she told me the news.

"Tomorrow evening the Mellons are hosting a gathering of the producers and the show's cast at their city apartment at the Hotel Navarro on Central Park South."

"Good God!"

"What?"

"I said, 'Goody!'"

"That's what I thought you said. Anyway, you and Bobby and Aleck are invited to come, too!"

"It's sure to be a wing-doodle, all right."

"What?"

"I said it's sure to be the thing to do tomorrow night."

"That's what I thought you said, Dottie, stop mumbling and speak up."

"Right."

"What was that?"

"We'll be there, all right."

"That's what I thought you said."

"*Ta-ta!*" she signed off.

"What's all this '*ta-ta*' crap everybody's throwing around these days? It's all your fault, Mr. Benchley."

"Always you point to me when there's something you don't like."

"And who else could I rely on to take the blame?"

"I mean that much to you, don't I, my dear? Well, you can always rely on my being here when you feel the need to strike out."

"Oh, Fred, you're swell."

"Let's get back to what has got to be done over the next day."

How best to proceed needed planning and the help of a couple of friends willing to really step out on a limb, so to speak. And no one I knew of could better fill the bill in theatricality, daring, and just plain chutzpah than our devilish pranksters, the Marx Brothers.

Mr. Benchley and I arranged to meet the boys at Tony's, a dozen blocks south of our destination, to go over our plan one final time before setting events in motion. Harpo was ten minutes late and came through the guarded door of the speakeasy winded. "Sorry, I had trouble finding a parking space; traffic is brutal."

"Finally!" said Groucho. "He's bought a car at last!"

"What are you talking about, a car?" said Chico. "He got a horse!"

"I wouldn't say 'got' a horse," said Zeppo.

"What would you say?" asked Groucho.

Groucho had been out of town these past few days, romancing a girlfriend on the Jersey Shore, so the situation needed explaining. "What? He got a horse and wagon, or not?"

"No wagon," admitted Harpo.

"No wagon, didn't 'get' a horse . . . . Don't tell me you *stole* a horse."

"It was she stole my affections!"

"Not again! That's what you said about that gorilla you met at the zoo last spring," said Groucho, "and look how that turned out!"

"This is different," said Harpo.

"That's what you said the last time and the time before that. Let me see, first it was that cow on Will Rogers's ranch—"

"Please refer to her as Henrietta; and she wasn't just any cow you'd meet on the street."

"That's right," said Chico, "she was in a meadow."

"And before that it was Wally Dunkin's trained Vaudeville seal."

"All right, but I didn't know that Georgie wasn't a girl."

"That's right, you were taken in by the fancy fur coat and the way she batted those long eyelashes, I remember that," said Groucho. "But, when you learned the truth—"

"He was devastated," said Zeppo, "weren't you, Harpo?"

"Please don't mention her—*his*—name again!"

The afternoon escapade had been carefully choreographed so as to break as few laws as possible.

Although there was always a risk of felony charges, I thought most would be considered misdemeanors—if we were lucky. After all, we were gathering a dangerous crew—all four of the Brothers could wreak havoc when loosed upon a city with a mission to fulfill.

We repeated our assignments and went through a checklist of props. We synchronized our watches and left Tony's for our destination. We had one plan in mind, and that was to find out the name of the woman murdered on the Midnight Owl.

She had been wearing a brooch, one created by a brilliant jewelry designer and sold at only one store in the world. The records, a register of sales of such extravagant items, were kept confidential and guarded. But with the help of our Marx Brothers we would prevail in our search and discovery of the name of the woman who had purchased the pin. If we didn't succeed, we'd appeal to the judge.

They descended like a pestilence over the city, and when they arrived at the most famous jewelers in America, I could almost feel the trembling of a thousand loose diamonds lying in their velvet-lined trays, locked beneath the counters, and hear the tinkling shiver of fear from the precious bracelets and necklaces at the very prospect of an assault. Mr. Benchley and I had brought bulls into a china shop, and that china shop was Tiffany's.

Mr. Benchley and I walked in through the entrance, which was guarded by two very big muscled and liveried guards who doubled as doormen. The showroom was large, and the views of all the counters were unobstructed by any barriers, helping to prevent shoplifting as well as presenting a clean, elegant venue where the sparkle of the merchandise would not be upstaged by the décor. The rows of expansive glass counters were free of objects other than adjustable countertop mirrors, and the lighting was such that the jewels seemed to dance gaily on the trays below and could be seen to best advantage. As one walked between the displays, it was like walking among a thousand constellations of brightly twinkling stars.

We found the display we wanted. The designs within the case, executed by a noted artist and exquisitely rendered in diamonds, all featured either a single blood ruby or a cashmere sapphire or the deep Brazilian-rainforest-green emerald. The exotic-bird brooches lay like gracefully recumbent creatures, the light imparting to their bodies of cold stones set in platinum a fiery and vibrant life of their own.

"May we see the bird on the left," said Mr. Benchley, when the impeccably dressed clerk asked if he could be of assistance. He unlocked the counter with a key, and slid the glass open, lifting out the large work of art and placing it on a flat velvet cushion before presenting it to me to behold its flashing glory.

"Exquisite!" I said, "But, don't you think it might be a bit much for a Quaker meeting, darling?"

I held the thing of beauty up near the neckline

of my black dress, adjusting the standing mirror to admire the piece. I also observed Groucho, wearing his usual four-season black tailcoat and carrying an attaché case and escorted by his handsome brother, Zeppo, dressed in the uniform of a Brinks Guard, as they entered from the street. Attached to the attaché case handle was a chain and cuff, and the cuff was around Groucho's wrist. Zeppo played the role of security guard to the hilt, looking around the store for those who might want to remove the case from the wrist of his brother. That the guards let the men pass into the store was a wonder, but then, Groucho was a master at assuming a stance that demanded a certain amount of respect—if not confusion. The twenty-dollar bill slipped into the handkerchief pocket of the guard didn't hurt, either. They were right on time, as planned, and were headed for the manager's office behind shiny birch-wood-paneled doors at the back of the store, while being followed by the ever-suspicious eyes of a store detective or two. While Groucho asked to see the manager, I pretended to admire the jewel-encrusted brooch and then turned to Mr. Benchley once again.

"The problem is, darling," I commented, just as Harpo, his short brown hair neatly combed, and dressed in a suit and tie, a raincoat over his arm, entered the store humming a tune. He walked to the silver cutlery counter along the wall, inside which were displayed the magnificent sterling-silver patterns that graced the finest tables on the East Side and were the preferred wedding registry gifts of brides all over the country.

As a clerk saw to Harpo's request to see this fork and that spoon, I continued: "The problem is, darling, as lovely as this brooch is, it is possible that a dozen other members of the Rotary Club could be wearing one just like it."

The clerk fervently assured me that each creation was a one-of-a-kind design by the artist, and each diamond bird unique.

That's when Chico arrived, pulling a dolly through the entry doors, over the objection of one of the guards. On it was stacked several boxes with the logo of Cartier Jewelers. They tried to stop his progress, but he began talking very loudly with his phony Italian accent, and this called the attention of several of the clerks and brought about the arrival of one of the floor detectives at his side.

Within a few seconds, the manager—a pencil-thin fellow with a pencil moustache, a persnickety attitude, and a bowtie that looked like it was strangling him, making the protrusion that was his head appear like an angry red pimple about to pop—entered from out of the offices at the rear of the store. Sizing up this new arrival, Groucho waylaid his victim by grabbing the fellow's hand to shake with his briefcase-tethered hand, which served only to slam the poor soul in the groin. To add insult to injury, Groucho apologized, and then reached up in an attempt to straighten the man's tie, which had been knocked askew. The atta-ché case slammed a frontal assault on the manager's chest. Groucho had managed to disarm, dishevel, and unravel any officious stance the man could assume, all this while announcing that he had arrived with the cache of gems that Mr. Tiffany had ordered.

As a little ruckus between Groucho, Chico, a guard, a detective, and the store's manager ensued, I asked the clerk to show me "that one, the brooch with the emerald eye."

"Oh, you like the chicken?" Mr. Benchley asked me.

"Sir, *that*, if I may correct you," said the clerk, "is a *pheasant*."

"Looks like a chicken to me . . . ."

"Pretty, but not quite right for me," I said, plac-ing the pin back onto the velvet cushion. "Ah! Now *that* is quite lovely," I said pointing to another.

"Well, that's a chicken, for sure."

"A *partridge*, sir," said the clerk, unsuccessfully trying to suppress his condescension.

"*Hmmm*," said Mr. Benchley, ignoring the little scene playing out with Groucho and Chico. "Not a chicken, you say . . . ."

The boys were flanking the manager, each talk-ing at the same time, spouting nonsense into the ear that presented itself: a torturous sight. I know from experience what it's like having just one Marx Brother bend your ear. I can't imagine two brothers, both ears.

"I have to deliver these gemstones immediately," said Groucho, holding up the case attached to his wrist. "My man here," he said, referring to Zeppo, "from the Secure Security Company, has to unlock these chains that bind me upon delivery of the goods . . . and boy, do I have the goods!"

"No, Mr. Manager," said Chico in broken English. "I god-a da goods right-a here!"

"Yes, but those are for Cartier's down the street," said the manager, pointing to the competitor's name and logo on the boxes, his pimple-head growing redder and redder. "You've come to the wrong place."

"I no comma to da wrong-a place," said Chico. "I comma to *here!*"

On the other side of the store, Harpo was being shown dozens of patterns of silverware, all lined up across the rolled-out length of black satin, and when I turned to look at him, he was asking the clerk to please bring down the sterling-silver coffee service. When the clerk turned his back to fetch it, Harpo inconspicuously moved a spoon at the end of the lineup of silverware patterns off the counter and into the coat hanging over his arm.

"Darling?" said Mr. Benchley calling my attention back to the brooches. "What about that one, the pigeon?"

"I'm sorry sir, you mean—it's a rooster."

"I thought you said there were no chickens, and now you are pointing to the cock, which is a chicken, after all! Young man," said Mr. Benchley with feigned annoyance, "That one over there? Now, don't tell me that is *not* a chicken!"

"It's a swan, sir."

"Water fowl. Close enough. We'll take it!"

"No," I said right on cue. "None of these are what I had in mind. Do you think I can have a design created just for me?"

"The designs are one of a kind, Madame. You will be the only person owning this particular brooch."

"Look, here is what I want," I said, taking out a sketch of a design I had fashioned myself, similar to the one I saw in the drawer of Featherstonhaugh's hotel room. "It's an egret. A bird on the wing. Can one be made for me?"

"Madame, the artist—well, something very similar to this has—I believe one has already been fashioned and purchased by—"

Frowning, he hesitated, turned, and pulling out his keys unlocked a drawer in a sleek, low wooden island counter behind him, removing a narrow black book consisting of no more than ten or twelve pages of designs. Flipping to the back of the book, he ran his finger down the page, following the handwritten accounts with his index finger. Finding what he was looking for, he then flipped several pages toward the front where there were photographs of the various designs.

He murmured, "Three egrets: walking, at attention, in flight."

He looked up at me, and then at Mr. Benchley, and was about to speak when I gave the signal. "Oh, I feel faint!" I said, as I fell back into the awaiting arms of Mr. Benchley.

"Someone, bring a chair and a glass of water!" ordered Mr. Benchley in a thunderous voice, setting everybody into action.

The clerk placed the book on the counter, and then as trained, returned the prized brooches back into their cushy velvet beds below the glass. Mr. Benchley knocked the black book to the floor on our side of the counter.

At the same time, just twenty feet to our side, Groucho, cupping his chin in his hand, stood leaning the elbow of his cuffed arm atop the attaché case he'd placed on the counter. Finally, after listening to the rants of Chico's pseudo-Italian character struggling to escape the grasp of one of the store's guards, Groucho had had enough. He took a swing at his battling brother with his tethered fist. The case flew open, releasing hundreds of gemstones, as fake as Woolworth's did sell, in an awe-inspiring rain that fell and rolled and tip-tapped on the surfaces of everything in sight.

Mind-numbing alarms went off; and the few genuine customers dropped to their hands and knees.

As if this was not sufficient distraction for our purpose, on the other side of the room, the clerk assisting Harpo was instantly alerted to attention by the alarm and interrupted in his task of counting the diminishing number of spoons he'd laid out before his customer. Several times he looked up from the count, and then, upon returning his eyes to the counter, began a recount of the silverware. He appeared nonplussed by the skirmish of clerks and customers diving onto the floor to collect, and possibly pocket, what appeared to be priceless gemstones.

Harpo turned abruptly to leave the store, and from his raincoat pocket escaped a knife, which clanked loudly onto the floor. He stopped in his tracks, and, when he thought his stash was secure, took a step. Out slipped teaspoons to jangle and scatter along the aisle.

"Sir!" said the clerk, ending his inventory on the counter when he realized the inventory was clattering all over the marble floor.

Harpo turned to face him, and then, as he spun back around to make a dash out of the store, a dozen knives, spoons, and forks clanked with each step he took. The silver clerk pressed another alarm button, setting off another series of bells and squawks, which sent Harpo into a jog.

But after Harpo stopped to retrieve a ruby the size of the Hope Diamond, which he inspected, flipped into the air, caught, and then pocketed, out slipped a sterling trophy bowl resounding on the floor like the deafening *gong* of the Liberty Bell. This he picked up and offered to a well-coiffed matron who was crawling on her hands and knees collecting treasures.

Mr. Benchley knelt down, retrieved the book at his feet, and flipped to the page of names of customers to which the brooches had been sold.

It was time to get out of the store. Not only were the bell alarms making my head ache, but the scheme was unraveling and our escape could be blocked at any moment if the doors were suddenly locked to bar our exit.

Harpo, free of the weighty silver, held open the door for Chico, Zeppo, and Groucho, who managed to crawl away unseen from the frenzied treasure hunters combing the floor for their fortunes. Mr. Benchley and I returned the book to the counter and, unnoticed, calmly walked out of the greatest American jewelry store in New York.

Harpo now shook out his raincoat and out fell a flurry of fruit knives and demitasse spoons. Then, for the finale, the elaborate samovar, last of the family silver, was sent crashing down in a deep, echoing thud on the marble floor.

Chapter Eleven

Aleck arrived at my door dressed in a summer ensemble of white linen accessorized with powder-blue shirt, tie, and pocket kerchief, with white buckskin on his feet and a white panama hat atop his head. He looked very like a Jamaican plantation owner. One fiery glare at Woodrow, as he hesitated in crossing over the threshold, was enough to stop any ideas my pup may have had of jumping up and laying paws on the white trousers. Woodrow slinked away and settled down in the corner.

Aleck's foul mood of the past few days since his return from his summer island retreat in Vermont appeared to have lifted somewhat. Aleck loved a good party where he would be surrounded with theatre people who hung on every word he said. After all, he was the most prominent theatre critic in the country, known as "the star maker"; finding a place in his good graces was the most important thing a young actor could do for his career, besides being able to act. And

tonight the Mellons' apartment would be crawling
with actors.

"Why aren't you dressed?" he asked, after I bade
him enter and poured him a scotch on the rocks.

"I really don't feel up to going to the party tonight, Aleck."

"Are you ill?"

"I will be if I go."

"Nonsense! Get dressed," he ordered, and just
sat there frowning at me. I took a long drag on the
cigarette before stubbing it out to answer the knock
on the door.

Mr. Benchley stood leaning on the doorframe,
dressed in a royal-blue suit and sporting a peppermint-
striped bowtie. Instead of his usual evening top-hat,
he was carrying a buff-colored grass fedora. On a
man of smaller, slimmer stature, the effect would
have been Runyonesque, but on Mr. Benchley, it was
daring with a touch of class. The two men eyed one
another's attire.

"Well, we look wonderful, don't we, old sport,"
said Mr. Benchley to Aleck, as he bent to pet Woodrow, who'd come over from his corner to greet and
jump on him, and to receive the stick of beef jerky
extracted from the coat pocket.

"You look very . . . carnival barker, Bob," said
Aleck.

"And you, Aleck, remind me of an overstuffed

Southern cracker in all his ponderous splendor." And then, looking over at me: "And you look like the second gravedigger. And why aren't you dressed?"

"She thinks the party will make her ill."

"Just sick and tired, I suppose," I said, dropping down on the sofa. I took a swig of my scotch, and when I heard no reply from the usually loquacious Aleck, I turned to face that big man, as cool as an ice cream sundae melting in the plush chair. But still he remained silent.

Mr. Benchley poured himself a drink and sat down next to me. "I just met our socialist friend down at the bar. He was giving Bunny an earful about conditions in a shirt factory in upstate New York. Bunny talked about all the fun stuff happening in Russia, making a labor movement moot. I left them to it."

"How very generous of you," I replied, mindlessly tapping down another cigarette. Mr. Benchley lit me up and said, "Yes, we had a very interesting talk."

"*Aaaaannnd?* What was so very interesting that you might share with me?"

"Oh, I think you should ask our socialist friend yourself, my dear, as he's going to tag along with us to the Mellons' soirée."

"Slumming, is he?" I said, my laughter hollow. "Fraternizing with the capitalist class? I don't know what's worse: the smugness of the socialist or the heartlessness of the rich capitalist."

"Please, Dorothy, dear, don't bore me with politics. You *do* know there will be caviar and champagne?" said Aleck, offering culinary inducements. I could see him salivate. "Bluepoint oysters, filet mignon, and for dessert—"

"And Tallulah wants you there," said Mr. Benchley.

"She won't in the least miss me."

"*Au contraire!* She depends on it."

"But, why did you invite *him?*" I asked. "Why on earth would he want to come and spend the evening with people he has contempt for?"

"You do it all the time, my dear, fodder for your stories. And . . . because you'll be there."

"What are you saying?"

"I think he plans on writing an exposé on wealthy Americans, how the other half—no—think again, that would be how the *one percent* live. Distribution of wealth, and all that. Don't worry; he won't pose any danger tonight."

"Oh, very well, give me ten minutes."

———•———

The Hotel Navarro on Central Park South was built only a couple of years before, and its art deco appointments offer luxury living, with spectacular, unobstructed views of Central Park from its southernmost border at 59th Street to its northernmost one at 110th Street. The spacious rooms of the Mellons' penthouse were already teeming with the vivacious rabble of theatre people, and the apartment was brightened with lamplight as the sun dipped down in the west, gradually leaving the park in darkness.

Piano music greeted our arrival, as did Tallulah, practically knocking over the butler who opened the door to us. Thirty or forty Broadway hopefuls were plowing into the spread at the buffet table, or lounging about on sofas and chairs, or leaning on the piano and swaying or singing along with the show tunes issuing forth. There was always music at such gatherings of showpeople. The musical accompaniment provided an opportunity for a young chorine to lend her voice to a song, perhaps to be heard by the likes of a Gershwin or a Richard Rogers or an Irving Berlin as an informal audition. You never knew who might drop in looking for a charmer like yourself to fill the very role he's trying to cast in his next smash hit!

I had brought Woodrow, who wore a red-satin bowtie made for him to wear at last year's Actors Equity Halloween party. He was fussed over and offered pâté. He loved being the center of attention, and he was my excuse when the time came that I wanted to escape the party: Dogs do not adhere to the social graces.

I could hear Hermione's distinctive bray over the music, from somewhere deep in the apartment.

At least, I thought, *when her voice becomes louder it might serve as a warning of her approach*, and if lucky, I might be able to avoid contact with her altogether, ducking away before I was caught.

No such luck with Roger, however; he was at my side before I knew it, begging introduction to Aleck, who beamed his pleasure when Roger said that he always counted on reading Aleck's thoughtful Broadway show reviews and that he was undoubtedly the best-known figure in America, better known than Calvin Coolidge. Our socialist friend nodded agreement and then turned to me and Mr. Benchley with, "And who isn't? 'Silent Cal' never entertained a thought or expressed an opinion in his life, so God only knows who's really sitting in the White House."

Hermione caught me—I was trapped, wedged between the show's director and the playwright wanting to discuss with me the possibility of consulting on a scene of dialogue in the play's second act, when she snuck up on me. She took me by surprise, and I must have looked startled, staring at her bared breasts—she was a foot taller than me, and her décolletage exceptionally low. I halted in my reply to the playwright midsentence as I was thus struck in the face, and then took in the rest of what there was of her dress. And it wasn't that I felt dowdy in my beaded sleeveless coral-silk shift with the Delmonte clips, standing next to this siren. Well, of course, I did; but it wasn't the comparison that had me reeling.

I marveled at her brazenness, or was it just plain careless stupidity on her part?   She excused herself for interrupting, and then, turning me by the elbow to look at the partygoers on the other side of the room, said: "I see you're with that socialist, tonight."

"He tagged along. Just slumming. Want to meet him? I'm sure you'll be charmed."

"I didn't know you were a—"

"Socialist? Not quite."

"Pity!"

"Why's that?"

"It would be fun to have a socialist friend."

"Barrel of laughs."

"Is he?"

Mr. Benchley appeared from out of the crush. Having arrived at my side, his eyes widened when he took in, first the bosom, and then the dress. But it was his double-take that almost gave him away. "Delightful gathering, Hermione," he choked out to avoid appearing speechless.

"Yeah, thanks, Bobby." She took a deep drag off her cigarette holder, and when she exhaled down her nose the effect was that of the mists settling over the twin peaks of New Hampshire.

"I understand this is your first venture into Show Business?" he asked.

"I told Roger, 'Roger, wouldn't it be the thing

to put some cash on a Broadway show?' and he said, 'Sure honey!'" she giggled. "But, I thought that that dreamy John Barrymore was going to be in the play, too. I was disappointed to hear I was wrong about that. It's that grumpy Lionel who's in it, instead."

I pointed to Lionel Barrymore, who was across the room, doing a little soft-shoe with a girl on each arm. "Doesn't look too terribly out-of-sorts to me."

"Oh, don't be an Airedale, Dot!"

Mr. Benchley caught my eye and said, "Has Hermione met Aleck?"

"Oh, you mean that roly-poly little man over there scooping up all the caviar garnish off the poached salmon plate?"

"She's met him," said Mr. Benchley. "How about my friend over there?"

"I was just asking Dot about him!"

"Come, I'll introduce you."

Before she could answer, the butler appeared with news that his mistress had a telephone call. "I'll take it in the study, she said, and smiled and excused herself, leaving me and Mr. Benchley alone with each other—but, not for long, because Mr. Benchley was whisked away to the bar by an old friend before we could discuss our next move.

The room was buzzing with music, gay conversation, and laughter. *A good distraction*, I thought, as I cut through the crowd, zigzagging my way, head down, hoping that no one would stop me. I figured that the bedrooms were on the upper floor, atop the curving stairs. I took the opportunity to slowly weave my way up, and when I was stopped by an actor I had known while growing up on the Upper West Side, I just handed him my empty glass and asked if he could get me a refill. A couple of women were coming out of the bathroom and I pretended that that was my destination, taking the door which they held for me and then, when they were gone, moving back toward the bedrooms.

I knew it was her bedroom when I entered it because of the perfume that clung in the air—a familiar perfume by Guerlain. *How vanity could give it all away*, I thought.

Quickly, I assessed the space, and then made straight for the dressing room, its door slightly ajar, a light glowing, revealing a glimpse of the many furs and racks of shoes and designer gowns within. That's when I heard the familiar padding footsteps, and when I looked around, there was Woodrow.

"Naughty boy," I scolded in a whisper, annoyed that Mr. Benchley had let go his leash. He followed me into the dressing room, where my eyes scanned over the many boxes on the shelves, looking for a particular box—oblong, bearing the distinctive name of *Madame Charlotte Chapelier*. I found what I was looking for and, stepping up on a little footstool, pulled the box down from its perch on the shelf. I knew what was inside, and with hands shaking I removed the lid.

I was not rewarded with the find I had expected, however; the box was empty. And I didn't have much time to think about where it might be hidden because all thinking stopped with the realization that there was a gun in my back.

"Did you really think I was stupid enough to keep the hat?" said Hermione, her voice uncharacteristically deep. "After the fuss you made about it on the train, telling that stupid detective that you'd *kill* for such a hat?"

"That was *Ruth's* big mouth," I stuttered out. *She'll not shoot me in here. The blood would get all over her pretty clothes, and those satin shoes over there on the rack — it would never wash out.*

"Don't worry, Dorothy, I'm not going to kill you here," she said, reading my thoughts. "Although, there is so much noise downstairs that even if anyone *did* hear the shot, they'd just think it was a champagne cork."

"And it would make a bloody mess of your things, of course."

"How did you know?"

"You may have been smart enough to get rid of the hat, but you were stupid enough to wear that brooch — that goddamn monster of a diamond brooch."

"You mean this pin?" she said, her eyes darting down toward her ample bosom. "I thought it was—"

"You thought it was the hat that gave you away? Yes, and the fact that you are not a natural blonde."

"Who is these days?" she said, with a hard, snorting laugh.

"But I found out that the real Hermione Mellon had turned prematurely gray in her early twenties. Before that strip job of yours your hair was *brown*, Joan Trombley! And before I met your husband, Freddie, and learned that he sent your cousin, Charles Fanshaw, to find you, I noticed something about that portrait you conveniently showed me in your sitting room at Last Call, the one of you and your sister—with your mother? I am aware that blonde little girls sometimes turn dark-haired at adulthood, so it wasn't your dark roots my—our— hairdresser Loretta had to bleach that caused me to notice that there was something very odd about that painting."

There was a noise in the hall and then voices at the door. She shoved the gun barrel deeper into my spine and pulled me back further into the dressing room, pulling the door closed. A couple of kids had entered the bedroom and were singing as they danced through and then out again in their romp through the house.

"We're going for a little ride, Dot."

"Don't be an Airedale, Hermione. How do you figure you can get away with this?"

"Easy. Freight elevator."

"No! I mean get away with killing me?"

"Who says that I'm going to kill you?"

"What, we're going to a sale at Klein's?"

"No, I'm going to have someone else kill you. This way," she said, pushing me out the dressing room door. Spotting Woodrow peeking out from behind a floor-length mink, she said, "*and your little dog, too!*"

"Can't we just leave him here? He won't bark."

Pointing the gun at my chest, she told me, "Pick up the dog!" She led me through the bedroom, gun aimed at my back, and peeked out of the bedroom door. I was trying to figure out if I could knock her in the head with a heavy candlestick or vase or something, but there was nothing handy to grab. "Let's move," she hissed.

She hustled me along the hall and down a short staircase ending in an alcove between the kitchen and a butler's pantry. The kitchen was too busy with caterers and waiters getting the food out to the partygoers for any of them to notice us as she pushed me out the service door. Down the elevator to the basement we went and, after peeking out of the gate, she led me along a maze of pipes to another door, which opened onto Central Park South. I clutched Woodrow to me.

"So where does this little expedition end, Hermione?"

"Get in the car," she said when we had arrived at the chauffeured Rolls parked on the street. Her liveried man opened the door, wrenched Woodrow from my arms, and threw him to the sidewalk before shoving me in the backseat. "Woodrow!" I screamed.

"Hermione" hopped in next to me, slamming the door.

I was horrified for Woodrow—alone on the sidewalk facing the busy thoroughfare of Central Park South. But, the doors were locked and I couldn't escape. Why, oh, *why* had I allowed myself to leave the relative safety of the apartment? I could have broken away. She never would have shot me, not with a hundred witnesses to see her do it! Lesson learned: Never let them take you to another location where it would be easier to kill you! *Too late!*

These panic-ridden thoughts raced through my head as the driver pulled away from the curb and into the slow stream of traffic. I could feel the rush of adrenalin course through my veins like a drug. I was poised to do something, anything, to get free, but I knew not what. I craned my neck to look out the back window—there was Woodrow, barking from the curb, and then he jumped off it and into the busy flow of traffic. I heard the screech of tires and the blast of a horn, and closed my eyes against the inevitable disaster waiting to befall my little pup. As any mother would grieve for her child, I reeled at the thought of his death under the tires of an automobile!

And then I thought, *I'll never be a mother; I'll never have the child I've always wanted. I would have been a good mother, I would've!*

"You'll get over it; it's just a dog," she chuckled. "I suppose you believe in the afterlife, Dot? If so, you'll be seeing the little fellow soon enough."

I wanted to hurt her, punch her, pull out the bleached hair in great chunks from her skull. Instead, I cringed at her heartlessness, and in the face of it I realized that the only way to fight such evil was to keep my wits about me and to stay calm when I wanted to strike out. For that was all I had left, my wits, my ingenuity, because only God knew where the hell they were taking me to finish me off!

At last I found my voice and I tried not to let it quiver as I said, "I see you've a hired man. Does he do your killing for you?"

"I'm a modern girl, Dot; I can do my own killing when I want to."

"I hope you're paying him enough," I said loudly for the man to hear. "After all, he could be a witness against you, you know, or blackmail you blind."

"Shut up!"

"Clever retort, Joan. You must know that people at the party will miss us there, that someone must have seen us when we left the building."

"Well, you were sick, fell ill, and I insisted on having my driver take you home, and I decided to make sure you were tucked in bed, like a good friend would do for a good friend. But, you wanted to ride around for a while, till your stomach settled—a ride through the park, you suggested—"

"Making it up as you go along, is that it? How will you explain how I went from a car ride to a bullet through my head?"

The evening traffic was sluggish as we approached the Grand Army Plaza, the corner of Fifth Avenue and 59th Street, where traffic finally came to a halt. We were only a short distance from where we had started out. The Plaza Hotel stood to the right, and any chance of signaling for help through the closed window was futile as Joan was on that side of the car.

The window on my side of the car faced the lane of traffic going in the opposite direction, going west toward Columbus Circle. On that side of the road, near the park entrance, oncoming traffic was lighter and moved briskly. Through the gaps in the flow of cars, I could see the horse-drawn carriages lined up, a favorite romantic attraction for tourist rides through the winding roads of Central Park. And that's where I caught sight of a familiar face, the face of a friend who just happened to look across the street at the same time I saw him. I knew that he recognized me, pawing frantically at the raised window, but then his attention was suddenly diverted and I didn't have a chance to make any further gesture to communicate that I needed help. The limo was moving again, and then suddenly turned north onto East Drive, the long, winding road that cut through Central Park. I slunk down in my seat, defeated.

The park was dark, except for the occasional lampposts lighting the road's periphery. The automobile's headlights sliced wedges through the blackness, and, except for the few times when we occasionally breezed past one of the slow-moving carriages, there was no one who might see my predicament.

"I'm not the only one who knows you and your darling 'husband' Roger are murderers," I said, hoping that knowledge would put an end to this madness, but after the words passed my lips I regretted having made the profession, because that knowledge would put my friends in danger.

And I was right to think that because she said, "Roger will take care of your Bobby Benchley, Dot. He'll have a little accident."

Before I could scratch out her eyes, the car slowed and turned off East Drive and onto a bridle path. A few hundred yards later the car came to a stop. The driver shut off the engine but kept the headlights glowing. Then, he got out, came to the driver's side passenger door, opened it, and grabbed me by the elbow, roughly pulling me out of the car. Hermione was at my side a second later, and while the chauffeur held me firm, she walked off a little way to look over the terrain.

The moon had risen in the east, and I turned away from the glare of the headlights, allowing my eyes to adjust to the natural light shed onto the darkened woods around us. Moonlight glinted off a high spot where a soft ring of illumination glowed in the distance over the tree-line. I instantly identified the landmark: the obelisk, "Cleopatra's Needle" we used to call it when I was a child, even though Cleopatra had nothing whatsoever to do with the Egyptian-style monument erected not far from the rear of the Metropolitan Museum of Art.

I could smell water. To the west lay the Croton Reservoir—that great expanse of fresh water that poured through the taps of the millions of homes on Manhattan Island. I knew it well. I knew the park like the back of my hand: the rambles, the Menagerie, Bethesda Fountain, Vista Rock, atop which sits Belvedere Castle, the Victorian "folly" built of stone and now used as headquarters by the United States Weather Bureau.

This was my playground when I was a child—*all* of Central Park was my playground. And I made a bet with myself that these two fly-by-night pippins hadn't the foggiest idea where we were. If I could make a break into the darkness of the trees, I'd have a chance of escape. I had to try; the alternative was a bullet in my lovely little head.

To break and run toward the obelisk would bring me to the museum and quickly to the street at Fifth

Avenue around 80th Street. But the area around the obelisk was open, mostly, and lit to be seen to best advantage, as was the grand edifice of the museum. I might get away, but they'd see me and most likely the big guy would catch me. Result: a bullet in the head.

But to break away off the bridal path and hit the low brush bordering it might be my best escape route. From there I could keep off the paths, move stealthily between the tall trees, and make it to the reservoir. They couldn't take a vehicle there. I could get through the darker regions guided only by moonlight and the water line, even get to the shelter and safety of Belvedere Castle while they searched aimlessly for me. From the castle I could put out the alarm.

All these plans were running through my mind over the course of half a minute while the Big Blonde tried to figure out her strategy. I had stopped struggling in the grip of the Big Dope, which served to lessen the firmness of his handhold.

"What do you think about down there? Just off the path and close to those bushes?"

"Good a place as any," said the Big Brute. "We can roll her body into the underbrush."

"They'll find her too quickly, once daylight comes, don't you think?"

"So, we'll put her in the trunk and drop her in the East River. It'll look like the Mafia hit her."

"No! We want it to look like the *anarchists* got her," said the airhead.

"Now, why in hell would the anarchists want to kill me?" I asked, and she told me to shut up. Which I did—after all, she had the gun, and I didn't want her to be facing me when I decided to run. I should not call her attention to me again.

That's when I heard the *clip-clop* of horses' hooves in the distance. A horse-drawn carriage was going by. They wouldn't shoot if there was anybody nearby to hear the gunshot.

I dug my heel into the Big Jerk's instep, and when he hollered I turned and poked his eyes with two fingers. I grabbed the opportunity to escape by sinking down toward to the ground and wriggling out from under his encircling arms. He turned to grab me as I began to run for the brush. Then the thunderous blast of the gun's discharge sounded. I made it to cover, and only then, while remaining very still, did I realize that in her moment of panic Joan had shot her sidekick.

There was much ado from the fellow as he lay there moaning and whimpering and yelling obscenities about the bull's-eye strike to his nether regions. I made my way through to a stand of trees and their voices faded.

Then I heard the roar of the car revving up, and when I glanced toward the direction from whence I'd come, I saw the headlights glimmering through the trees at a distance. I watched as they turned north, away from me. I sighed with relief, stood to my full height, took deep breaths, and considered my best choices to exit the park. I was just about to walk toward the museum when suddenly I saw tiny specks of light in the distance, flickering between the trees, and heard the hum of a motorcar getting closer and closer as the headlights shone bigger and brighter on the approach. East Drive was not in that direction, I didn't think.

The flickering lights became bigger and bigger until they were large spheres, and I knew they hadn't given up the plan to kill me. I was in greater danger now because Joan Trombley was angry and desperate. As careless as she was, she wouldn't refrain from any rash decision about where and when to kill me.

The car stopped, the headlights were killed, and I heard the sound of a door slam. As I looked out blindly, my eyes slowly adjusting to the sudden darkness, I caught the striking glimmer of diamonds catching the rays of moonlight. She was standing only a few feet away.

I held my breath and took a step back, but she must have heard the sound of a twig cracking under my foot, for the gun went off with deafening thunder and I could even see the spark of the shot coming out of the barrel. I ran!

Now there was another kind of light bobbing along the tree branches and I realized she had a flashlight, and she was coming up behind me. I ran for cover, and as I was about to dive behind a boulder I again heard the loud report of the gun. I was now between a rock and a hard place.

There was a muffled sound of something getting closer on the grassy knoll where I stood frozen and listening in the dark gray of the night. It was the snorting breath of an animal coming closer and closer. With my heart in my mouth I turned toward the direction I thought the animal was coming from and my throat choked off a futile scream.

Was it a coyote? Or a wolf? They still lived in the park. I expected the end, and my life was flashing before my eyes when in front of me rose up a great black shadow waving its head at me! I immediately mourned that I could have done things a little differently and lived a better, a finer life. I could feel the heat of the beast's breath on me and closed my eyes before I was mauled.

Instead, I was hoisted into the air by a strong, muscled arm and found myself bouncing on a galloping horse, in a most unbalanced position on my stomach, into the moonlit clearing that was the reservoir.

The horseman of my near-apocalypse slowed the horse to a canter and unceremoniously told me to reposition my weight, spread-legged over the animal's rump, and ordered in no uncertain terms: "Hang onto my waist!"

Harpo and his "Maggie" maneuvered carefully along the narrow path bordering the big lake. The full moon reflected on the still waters, and to the east and west, beyond the meadows and woods of my beloved park, stood the window-lit buildings of the exclusive apartment houses.

Then came the roar of a motorcar engine, close, where a car was not meant to travel. The headlights bounced wildly as the automobile hit the small mounds and rocks along the grassy spaces as it made a beeline toward us. Before I knew it, Harpo had taken us off the walking path and onto the bridal path at full gallop. Within just a few seconds it seemed our road was being brightened by the glaring headlights coming up fast behind us.

"Hold on, Dottie! Just close your eyes and hang onto me."

The next thing I knew, my behind was off my perch, in the air, and my heart fell into my stomach, for we were flying forward at a great speed and I had to struggle for a stronghold as Harpo was escaping my grasp. I felt weightless for a time. I imagined that now was to come the moment of my death, and I didn't want it to end this way.

My bottom smacked down hard again, landing on solid horseflesh, and Harpo returned like a welcomed slap against my chest. I hadn't closed my eyes as I was told, and now I felt lightheaded and faint, having watched from my vantage point the great leap we—Harpo, me, and Maggie—had just taken off the bridal path over a wall of boulders and down into a grassy ramble.

"Did we make it?" asked my friend.

"You can open your eyes now, Harpo," I said.

"Thanks!"

"But I wouldn't slow down."

"Well, there's a bridge up ahead, I think, off the bridal path we were on, and I see lights. She may be heading there to get an open shot at us as we ride under the arch."

"Go where you must, Harpo; we'll cross that bitch when we get to her."

"Must you joke?"

"It's expected of me."

She was out of the car and waiting for us on the bridge, aiming the gun with both hands. It looked like she'd been hurt sometime during the chase, because she was having trouble getting a firm grip on the weapon.

There was nowhere for us to go—walls bordered the road, so Harpo kicked Maggie into a run, and just as we entered the momentary shelter of the bridge, the gunshot echoed wildly within the archway.

She hadn't time to maneuver around to get off a shot as we exited the archway and rode off into the night. But soon the sound of the engine roared at our back and we knew she was on the move again, unrelenting in her mission to see us dead.

Belvedere Castle sits like a queen on the second-highest point in Central Park. Joan would have a hard time getting her motorcar to the castle, which is at the southern foot of the reservoir. She'd have to abandon the auto and circumvent the woods and marshy glades on foot, or walk over the footpaths leading to the building, where she might herself be ambushed. I didn't doubt she would try to get to the castle.

Harpo guided Maggie more slowly now that we were a safe distance from Joan's pursuit on foot, and in just a few hundred feet he brought the horse to climb the rock where it leveled out for us. We—Maggie, that is—rested a minute while we took in the view below. To our north and east was the great reservoir, sparkling in the dark and mirroring the cumulous clouds, white and low against the black sky. The castle was lit with floodlights on the outside, but the windows were dark squares, indicating no one was there. We thought it best to make our way toward Central Park West. She must have stopped and killed the headlights. She would now be on foot, coming toward us on a walking path around the lake. We agreed, too, that our best course of action was to make it to the busy thoroughfare to our west. First we would go south, off the walking path, through another ramble. We wasted not another minute as Harpo guided Maggie back down off the rock ledge and onto the soft turf toward the exit from the park at 77th Street.

But as we arrived at the footpath out of the park, headlights, close by and on the meadow, flashed on, and we could see her walking toward us in silhouette, her dress rendered a sheer, gauzy film about her figure by the backlighting, as she once again lifted her arm to aim the weapon at us.

A shot was fired and suddenly she disappeared, our vision obscured by the hazy lights shining in our eyes. We watched as a figure, a man, walked toward where she had stood before falling down next to the lump that was Joan Trombley on the ground.

Harpo brought Maggie out of the direct glare of the light, and now we were able to see Freddie Trombley, rocking and moaning over the body of his wife. From out of the distance, down the dimly lit walking path, came a horse and buggy, clip-clopping along. I heard the familiar bark of a dog—my precious pup!—and in a moment I was plucked from my perch on Maggie by the sturdy arms of Mr. Benchley, and set down firmly and held in his comforting embrace. When I broke away, Woodrow Wilson leaped into my arms and licked away the tears rolling down my cheeks.

Belvedere Castle

The Final Chapter

We had gathered at a long table on the canopy-covered garden patio of Bernardo Castelli's Italian Restaurant in Little Italy. The strings of lanterns shone warmly and the night was refreshingly cool for the beginning of September. The wine was red and ever flowing and the conversation as varied and interesting as the dinner fare.

The Italian restaurateur, Bernardo Castelli, the man who had helped Lamberto Maggiorani make his start by opening the bakery for him next-door to the restaurant, had heard about how Mr. Benchley and I and our socialist friend and the Marx Brothers had helped protect young Giusto's life, and he insisted on hosting a party for us. The Maggioranis were there, Lamberto, Lianella, their little boy, Enzo, Papa Corelli, and Giusto, along with me, Mr. Benchley, our socialist friend, Heywood, Ruth, Tallulah, Harpo Marx, and Aleck, who insisted on coming "to review the food for the *Times*." This he did do, to the glory of

Bernardo Castelli, who consequently had to expand the restaurant into the adjoining building's storefront to accommodate the crowds who flocked in to try the *saltimbocca*, the tender *calamari*, the octopus salad, the exquisite Bolognese sauce, the mouthwatering *pasta con la sarde* with wild fennel, and the stuffed leg of lamb, not to mention the numerous vegetable dishes prepared by the divine hand of Signor Castelli himself! We had feasted for two hours, and the food kept on coming. The espresso was being poured, and aperitif glasses filled with anisette. And now, we were to experience the delectable little masterpieces of Italian pastry prepared by the Maggiorani Bakery next door.

I bit into a *cannoli*, and moaned. Aleck was happy, I could tell, because he was sipping his *demitasse* with his pinky-finger extended. Mr. Benchley was well into a napoleon, and the others paid rapt attention to the little lecture given by our socialist friend (whose Italian is fluent, and used only to clarify a point for Giusto's benefit).

"Nobody wants the anarchist, because the anarchist believes in no interconnections," he said. "He refuses to answer to the bosses, to the labor leaders, to *any* governing power at all, so he isn't under anyone's control, you see. He refuses to take a political stand—won't pledge allegiance to any nation, and so he won't go to war and fight for whatever it is that the nationalistic powers want him to fight for. The politicians ask, how can you win anything—the land, the power, the oil, the coal, if these unpatriotic crazies refuse to fight for us? The Reds hate them. The social- ist and labor leaders see anarchists as crackpots, loose cannons who only *undermine* the work their organizers are doing. The anarchist does not see the big picture, which is that you can't just demand from the bosses better pay and working conditions and expect that you'll get much without the threatening weight of a union behind you."

"True," said Heywood. "You have to form an army of sorts, a union of men, or the special interests will run your life."

"But that is like war, like fight in war and to play the game with the capitalists!" said Giusto.

"But, Giusto," asked our socialist friend, "think about this: If Vanzetti had allowed any of his fellow anarchists to *organize* a real movement to free them, do you really think they'd have ever been executed, or even jailed?"

Giusto nodded, but I doubted he was convinced. He said: "They die for the princ-apple."

They died to keep their principles, the principles of their cause, and fighting would have been a betrayal of all they believed in.

I looked at young Giusto and thought about how, when one is young, one's political philosophies might often change, perhaps shifting from right to left; these philosophies were the reflection of one's conscience and experience. How would he feel about things in ten or twenty years from now?

Aleck ignored the political talk and instead turned to ask Bernardo Castelli if he could take home an order of the *scampi*, and to make him a reservation for eight the following Sunday evening.

The conversation had turned to the events of the past few days when Ruth asked, "Why didn't Roger just divorce Hermione? Why kill her?"

"Money. In a divorce he would have gotten nothing, and it was she who had the great fortune," I said.

Ruth asked, "What was it about the portrait in Hermione's room at Last Call that made you suspect she wasn't the real Hermione?"

"Well, I didn't put it together at first," I said, "But then I remembered that Hermione told me her sister died, and Johnny, the kid at the party, said it was a *twin* who had died, 'when she was just a little kid.' The two girls in the painting were in their early teens. Heywood made inquiries and found out the child had drowned around her eighth birthday. So the painting wasn't quite right, you see. And then I remembered Tallulah saying that Hermione had had her black roots bleached—remember that day we went to have our hair done, Lulla, at Loretta's salon?"

"That's right; Loretta said she had to bleach Hermione's black roots—but what does that—"

"The real Hermione was prematurely gray-haired, and I remembered that boy, Johnny, at the Mellons' party, saying he was surprised she wasn't an old lady, and that with her pretty blonde hair she looked like a movie star."

Mr. Benchley added, "It was the *old-lady* remark, and the fact that Freddie Trombley said the dead woman in Bedroom Two was gray-haired, whereas his missing wife was a brunette."

"Also, the odd statement you made, Tallulah, that she had been to Henri's beauty salon and found it pretentious, as you mentioned she had said to Loretta; that seemed strange, considering she'd never been to the States before and had been in town only one day before going to Loretta's to get her hair done."

"So, you think she had been here in New York before," said Tallulah.

"Well, the brooch," said Mr. Benchley. "It was a one-of-a-kind creation, no others made. If it had been purchased by Roger Mellon last June, as we discovered when we looked at the sales registry at Tiffany's, thanks to the help of Harpo and his brothers, why, then, was it on the veil of a hat worn by 'The Dead Woman in Bedroom Two'?"

"Look, Mr. Benchley, darling friend: I am not going to write about this whole fiasco under the title, *The Dead Woman in Bedroom Two,* as you would have me do. I won the coin-toss, remember? I have *another* title in mind for the day I am ready to sit down and write about it," I said, picking off the edge of an anginette cookie and feeding the morsel to Woodrow, who was lying beside my chair.

Mr. Benchley ignored me and continued on: "Roger met Joan Trombley when he was living in Paris, while she was taking a shopping vacation away from Freddie, it seems. Hermione was in a sanatorium in Switzerland, giving her husband, who'd obviously married her for her inheritance, a chance to fool around in 'Gay Paree'! He couldn't divorce the real Hermione; her fortune would be gone with her if he did, so what better than to kill her on the train? It would be easy for Joan to assume the role of Hermione, as no one, other than a few people in Kenya, had ever seen the real wife."

"And the bomb was just a handy diversion, the only clever part of the scheme to send us off on a wild-goose-chase looking for anarchist bombers," said Heywood.

"Yes," I replied, "getting poor Giusto involved in the madness, using to their advantage the prejudice that follows the newly arrived immigrant once he gets off the boat."

"That fake bomb on the train, the one that was found in the dead woman's room? Well, it was part of Roger's and Joan's plan to make the murder appear to be the work of anarchist conspirators," added Mr. Benchley. "He ran a munitions factory during the war, remember. Typical Sherlockian ploy: Distract Holmes with a fake crime, while Moriarty commits the real one."

"I see," said Ruth, "Fake bombers, real bludgeoners!"

"Charles Fanshaw came to the States on the same ship Roger and the *real* Hermione had sailed on from England. He was on the trail of his cousin, Joan Trombley, after he discovered that it was Roger she had been having an affair with before she ran off. He thought Roger would possibly lead him to her, but to his surprise he spotted Joan on the Midnight Owl. Later he must have figured out the scheme, and he confronted the killers at Last Call, where they knocked him off, too."

"By the way, Tallulah, you were right, you know," I said. "You did see a couple embracing on the bench when you slithered back to the bungalow at dawn, night of the party."

"I object to the term, *slithered!*"

Mr. Benchley nodded: "You interrupted Joan and Roger while attempting to retrieve the dead body of her cousin in the shed, and which they intended stuffing in the roomy, oversized trunk of the Mercedes! They posed him on the bench when they heard your callywogging—"

"What the hell is *callywogging?*"

"Your *singing*, my dear girl. What looked like

a lover's embrace was simply Joan trying to keep Fanshaw propped up and from keeling over to the ground!"

"But," asked Lamberto, "why drag Giusto into the crime?"

Mr. Benchley said, "I suppose Joan and Roger wanted a fall guy for the murder, one carrying a note and cash. They would throw suspicion off themselves by making it appear the dead woman was in cahoots with the bomb-throwing anarchists."

"They were clever," I said. "They wanted Giusto to be spotted by me or Mr. Benchley. Why, it was probably Roger knocked on my door to wake me up, so I would look out and see Giusto in Bedroom Two at the appointed time as directed in the note."

"So, both Hermione and Joan are dead," said Ruth, "and I hear the chauffeur survived being shot in the ass. Now, what happens to Roger?"

"He confessed to me the whole scheme when I knocked the gun out of his hand," said our socialist friend. "He'll go to jail, the jury will find him guilty, and he'll be executed."

I smiled at him in gratitude for what he had done to save Mr. Benchley while I was galloping through Central Park with Harpo. "When Roger discovered Joan gone from the apartment and he saw the hatbox from Madame Charlotte's *Chapelier* tossed on the floor of the dressing room, his fears were realized, especially when Mr. Benchley, who was looking for me, asked if he had seen me anywhere. Woodrow, dragging his leash and wandering around the sidewalk outside the building, brought Harpo to the apartment door. Harpo knew something was wrong when he saw me in a big car turning into Central Park's East Drive, and Woodrow barking after the car.

"Harpo and Mr. Benchley ran out of the apartment without telling Aleck, Tallulah, or our socialist friend what was going on. But our socialist friend saw them leave and the expression on Roger's face as he stood at the top of the stairs leading to the bedrooms prompted our friend to follow him into the den, where he saw Roger take out a gun from his desk drawer. He followed Roger out of the apartment, and somewhere between the elevator and the lobby, wrestled the gun away from him."

"You thought I was the killer, didn't you, Dorothy?" said our socialist friend.

I blushed, but then I decided to answer his question with directness: 'Yes, for a while I did. I saw you in discussion with Fanshaw, in the corridor of the train. Fanshaw was following me, or so I thought, and when he wound up dead—"

"And then you were seen by one of the Harvard boys knocking on the dead woman's door not long before the body was discovered, and—"

"There was a good reason for that—"

"Let me finish!" I said. "And you were the only person who knew where Giusto and his family lived in Little Italy. After Giusto was shot, I realized that you were the only person, other than myself and Mr. Benchley, here, who knew where to find the young man. It was a perfectly understandable conclusion. Anyway, I'd still like to know what you were doing visiting the woman's room middle of the night?"

"Actually, I had come to see you. When I saw you in the hall earlier in the evening, you appeared to have just come out of that room, Bedroom Two. I thought it was your room. I was mistaken."

"But," I stammered, "what did you want to see me about?"

"To apologize."

"What for?"

"Being a bit of a bore. No! Don't pretend I wasn't; all my stuff about rubbing elbows with capitalists—"

"I don't remember that, and I wasn't going to object to what you said about your being a bit of a bore. I thought you were, actually. I suppose it had been a harrowing sort of a day, as we all know and will never forget."

He chuckled good-naturedly.

And I thought that *now* I could answer Mr. Benchley's query as to why I didn't like the man, when we had stood outside the Gonk after luncheon:

He could effect change for the better in this crazy world of ours. Through his insightful books he could effect change when I could only make fun, make jokes and write sad little poems about the inequities of life. For once, I'd been attracted to a man who was too good for me, a man I didn't feel worthy of, and that made me afraid. So I turned away.

"And that poor man, Trombley?" asked Ruth. "He shot his wife to death in a fit of passion!"

"Well," said Harpo, "he shot her in the nick of time, just as she was about to shoot at me and Dottie, point blank. And let me say, if he *hadn't* shot his wife, one of us, or both, might not be enjoying this lovely, cool September evening. I have the feeling that Freddie will get off scot free!"

We were leaving the restaurant, saying our good-byes and thank-yous to our new Italian friends, when I asked Harpo how his horse, Maggie, was faring.

"She's doing great! She can't live at my place, and Frank said I had to get her out of the hotel, so I found a stall for her at the Westside stables. She likes you, I know it! She's right outside, Dottie, come and say hello."

"You know, Harpo," said Mr. Benchley, as we walked out into the night to visit the horse tethered at the lamppost, "I am eternally grateful to you and Maggie for saving our Mrs. Parker."

"Don't mention it. She needed to stretch her legs after all that time sitting in a hotel room—Maggie that is."

"But, I have to tell you something, Harpo, something you may not like to know," I said.

"About Maggie?" he said, "She's not a boy horse; I checked! What could be so bad?"

"Harpo, Maggie lied to you. She's not a Lipizzaner, she's a Quarterhorse."

Harpo looked taken aback at the news. He considered the consequences. Nodding, he replied, "That's all right, Dottie—I'm five-quarters Jewish. Our love will see us through."

"Harpo, you have to return Maggie to her policeman. You can go to jail for that, you know?" said Mr. Benchley.

"Well, I could go to jail for a lot of things," he said defensively, "But I'm not giving Maggie to the cops."

"Why not?" I asked.

"Because she belongs to an actor playing a Canadian Mountie in that production of *Rosemarie*, over at the Hippodrome. He stole my gal; I stole his."

"Oh, Harpo, you are a character!"

He threw me a wily grin, patted Maggie on the nose, and ran a loving palm down her mane.

Turning to me with wide-eyed innocence, he asked: "You don't think there's any Irish in her, do you?"

The End

In business!

These two Italian cousins turned in their pushcarts for a fruit and vegetable store.

Lamberto's bakery

Bernardo Castelli hosted a dinner for us in his restaurant in Little Italy.

Afterword

Dorothy Parker and Ruth Hale were in Boston during the weeks before the executions of Nicola Sacco and Bartolomeo Vanzetti, organizing and marching in demonstrations at the State House. They were arrested during their peaceful march, and they really were watched by the feds, and suspected, too, of planning to set off a bomb. Whether or not they returned to New York City on the Midnight Owl is unknown.

In his column for Pulitzer's *World*, Heywood Broun questioned the fairness of the trials, appeals, and death sentence, as well as the integrity of the powerful political machine—citing prejudicial conduct of the Judicial, the police department, the district attorney's office, and the governor's office of the State of Massachusetts, which doggedly brought about the murder convictions and later stonewalled numerous appeals for new trials and for commutation of the death sentences. His publisher told him he would not accept another column on the subject. Broun resigned.

Robert Benchley became involved in the case through an affidavit of prejudice on behalf of Bartolomeo Vanzetti for a new trial to Governor Alvan Fuller of Massachusetts in May 1927. In it, he tells of a conversation overheard in 1921 and relayed to him by his friend, Loring Coes, in which Coes, in the locker-room of the Worchester Golf Club the day that Benchley picked him up from the club, overheard Judge Thayer refer to Sacco and Vanzetti as "those bastards down there," and say that he "would get them good and proper." As for the "parlor radicals" who were defending the men, he would "show them and would get those guys hanged." He "would like to hang a few dozen of those radicals, too." As Coes never came forward as a firsthand witness to these statements, as Benchley expected him to do, during the early summer of 1927 Benchley followed up on the issue and went as far as an interview with Governor Fuller, who suggested his statements were embellished to make a better story of it.

On August 23, 1977, the fiftieth anniversary of the executions, Governor Michael Dukakis of Massachusetts issued a proclamation that stated that Sacco and Vanzetti had been unfairly tried and convicted. Without asserting the men's innocence, a subject that has been in constant debate over the years, the proclamation was made that "any disgrace should be forever removed from their names."

Praise for *Dorothy Parker Mysteries*

Those of us who since childhood had wished there was a time machine that could let us experience and enjoy life in other periods, should read Agata Stanford's "Dorothy Parker Mysteries" series. They wonderfully recreate the atmosphere and spirit of the literary and artistic crowd at the Algonquin Round Table in the 1920s, and bring back to life the wit, habits, foibles, and escapades of Dorothy Parker, Robert Benchley, and Alexander Woollcott, as well as of the multitude of their friends and even their pets, both human and animal.

— *Anatole Konstantin*
Author of *A Red Boyhood: Growing Up Under Stalin*

Agata Stanford's "Dorothy Parker Mysteries" is destined to become a classic series. It's an addictive cocktail for the avid mystery reader. It has it all: murder, mystery, and Marx Brothers' mayhem. You'll see, once you've taken Manhattan with the Parker/Benchley crowd. Dorothy Parker wins! Move over, Nick and Nora.

— *Elizabeth Fuller*
Author of *Me and Jezebel*

Dorothy Parker and the Regulars of the Algonquin Hotel Round Table are alive and well in Agata Stanford's *The Broadway Murders*. Descriptions are fantastic in this who-dunnit as Stanford writes very colorfully. This is an adult's picture book, too, which in the end turned out to be pretty terrific.

—*Terri Ann Armstrong*
Author of "Medieval Menace" for *Suspense Magazine*

If you like murder mysteries, the fast-paced action, witty conversation, and glib repartee of the flapper era, you will love Agata Stanford's recreation of the atmosphere of the crowd at the Algonquin Round Table in the 1920s.

—*Mr. Tomato*
for *TheThreeTomatoes.com*

Dorothy is presented with wit and sarcasm sprinkled with tremendous insight. The life she lived is believably recreated, including the escapades of the Marx Brothers, the late nights of theater and dinners, even the famous speakeasy they drank at; all serve as backdrop to the investigation. The writing style affects the breezy language and popular slang to further transport you to that era when jazz artists and flappers coined modern terms. It is a heady mix and an escapist pleasure.

—*A.F. Heart*
for *Mysteries and Musings*

About the Author

Agata Stanford is an actress, director, and playwright who grew up in New York City. While attending the School of Performing Arts, she'd often walk past the Algonquin Hotel, which sparked her early interest in the legendary Algonquin Round Table.